Albion Lost
The Exiled Fleet Book 1

Richard Fox

For Dan
Ever a good man

CHAPTER 1

A tremor passed through the deck plates and into Captain Jimenez's chair as his ship came out of slip space. The air vents feeding the bridge blew a gust of hot air over Jimenez and his crew, all of whom opened their shirts and began cursing the chief engineer who'd promised the air conditioners were fixed.

Glancing at a screen attached to his chair, Jimenez saw green and amber conditions across the board. None of the systems on the *Cabo* had failed during the translation from faster-than-light travel, which was a significant improvement from the last engineer's performance.

Maybe he wouldn't space the engineer just yet.

As the ice world of Sevastopol shone like a full moon through the bridge's windows, his metal left hand twitched at the memory of working the mines as a child. Jimenez brought his oversized, spiked cybernetic hand to his collar and popped the top button with a flick of thorn-tipped nails. That he'd lost the original to frostbite on that godforsaken planet was a secret. He preferred his crew—and anyone else who ever heard of Iron Hand Jimenez—to come up with their own story as to how it happened; the imagination did wonders to build fear.

As a pirate, Jimenez preferred to work smarter and not harder; it was much better for the bottom line and life expectancy. Hailing a targeted ship and looking the part of a pirate willing to carry out a promise to space every last man, woman, and child on a civilian transport if his commands weren't followed made his job easier.

"Get Medived on the line," Jimenez said. "That old bastard owes me money. I'll have his hide and his mine if he doesn't explain all the slip traffic coming through here over the last few days."

"Sure thing, boss," said the sailor at a workstation to his right. Tarka sniffed hard and leaned closer to the fuzzy holo screens in front of her. "Would if I could, but Medived's spot isn't broadcasting on the net."

"Then raise Orlaf." Jimenez shifted in his seat as sweat ran down his back.

"Nobody's online," she said. "No ore tenders, no nothing." The rest of the bridge crew craned their necks toward Tarka's screens.

Jimenez curled his metal fingers into a fist and let it fall onto his chair with a clang, snapping the crew back to their duties. He unbuckled from his chair and leaned next to Tarka.

"Bull," Jimenez said quietly. "The slip lines have been humming for days with ships coming in and out of Sevastopol space. No one's got the balls to lay a finger on Orlaf's claim; he's with the Wyverns. Last time I saw movement like this was when some Cathay admiral decided he wanted his own empire in wild space. This place should be full of refugee ships carrying all their worldly possessions and marketable bodies."

"Radar's clean except for some debris in a decaying orbit over that snowball and comm channels are dead, sir." Tarka tapped a control panel, brought up a feed from the forward cannons, and zoomed onto the planet's surface. Jimenez reached over her shoulder and tapped in coordinates.

The camera shifted and settled on an open wound on the planet's surface. The strip mine was almost a mile wide, surrounded by refineries and ramshackle buildings. Blown snow filled the streets and covered the roofs. Jimenez shifted the view to Olaf's headquarters, which lay in a smoldering heap. The metal spires that once lorded over the city were blasted apart.

"Conn…pull a route from the grav buoy back to Sicani. Get us the hell out of here," Jimenez said as he went back to his seat, walking too fast for anyone to think nothing was amiss.

"Got a radar hit," Tarka said, "but this can't be right. Must be some kind of jamming. Nothing's this big." A track appeared on her holo screens coming around the planet's dark side. Three more came after that, then a flood of unidentified ships, each larger than any warship in wild space.

"Conn?" Jimenez strapped himself in and slapped his metal palm against the armrest.

"Something's coming through slip space right on top of us," the conn officer said. "I can't form a sheath to—"

The star field above the *Cabo* vanished, replaced by the circular underside of a massive spacecraft.

Jimenez stared at the behemoth, his jaw slack. His crew panicked, screaming orders at each other as their captain remained frozen in shock.

Six energy beams burst from the massive ship and ripped the *Cabo* apart within seconds.

CHAPTER 2

Salis closed her only piece of luggage and waited for a hiss of air as the case sealed itself shut. The case held little more than a few sets of clothes and essential toiletries, the sum total of everything she owned. She was used to getting by with little to nothing, but after three months traveling through slip space, she could understand why her fellow travelers carried significantly more worldly goods with them.

"Attention, all passengers," came from a speaker in the ceiling, "please disembark at your nearest gangway. Mandatory customs and immigration screening is required by New Exeter authorities regardless of your final destination. Please have all your documents ready for inspection."

Despite three months of recycled air, passable food, and a cabin slightly more robust than the steerage decks, she was hesitant to leave the *High Sierra*. She ran her fingertips along her forearm, feeling the slight mass of an implant near her elbow and the connecting line of neuro-wire running to another implant within her wrist. That the doctors on Geneva swore her augments were undetectable by anything less than a full bio scan should have put her mind at ease, but they weren't the ones about to come under scrutiny. Albion, like most civilized star nations, had strict laws against voluntary biological augmentation.

The neuro-wires tacked on to the rest of her nervous system sent a shiver through her body, and an ache for something missing, a phantom itch for a part of her body she'd never had, scratched at her mind. She'd have her gestalt soon, and then she would finally feel whole.

Salis tapped out the address of a hotel onto the smart tag attached to her luggage and walked over to a floor-length mirror next to the cabin's door. With her hair in loose waves, a silk blouse that flowed from her shoulders to below her waist in the latest style from Toulouse, and pants that ended above her ankles, she was every bit the young low-level executive and not at all her true self.

Why she had to travel under an alias and under cover was never fully explained to her, and she hadn't pressed for more answers. On Geneva, and especially in the Houses, the apprentice does not question the master.

Salis picked up a small briefcase next to the door and brushed her fingers against a sensor on the frame. The door slid open to a corridor full of passengers bustling toward a bright opening farther down the passageway.

Natural sunlight stung her eyes for a moment. Albion's star was a bit more luminescent than Geneva's, something Salis knew she'd have to get used to during her long stay. She peered down both sides of the corridor, keeping an eye out for one person in particular, then stepped out of her cabin.

After three months aboard the *High Sierra*, everyone but her seemed overly anxious to get the hell off the ship and onto Albion. That the transit had taken a week longer than advertised hadn't gone over well with the passengers in the more expensive staterooms, but such were the hazards of slip space. The gravity tides between stars could stretch or compress the faster-than-light travel times, and the *High Sierra* had the misfortune of catching un-fair winds after it weighed anchor from Uttar.

Uniformed ship's crew went flush against the bulkheads to make way for the rush of people making for the exit. The crew's faces looked more relieved that the ship had finally made landfall than most of the paying passengers. Salis traded nods and smiles with the butlers and stewards. One would eventually make it to her room and see that her suitcase got sent to an Exeter city delivery service and then on to her hotel.

"Fiona!" came from behind her, and Salis bit her bottom lip in frustration. She'd been so close to avoiding him.

"Wait up…" A heavyset man with a shock of red hair and whose skin was burnt orange from tanning treatments elbowed his way through the crowd.

"Reginald…I thought you would have disembarked sooner with the rest of first class," she said.

"Well, you didn't answer the message I sent you last night. I have to know if you're still interested in that cove whale tour. They really are spectacular creatures— you must see them." He ambled just ahead of her and used his sturdy frame to help ease her passage toward the open doors a few yards ahead. Salis had come to the much older—and by his own boasts, much richer—man's attention as they neared Albion. While she'd rebuffed his every polite attempt to gain her attention, the man was persistent.

"I need to adjust to Albion's day-night cycle, so I turned in early. Very sorry, my dear Reginald."

Stepping around the exit and onto the gangway, she moved through the environmental force field separating the ship from Albion's natural air with a gust of air and found her senses under assault. Hot, heavy air laden with the smell of sea salt clung to her like wet clothing. Her first breath was almost a struggle.

She came to a sudden stop and took in her assignment, her home for the next twenty years—New Exeter. The city filled the inner edge of an ancient impact crater nearly fifty miles around. The western third of the crater wall was lost to the ocean that spilled into the crater and formed a harbor. A bridge connected one edge of the harbor wall to the other, and sunlight from a pair of setting stars made the glass and composite-metal construction glint like jewels.

"That's the Boadicea Bridge," Reginald said. "The

sunset views are quite spectacular…"

"Is the air on the bridge like—" She took a short breath and wiped sweat from her brow. "—this everywhere?"

"What? Humid? I thought the main city on Durongin was tropical."

Salis sucked the damnably thick air through her teeth. She'd spent her entire life on Geneva, a cold, rocky world. Her cover story had a more varied history.

"There's humid and then there's this soup." Salis hurried down the gangway to a waiting tram. She gripped a sweating metal bar and stayed on her feet as more passengers filed into the wide-bodied vehicle.

Reginald tapped on a window, then pointed to the first-class tram with tinted windows and a smiling spaceport worker offering water bottles at the entrance. He mimed sending a text message and gave her a wide smile. She nodded quickly and breathed a sigh of relief when he finally turned away.

Screens along upper luggage racks played video footage of a devastated coastal city, forests on fire, filthy refugees—all with dark hair and features unlike the average Albian—fleeing the city on foot.

"What happened?" she asked.

"Some nearby unaligned world decided to mine out an asteroid in low orbit," Reginald said. "Guess Albion sent a fleet to help them out. Shame they'll miss the holiday because somebody got careless a couple stars over."

"Such a shame." Salis looked across the tarmac, noting the obvious security vehicles and armed personnel forming a loose cordon around the *High Sierra*. The guards carried holstered sidearms, their focus on the disembarking passengers, not the luggage coming off the ship where robots sorted the bags into waiting trucks.

Wires ran from behind a curved mirror in the back of the tram and into the overhead storage spaces. Salis used the mirror as she adjusted her hair while mapping out the surveillance setup that ran through the tram. She spotted at least five subtle camera lenses and DNA screeners within the air-conditioning vents.

By now, the Albion security forces would have her fingerprints, gene-code, iris scans, X-rays, and infrared of her entire body. A decent screening system, but one that could still be beaten.

The tram driver stood up from behind the wheel and rapped his fingers against a metal bar.

"Hello and welcome to New Exeter spaceport." He paused to wipe a handkerchief over his face. "Lovely weather we're having for you all. I know you've been on a long void transit, but one last bit of administration and you'll all be free to enjoy this fair city."

He droned on about duty-free shops and customs declarations. Salis noted the weapon concealed within his coat, and how the tone of his voice changed suddenly while talking. She'd bet money he received instructions through a subdermal earpiece as he rushed through the last of his speech.

A drone the size of a dinner plate floated around the outside of the tram.

Salis tapped a finger against the balance pole, feigning annoyance. Security was far too high for something as routine as a cruise ship arrival.

Act natural. Act like you're supposed to be here, she thought.

The tram lurched forward and zipped across the landing pad. One security vehicle followed close behind.

The roar of ascending spacecraft shook the windows as a cargo lighter rumbled overhead. A pair of ground-to-void fighters sat outside an open hangar, missiles on their wings and pilots in the cockpits. Drone carts carrying luggage and fuel cells zipped around the spaceport. Given the sheer number of moving pieces, Salis guessed the New Exeter port authorities sprang for a top-of-the-line AI manager.

The bus stopped outside a round building

connected to the main port.

"Customs and immigration," the driver said. "Step into any privacy booth you like. Watch your step as you get out."

Salis did not enjoy her brief foray back into the city's raw weather as she went from the tram into the immigration building. Inside, rows of circular booths with semi-opaque walls, each the size of an escape pod, waited for newcomers. Salis felt herself sweating despite the welcome embrace of conditioned air as she walked into the nearest booth and shut the waist-high door behind her. The interior was nothing more than a ring of padded seats and a small desk in the center. The walls switched to a landscape view from the center of the city's harbor.

A pleasant-looking woman appeared on the interior wall and bowed slightly to Salis.

"Hello, you can call me Cynthia. I am a virtual intelligence representing the laws and regulations of New Exeter and Albion. Please have a seat."

Salis felt a flicker of hope as she sat down and withdrew her passport slate from her purse. Virtual intelligences handled routine matters and had little capacity for anything beyond the norm. If she was under any additional scrutiny, a real person would be speaking with her.

Swiping a finger over the screen, she opened her passport.

"Thank you…Ms. Salis. What is the nature of your visit?"

"I represent Sook Mining Limited. We're interested in expanding operations to this sector." Salis added a slight smile as she finished. Rarely did a free-market economy like Albion's ever say no to a capital injection.

"You are not listed as having a hotel reservation anywhere in New Exeter City. Would you care for a recommendation?" The faux-woman's image shimmered briefly, and Salis' hand curled into a fist as her heartbeat accelerated. The video error undoubtedly meant an operator within the VI system had just taken over.

"I wanted a room with a view of the migrating whales…the ones with the bioluminescent algae. Given that my arrival date was a bit fuzzy, I thought I'd wait and see if the whales were even around before I spent a fortune for a room looking out at a whole bunch of nothing."

"You arrived just in time. A pod of prism whales is on the way to the harbor and should arrive just after sunset. I can send available harbor-watch charters to your data assistant and recommend several hotels."

"Please."

The VI's head cocked from side to side. Her mouth became pixelated as she spoke again.

"Albion is a signatory to the Vitruvian Accords. Any cybernetic augmentations beyond those required for minimal quality-of-life standards are subject to inspection and possible sanction. Do you have anything to declare?"

The corner of Salis' mouth twitched before she answered. Her neuro-wires were dormant, practically invisible to all but a full-spectrum scan, and utterly useless as an augmentation so long as she was without her gestalt. Admitting to the neuro-wires would mark her out as something far from a simple corporate scout. But if the security service already knew about her augmentations...

"Nothing to declare," Salis said.

"One moment please." The VI's features snapped from stern to pleasant, then froze solid.

Salis drummed her fingertips against her thigh and slid her passport back into her purse.

The holo walls snapped off, and Salis found her booth surrounded by police in light body armor and carrying carbines. There were three police that she could see, and certainly another behind her. More would arrive soon. None had their weapons pointed at her, but one had a hand on a shock pistol holstered to his chest. Salis' fingertips tightened on the edge of her passport as a quick sequence of attacks ran across her mind.

"Don't move," said a policewoman who pointed a knife hand at Salis. "You're carrying unsanctioned augmentations. You will come with us for further inspection. Any resistance and we will use deadly force."

"There's been some mistake," Salis said, sounding too calm for a simple civilian surrounded by armed guards. The police backed away and swung their weapons to a low and ready position across their bodies.

"No mistake," said a man with an accent Salis recognized as he stepped around a policeman. He wore a loose-fitting black jumpsuit with yellow and blue trim. His close-cropped gray hair and stern face put him in his late forties.

Salis stayed perfectly still, her body tense as a coiled spring.

The man pressed his lips together and grunted. He crossed his arms over his chest and pulled a sleeve back and up his forearm. Salis caught a flash of bronze chain mail and squares of armor the size of her palm layered over the mail.

"*Bainvegna, Grisoni Salis,*" he said.

Salis relaxed.

"*Tgau, Capitan Royce,*" she said.

"Someone want to explain this?" the policewoman asked.

"New recruit, lieutenant. I'll take it from here," he said.

The police lowered their weapons but didn't take their eyes off Salis.

"You could have mentioned she was expected, Royce," the lieutenant said. "Save us the trouble of getting all this crap on in the middle of a heat wave."

"If you'd have let her slip by, I would have you all guarding crosswalks in full gear for failing to follow protocol," Royce said. "But you should have pulled her before she ever got into the booth. Stay in kit until the end of your shift. We'll go over where you went wrong once the new team takes over."

"Yes, sir," the lieutenant snapped and directed the rest of her armed team away with a jerk of her head.

Salis stood up and saluted.

"Were you testing me or them by keeping my arrival secret?" she asked.

"Both. Come with me." Royce turned and walked toward a side door. "Why didn't you announce your identity and purpose once the police arrived?"

"My instructions were to maintain my cover and present myself to you at the palace. Just because I was due some additional scrutiny didn't mean I was going to give up."

"The med scans wouldn't have picked up your gestalt connections. You might well have made it through. But you broke your cover when you got ready for a fight. Businesspeople should panic a bit when confronted with guns—you became calm."

"I am trained to protect and defend, not to be a

spy. Espionage is beyond the remit of our contract. Does the King know this?"

"Of course he does." Royce pushed the door open and led her toward an idling air car double-parked in front of a cargo truck. "The King has never asked us to violate our contract. He has a capable spy service of his own. I wanted to test your composure under stress and see if the heightened alert levels were being followed. Complacency is a problem across the system. Albion has been at peace for too long."

The gull-wing doors on the air car rose up. Salis increased her pace and made for the driver's seat…then came to a sudden stop.

"Yes, you should be driving." Royce cited one of the oldest traditions of their order and stepped around her to sit in the driver's seat. "But you don't know where you're going. Just get in."

"Sorry, sir." The air car's front passenger seat had several more data screens than the few civilian models she'd ever been in. Salis found the air car's weapon systems with a few taps, brought the electronic countermeasure systems online, and powered up the rotary cannon hidden within the car's body. Data scrolled across the windows as the repulsor engines came to life with a hum.

"This electronics suite looks Cathay," Salis said. "I thought Albion and the Cathay Dynasty were still at odds over the settlement from the last war."

"They are." Royce brought the car up into the air, rising above the screening building. "Albion prefers to use their own tech wherever and whenever possible, but they'll hack a better system if they find it. That Albion has yet to reach a licensing agreement with Cathay is a state secret and not to be repeated."

The captain angled the car upwards and accelerated forward.

"Albion steals technology? Surprising."

"They have yet to arrange payment. The King

considers that an important distinction." Royce pointed toward a massive building built into the crater wall a few miles from the edge of the harbor. The structure was built into three tiers, the base a different kind of polished marble. Towers topped with exposed anti-aircraft cannons dotted each wall.

"As you can imagine, that's where the King and the royal family live, Castle Loudon." Royce joined a lane of air cars headed toward the center of the city.

"Security is higher than what I was briefed on. What's going on?"

"What do you know about the Treaty of Reuilly?" Royce asked.

"That it should have ended the second expansion wars decades ago, but the bombing that killed most of the diplomats kept some of the key star nations from ratifying it. No one took responsibility for the attack; everyone still assumes their enemies were behind it. The academy laid out a decent theory that a mercenary named Ja'war the

Black is responsible, but every crackpot conspiracy theorist over the last three decades has an idea."

"Ja'war the Black was captured," Royce said. "One of the King's agents found him deep in wild space. They brought his cryo-tube in nine days ago. Since then, there have been a number of…security incidents. We're not sure if it's related to Ja'war's capture, but we're not taking any chances."

"Still alive after so many years? That's puzzling. Ja'war's employer should have killed him after the attack— a fairly common occurrence after any high-profile assassination." Salis looked down, ogling the concentric layout of the city around the harbor.

"Ja'war is a Faceless, the only specified bit of technology expressly forbidden by the Vitruvian Accords, but the worlds in wild space don't hold to the Accords, or any extradition treaties. Explains why he eluded capture for so long. Small miracle he was caught."

"How did they catch him?" Salis asked.

29

"You've never been bonded to a gestalt before, correct?" Royce steered the car out of the lane toward the castle. A warning screen popped up over the steering wheel and he tapped in an authorization code.

Salis knew better than to keep pressing about Ja'war's capture. She was a fresh addition to Royce's force. She would be told everything she needed to know to perform her duties and she would expect nothing more or less than that.

"Correct, sir. The surgeons cleared me for immediate augmentation."

"I have two gestalts available. You'll take on Andrin's. The gestalt has had enough time to settle since the separation. You'll assume the rest of his contract as well, assuming the King accepts your oath."

"I…I thought I'd bond with a newborn. The benefits to both gestalt and body are—"

"We're on the fringe of core space, Salis, not some place days from Geneva. Your assignment here is well out of the ordinary for an oath-sworn company, especially since Andrin was a medical issue and not a casualty. His gestalt will serve you well. I'll have you fit soon as we land," he said, glancing at a clock on the dashboard, "and I supervise another matter."

Salis wanted to ask about the second gestalt but held her tongue.

CHAPTER 3

The jungle buzzed with the morning cycle of insect life. Cicada analogs flit between orchid blossoms atop eight-foot stalks of *daxmi* plants, each reaching for a patch of sunlight streaming through the canopy above. Neon-blue dragonflies dove through the swarm of cicadas, snatching their breakfast with a snap of chitin on chitin.

Commodore Thomas Gage moved along a narrow animal path, his active camouflage fatigues shifting with each step, the new pattern flowing down the tightly wound acti-cloth over his rifle. He tested each step carefully, avoiding dried clumps of dead grass as his stalk continued.

The man behind him wasn't so careful. He burst out of a patch of *daxmi* and stirred up a cloud of pollen that went straight to his face and eyes. Slapping a thick-fingered hand over his mouth, he fought back a sneeze, moved his hand away, then slapped it back as a terrible snort echoed through his sinuses. The heavy pack on his back jingled as loose straps bounced against each other.

"Bertram, I told you to double up on the antihistamines," Gage said.

"Aye, sir, that you did. You and the Master Chief were also most adamant about me not falling asleep while we're on this little hike. I take one too many of those purple pills and it's my snoring to worry about and not my sneezing."

Bertram looked at Gage with watery eyes and sniffed.

"Shouldn't be so bad making a bit of noise," Bertram said. "This is drop bear country. Best to scare them off a bit."

"We're looking for armed pirates," said Gage as he ducked his head around a bend on the path and found his Siam guide, Kamala, squatting next to a mud puddle a few yards away. "Best *we* sneak up on *them* than the other way around."

"You're assuming the drop bears haven't got to them first. Or the sabretooth pumas. Or a pollen fog. Those will smother a man sure as—"

Another man in camouflage came up from behind and shushed Bertram.

"Yeoman," Master Chief Eisen grabbed Bertram by the pack and secured the loose straps, "you're here to attend to the good Commodore. Making noise and complaining are not in that job description."

"Walking around the blasted drop-bear-infested forests hoping to shoot strangers is not why most sailors choose to be stewards." Bertram braced himself as Eisen finished fixing his pack. Eisen then grabbed Bertram by the shoulders and spun him around.

"Sir, may I have a word with this sailor?" Eisen asked.

Gage walked down the path to Kamala, leaving the senior sailor to convey whatever important bit of expletive-laced feedback Bertram needed.

The Siam scout squatted with his archaic rifle against one knee, his other hand hovering just above the mud. He wore a simple sleeveless khaki uniform, and a floppy hat hid the back of his head and sides of his face from view.

"Found something?" Gage asked.

"Two men, heavy," Kamala said in the local dialect, an incomprehensible stream of brief syllables; the translation came through Gage's earpiece. The Siam man flicked two fingers at boot impressions in the mud. He then picked up a blade of grass with small tufts of fiber at the end and touched a small indentation of a few toes and the ball of a foot.

"One girl."

"The village leader said the pirates came at night, took the women out of the emergency shelters. We're close?" Gage asked.

"There's a clearing a few leagues on," Kamala said. "A ravine big enough for a lander. Good place to hide."

"We've ten armed sailors with us. We can handle two pirates." Gage took a sensor pack from off his chest rig and brought it online with a shake. Error messages scrolled up the screen. "Still too many ionizing particles in the atmosphere. We're down to mark one eyeballs and ears."

Kamala rose up gracefully, as if he was made of smoke.

"Pirates come every so often," he said. "Most we catch. If we let one or two get away, they spread what happens to any light-eye that thinks we're weak. The disaster brought out the vultures, ones without fear. Come."

The scout went on, blending into the grass. Gage signaled to Eisen and a sheepish-looking Bertram to follow. They passed the signal to the sailors behind them.

"Albion bothers with prisons for pirates, yes?" Kamala asked.

"Hard labor on Uffernau, one of our ice moons. Why?"

"No prisons for murderers, thieves, or deviants on Siam. I'll show you what we do when we find them." Kamala ducked beneath a bent lotus frond and led them into a thinning copse of foliage. "Albion is here to help after the disaster. I see the divine in you, in your people. But Siam has her own laws. Remember this."

"I've dealt with pirates in wild space, seen firsthand what they're capable of," Gage said. "I know Siam's had issues with some of the larger bands. We came here for humanitarian reasons. The chance to deal with pirates is a bonus for me."

"Karma is just. Karma is patient." Kamala moved

along, his wide-bottomed sandals making barely an impression on the grass.

Gage felt heat rising as they travelled deeper into the jungle and onto a rocky slope choked with vines. The enviro-layer beneath his composite-armor body glove and active camo sent chilled fluid over his midsection and around the base of his neck, but sweat kept pouring down his face as the humidity became a steamy haze.

"Albion, you ever been to my world?" Kamala asked as he climbed up a boulder and onto a ledge.

"Transited through the system more than once to and from wild space," Gage said, struggling to keep his words level through the strain of climbing. "Never touched down."

"'Wild space,'" Kamala clicked his tongue, "those beyond call it 'free space,' where people can live without some mushroom hundreds of light-years away deciding what they can and cannot do. Wait here a moment." The scout stopped at the edge of a cliff and pointed to the fog bank that formed a gray abyss around them.

"For what?" Gage asked.

"Hunters, hikers…I used to lead visitors from Albion up here." Kamala's face fell. "We call this place The Word of Buddha. After the disaster, I don't know if we'll still hear it."

A whistle began in the distance, air rushing through treetops.

Kamala tapped the butt of his rifle against a tree beside Gage, then he tucked his hat beneath an arm and wrapped a hand into a vine. The officer gripped a vine and planted his feet against bare rock.

The ground quivered as a low moan rose through the air. A blast of wind rocked Gage from side to side as the fog danced away, fleeing down a canyon that had been hidden from view moments ago.

The air cleared, and Gage could see out to the ocean and Lopburi City along the coast—what remained of Lopburi City, at least. Entire neighborhoods were

39

smashed to rubble, crushed by a tidal wave almost a week ago. In the ocean, jutting up in front of the rising sun was a mountain peak not born from the planet, but a massive hunk of an asteroid that the Siam had brought into low orbit to be mined.

No one was exactly sure what caused the explosion aboard the asteroid because everyone involved with the operation on the rock was dead. But one of the larger fragments had crashed into the ocean and sent up a tsunami that killed almost a million people up and down the coast within hours. Fragments had bombarded much of the settled areas, setting fire to entire cities and kicking up enough dust that the planet would slip into a near ice age within years.

Lumps of burning meteors left long streaks across the sky as innumerable lumps of rock broken away from the mining station made their inevitable descent through Siam's gravity well. Deep bands of yellow and orange traced across the horizon, spectacular with the mega-tones of kicked-up dust diffusing through the atmosphere.

The planet's settlements were clustered along this coast. If they'd lived on the planet's second-largest continent where the body of the asteroid had hit, none would have survived. The sight of thousands of miles of burning forests and a dirty scar spreading through the planet's atmosphere had greeted 11th Fleet when they'd finally arrived to help.

"Blimey, that was something!" Bertram said. "Anyone get that on vid?"

Chief Eisen reached out and put a heavy hand on the steward's shoulder.

"Almost there." Kamala hopped off the rock and jogged to a small outcropping where he went prone. Gage crawled up next to him and peered over the ledge. Jungle spread beneath them in a wide ravine parallel to the canyon where The Word of Buddha had just swept through.

Gage watched as the trees swayed in the last of the

wind gust, then narrowed his eyes. The leaves of the thin trees on one side of the meadow shifted differently than the rest, almost lagging behind the sway.

"Camo tarps." Gage took an eyepiece from his belt and looked through it. He tabbed through infrared and ultraviolet settings but couldn't see through the false front.

"Chief…" He held the optic up to Eisen, who took a quick glance and grunted.

"Top-of-the-line gear," Eisen said. "Not your normal pirate hand-me-down crap that's decades old."

"That cruiser we chased out of system had decent acceleration," Gage said. "You think we're dealing with Harlequins?"

"Taking slaves and leaving their own behind isn't Harlequin MO. Totenkopf or Wyverns is my guess," the chief said.

"Totenkopf come to trade," Kamala said. "They stay in the star ports, behave themselves. Wyverns demanded tribute. It didn't go well for any of us." He rubbed a hand over a burn scar on his arm.

"Wyverns were mostly Francia military that refused to surrender at the end of the last war, but that was decades ago," Gage said. "Attrition…lack of spare parts after the Reich smashed their shipyards over Bordeaux…shouldn't be too difficult."

"You want us to sneak down there with ten armed sailors—not Marines who live for this sort of thing—and do what exactly, sir?" Eisen asked.

"I want to go down there with five men and Kamala. You set up the mortars and provide overwatch," Gage said. "All the interference in the atmosphere will degrade the autonomous targeters, but an IR designation will still work. We just have to paint the targets. Aim assist on the rifles should still work."

"We're looking at about five hundred yards from here to the target area," Eisen said, pulling the butt of his rifle out further. He slapped the bottom barrel and bipod arms swung out. "We can probably hit what's down there, just get rid of the camo."

"Judicious aim is appreciated," Gage said. "There are civilians down there. Don't take any risks with their lives."

"Aye aye," Eisen said and motioned for four other sailors to take up firing positions along the ridge.

"Bertram, drop your pack," Gage said.

The steward sighed and slipped it off his back. "Thank you, sir. I'll stay up here, make you some lovely tea and then—"

"You're coming with me. Move." Gage slapped him on the shoulder, then followed Kamala down the hillside.

Bertram followed after a hard poke from a sailor behind him.

"See if the man gets his tea after I come face-to-face with a Wyvern pirate. You know they have to kill their own mothers before they can join a raider crew?" the steward mumbled. "Plus, this has to be a drop bear thicket if I've ever seen one."

"Bertram," Gage said over his shoulder.

The doughy sailor continued on in near silence, grumbling nonstop.

Kamala led the Albion men off a main trail, over a running stream, and to a narrow path next to a large bush covered with white orchids and thorny branches stretched over the flowers.

Gage stopped and looked up at the canopy. The last time he'd tangled with pirates on solid ground had been years back, and he'd learned a lesson that day on Volera II that nearly cost him his life.

"Hold on…" Gage's words stopped Kamala in his tracks. Gage took his optics off his belt and did a quick scan ahead of them. A loose field of crisscrossing laser lines came up on the screen.

"Laser wire," Gage said. "They've been here for a few days. Makes sense that they've got alarms set. No cameras, at least."

"What happens if we trip them?" asked a sailor behind Bertram.

"Maybe they come out and look, maybe mines." Gage tapped his fingertips against his thigh as he thought.

"*Jigarra* plant," said Kamala, walking over and motioning to the nearly solid mass of brambles and thorn bushes. "Always wild hogs in here."

"We're here for pirates, not pigs," Gage said.

"Stupid to set up camp next to a *jigarra* bush," Kamala said. "Hogs forage during the day, hide at night." He took a small cylinder from his pocket and tapped out a toothpick. He snapped the tip and flicked it into the bush, then tossed out two more.

"Firesticks," the scout said. "Won't burn too long, but they'll smoke out the pigs."

"How do you even know they're in there?" Gage asked.

Kamala motioned up with a jerk of his head.

"Don't look, but there are two drop bears up there. Must have followed the hogs' scent here…waiting for one to break away from the group," Kamala said.

"How many?" Bertram backed up and bumped into a sailor behind him.

"Don't worry." The Siam took a spray bottle from his belt and spritzed Bertram twice. "Repellant. My wife makes it."

Gage's nose wrinkled at the pungent odor of ammonia and cut grass.

"Ugh, smells like cat piss," Bertram said.

"It is. You can smell like that or worry about drop bears."

"More please." Bertram held up his arms and got another spray.

Gage breathed through his nose as Kamala hit him with the repellant around his neck.

"How do I get this smell out of the good Mr. Gage's cloth—"

The bush rustled as gray smoke rose from where the firesticks had landed. They heard the pigs grunting as they meandered away from the smoke and toward the laser fence. Kamala grabbed his rifle by the barrel and rapped the butt against the thorns.

Pigs bolted out of the bush and through the pirates' perimeter…without the sound of an alarm.

"Quick," Kamala said, running after the dozen hairy animals as they bounded over the jungle floor.

"Stay low." Gage went after the scout, grasping what the Siam was doing. The laser fence would read a multitude of breaches. Their passage was just more noise for whoever saw the alarm go off.

Kamala came to a stop in a streambed with wet soil walls almost up to Gage's waist. He knelt beneath a snarl of roots spreading from a tall tree next to the embankment and drew a machete with a dark matte blade off his back. The Albion men took cover along the low wall.

Bertram's breathing was fast and shallow. Stress, not exertion. Gage put a reassuring hand on the steward's shoulder.

"Deep breath. We have the advantage—don't forget it," Gage whispered.

"Never seen a pirate in the flesh, sir. Never had to come up on another man that wanted to kill me. Sure, there was that time when Ol' Josh thought me and his girl were—" A twig snap silenced him.

Gage put his finger to his trigger and activated his rifle optics with a press of a button. Ballistic glasses slid down from his helmet and a small screen with the video feed from his weapon came up in front of his eyes. He slowly lifted the rifle up and panned it from side to side.

A man with an open shirt, leather pants, and thick boots tromped through the jungle toward them, a shotgun in one hand and a radio in the other. A giant fleur-de-lis tattooed on his chest and on one temple spoke of his allegiance: Wyverns.

"Kamala," said Gage as he lowered his weapon and looked to the side. The Siam was gone.

"Sir, take the shot?" a sailor whispered.

Gage looked at his suppressor-less rifle muzzle, then shook his head. There could be more pirates lurking around. Giving up the element of surprise for a single enemy was a poor tactical decision. They were through the perimeter. Once the guard reported on yet another pig incursion and went back, Gage and his men could sneak up on the main camp.

There was a splash downstream. A juvenile pig with white matted fur and black spots raised its snout in the air, then ran away.

The static and occasional squelch from his radio grew louder as the guard walked toward the stream. Gage pressed himself into the mud, placing his confidence in Albion, engineering to keep him hidden as his uniform aligned its colors to blend in.

The guard, a man in his late thirties with the build

of an ogre and the hygiene to match, stopped next to the tree and rested a forearm against it, holding his shotgun barrel down and dangerously close to Gage.

Gage stayed perfectly still as his heart beat so loudly he was surprised the pirate couldn't hear it.

The Wyvern raised his radio to his face.

"Rien. Encore rien." He moved the radio away and shouted, *"Ey! Casse-toi vous cochons!"*

Just then, Bertram sneezed.

The pirate's head snapped to the side. He frowned and cradled the shotgun in both hands. Gage pressed his finger to the trigger, ready to kill the Wyvern the instant he realized he wasn't alone.

He slapped his shotgun barrel against his palm, then spat over the edge of the mud ledge. The drop splattered atop Gage's boot.

The tip of Kamala's machete flicked up behind the pirate's shoulder. The blade slashed behind the man's neck and he gave off a startled huff. His eyes danced up and down and his mouth went slack. Blood poured down his neck and across his chest. Kamala reached around and plucked the shotgun out of his hands, then gave the pirate a nudge.

The man toppled over and fell across the stream. His head bounced against a rock and went rolling into the stream, bobbing like a cork as the water swept it away.

"Only one," Kamala said. "Poor security."

"Up," said Gage as he grabbed a shell-shocked Bertram and twisted him away from the corpse. "They'll come looking for him soon. Form a firing line and we advance on the camp. Don't shoot unless we're fired on or I give the order. Move."

Kamala wiped the bloody blade against the dead pirate's leg, then sheathed the machete.

Gage and the Siam guide hurried a few steps ahead of the sailors, who remained uniformly silent as they made their way through the jungle. Space combat was brutal, the work of energy cannons against hulls and shields accompanied by explosions that killed men and women instantly or promised suffocation in the freezing void when space suits were badly damaged.

Seeing your enemy bleed wasn't part of the equation.

On Volera II, Gage had come face-to-face with a Harlequin *mortir*, one of their cyborgs designed solely for murder. He'd seen the killing precision of a dedicated assassin firsthand. There were still nights he woke up in a cold sweat, remembering the glint of a blade as it drove at his neck. A shiver went down his spine. At least that *mortir* was dead. Probably dead.

"Got a crow's nest," one of the sailors said. "Two o'clock, see two of them up there."

"Take cover." Gage knelt behind a fallen tree and found the observation post. Two pirates sat in an armored pillbox mounted on a tree almost four yards in diameter. The now extinct Francia Expeditionary Legions had prized their modular technology for rapid landfall campaigns. A single lander could bring pallets full of armored walls and transform that cargo into a fully functioning forward operating base within ten minutes. That some of the old tech still found use with the Wyverns shouldn't have been a surprise, no matter how unpleasant it was to Gage.

The two pirates in the crow's nest busied themselves with data slates. The blast windows were up, allowing the morning breeze to circulate through the enclosure. One's fingers mashed at the screen, probably playing a game. The other had his feet up, half dozing as he looked at his slate. The four repeater blasters mounted on pintles gave Gage pause.

A beat-up lander lay a few dozen yards away, tucked against the tree line. Tall poles held up the active camo-nets overhead. The ramp was down, and open boxes full of scavenged electronics and gold-inlaid jade statues were piled around the base of the ramp. Each Siam family kept a shrine centered on the statues of a kneeling saint. They were never sold and were something of a collector's item beyond the planet. Gage made out two more pirates in the plane. One stretched, walked to the edge of the ramp, and relieved himself over the side.

"That's a Yennovo G9," Bertram said. "Needs at least three to fly. Can carry ten people, but they wouldn't bring that many if they planned on taking stolen goods up to their ship."

"There were four, maybe five, during the kidnapping," Kamala said.

"Where are the prisoners?" Eisen asked.

"They'll be in the G9 and restrained," Gage said. "They know the area, know where to go. The pirates don't. They won't let the girls even see an escape route. How long until that crate could be airborne?" he asked Bertram.

"Engines aren't even lit. Cycle time for those engines is almost three minutes."

Gage winced. Worst-case scenario, having around one hundred eighty seconds to disable or capture the shuttle from the moment the pirates realized they were compromised and could blast away was a tough challenge.

"We need to stop it from taking off," Gage said, "and without putting the girls inside at risk. If they get airborne, we'll never be able to track them with all the interference in the atmosphere."

Gage ran tactical scenarios through his mind. Not knowing the total number of pirates or if one was sitting in the cockpit ready to flip on the engines at a moment's notice added too much ambiguity to his options.

"I say we run up and shoot them all in the face," Kamala said.

"We do have surprise on our side...yes," Gage said.

"Sir, I was a boatswain's mate before I came to bat for you," Bertram said. "The power packs in a G9 are where the wings and fuselage meet. Enough bullets in there and that bird's not going anywhere. Her hull's as strong as tissue paper against our blasters, but I do suggest we get close, shoot at an upward angle to keep from hurting the innocents inside."

"Good suggestion, Bertram," Gage said. "Master Chief Eisen, ready the designator and paint the crow's nest. We'll launch our assault soon as the missile takes it out. Bertram, Clyde, you damage the batteries. Eisen, you and the rest lay down suppressive fire on anyone else that shows up. Kamala and I will get into the shuttle. We're not here for kills. Get the prisoners and get them to safety, understand?"

The sailors nodded. Eisen tapped a sailor with a laser designator on his rifle and the man aimed it at the crow's nest.

"Assault element, let's go," Gage said. He slid over the tree trunk and moved toward the shuttle at a crouch, Kamala beside him.

"How the hell did I end up on the 'assault element'?" Bertram whispered to Clyde, the other sailor with him.

"Maybe because you opened your big mouth

about knowing everything about the G9," Clyde shot back.

"Be helpful…get thrown into the fire. Got it. Very fair," Bertram muttered.

Gage glared fire over his shoulder and his steward sank a little deeper into his low stance.

They were fifty yards from the shuttle when a pirate with dreadlocks down to his chest walked onto the G9's ramp and peered into the forest. He held a radio up to his mouth and spoke.

"Down." Gage went to his knees and crawled beneath a fern with rainbow-colored fronds that shimmered with the breeze. The dead pirate must have gone overdue. The man with the dreadlocks hollered into the shuttle and two more Wyverns carrying rifles came tromping down the ramp.

"Bet they're going to come right for us," Bertram said. "Yup. I hate being right all the time."

"Eisen," Gage tapped the mic on his throat, "where's that fire support?"

"...connection...fixed. Splash, over."

Gage cocked up an eyebrow, trying to remember details from his basic officer course's field artillery familiarization training from almost two decades ago. "Shot" meant the round was in the air, then "splash" would mean...

A brief whistle filled the air, then the base of the tree holding the pirate crow's nest exploded into smithereens. Giant scales of bark snapped away as the trunk buckled and slowly tipped back into the jungle...directly for the Albion sailors.

As Gage lurched to his feet and ran straight for the camp, the question of whether the guided missile had missed the crow's nest or if the sailor with the laser designator had intentionally targeted the trunk crossed his mind.

He kept running as a shadow grew over his head. The groan of defeated wood roared in his ears, and he spied a circle of large rocks around a smoldering fire. He leaped into the circle as thin branches thundered down around him, tossing up a blizzard of leaves with the impact. The rocks took the brunt of the impact but still some whipped against his back and legs.

An empty bird's nest bounced off Gage's head. He looked up and saw a crawlspace through the downed branches, propped up by the rocks around the cooking fire.

Heat bore through the thin armor on his hips and stomach as he lay in a pile of still-burning embers. Gage scrambled forward, knocking up soot and ash that caked his rifle and covered his ballistic glasses as he moved. He crawled clear of the fire pit and branches and tried to wipe the gray sludge of ash and water away, only managing to make the mess worse.

Gage ripped his helmet off…and found himself looking eye to eye with two pirates standing a few yards away beside the crushed crow's nest. That he'd just crawled out of the fire and probably looked like some sort of Siam forest spirit might have been what kept the pirates flat-footed for a moment. He swung his weapon up and fired from the hip. The three-round burst kicked up dirt at the pirates' feet and shocked them into action.

The commodore took better aim and fired. His weapon made a deep buzz and an amber light blinked over the shot counter. Energy rifles had little in the way of moving parts, but the focusing crystals could be fouled, rendering the weapon unusable. Gage dropped the ash-choked rifle and drew the pistol on his hip.

Time seemed to slow as he sidestepped as one of the pirates fired, a blue bolt that snapped past Gage's face and left a wave of heat over his bare skin. Gage lined up the sights and hit the pirate twice in the chest. He swung the weapon toward the other target and found him already aiming at the Albion officer.

A red bolt slashed down and hit the pirate on the shoulder. His rifle went flying and he pitched to the ground with an ugly black burn against the base of his neck and one arm badly dislocated. Gage snatched up the fallen rifle and promised to award an extra day's shore leave to whoever made that shot from the cliff where Chief Eisen and the rest were on overwatch.

Engines chugged to life and a blast of hot air washed over Gage. The Yennovo, its ramp up and secured, was nearly halfway through the preflight cycle.

"Damn it!" As Gage ran toward the shuttle, he glanced to one side, hoping to see Kamala, and found nothing but a mountain of branches. No sign of Bertram and Clyde; they were either on the wrong side of the fallen tree…or under it.

Gage raised the pirate's rifle to his shoulder and aimed at the base of the wing. This weapon let off a slew of solid projectiles, and the kick nearly knocked him off balance and pulled the muzzle high after a few shots. He ran beneath the wing and fired again. Thin fingers of electricity and sparks broke into the air and one of the engines coughed.

He ran toward the front. The dreadlocked pirate was the only one in the twin forward pilot seats. He was shouting and bashing his fists against the controls.

Gage fired a round through the windshield over the man's head. The pirate looked at Gage and sneered.

The Albion officer pointed one hand at the still revving engine, then chopped his fingertips across his throat.

The pirate gave him the finger.

Gage shot him in the chest, the bullets shattering the windshield into fragments. Through the spider-web-cracked glass, the pilot lay dead over the controls, blood dripping down the back of his seat and off the console.

As the active engine wound down slowly, Gage turned his attention to the crushed crow's nest. The red smears against the glass spoke of what happened to the two men inside.

Kamala, his clothes torn and covered in leaves, limped over to the back of the shuttle. The Siam man pointed a bloody hand at Gage and shouted.

"Untranslatable," came through Gage's earpiece in a woman's voice.

"What? Are you hurt?" Gage looked over the man, who was bleeding from many small cuts.

"With your mother—untranslatable—and both dogs!" Kamala pointed to the other side of the cargo ramp. "Go trip the emergency release when I say so. Curse you and that cross-eyed diseased foreigner of yours that can't shoot."

Gage unsnapped a panel on the other side of the ramp and grabbed the orange handle within. Kamala nodded and they pulled at the same time. The ramp slammed to the ground and kicked up a cloud of dust.

Kamala jumped onto the ramp, screaming in his own language. Several female voices answered him. Four young women were chained to the bulkhead, all in nighttime clothes and crying almost hysterically. Gage's earpiece couldn't keep up with the rapid-fire Siam-ese as

Kamala spoke with them.

"Kamala? Kamala! How many pirates were there? We can account for six,"

Gage said.

"One more," the scout said. "He left when that first went to check on the alarm."

"Probably on his way back." Gage went back down the ramp and was met by Bertram and Clyde, neither of whom looked the worse for wear.

"Sir! Did you see the giant bloody tree that tried to kill us?" Bertram asked. "I never knew I could run that fast. Are you well, sir? You look like a ghost."

"There's one more pirate out there," Gage said. "Form a perimeter and keep an eye out."

"There he is." Clyde pointed over Gage's shoulder and sidestepped around the commodore with his weapon raised. Bertram, who barely came up to Gage's sternum, spread his arms wide and jumped between his officer and danger.

A tall pirate stood at the edge of the clearing, his arms held wide, a rifle dangling from one hand.

"Albion military!" Clyde shouted. "Drop your weapon or I'll—"

The pirate tossed his rifle aside and ran off into the jungle.

"Oh, all right then." Clyde half-raised his weapon to aim, then looked at Gage. "Shoot him, sir? Seems hardly fair what with him being unarmed."

"Forget him," Gage said, watching the pirate flee. "We'll get his weapon. He'll either make his way back to the village and surrender or…what is that? Up in the trees?"

A dark shape fell from the jungle canopy and landed on top of the pirate. A terrified scream ended abruptly followed by a low ululation that echoed through the forest, punctuated by the snap of bone.

"Drop bear," Kamala said from the top of the ramp. The four young women clustered behind him, each rubbing their wrists where they'd been bound. "They won't attack an armed man unless they're hurt or starving. Idiot volunteered to be lunch when he tossed his rifle aside. Such is life in the jungle."

"Is it still hungry?" Bertram slunk back behind Gage.

"It'll carry the kill to its nest, share with the other one I saw. They're predators, not trophy hunters." Kamala reached into his shirt and plucked out a leaf with a bloody stem. "How about you bring down your medic?"

"Yes, of course." He slapped Bertram on the shoulder and his steward turned away, one hand to his mic. "Are the girls injured?"

"Scared, few bruises," Kamala said. "Slaves are worth more than bodies. 'Intact' slaves…even more." Kamala let a half-smile spread over his scratched face. "They're lucky the pirates were more disciplined with some things than others."

"We'll call in our own shuttle," Gage said, "get

them back home and to a proper medical checkup."

The oldest of the young women spoke with Kamala, then she took Gage's hand and pressed his knuckles between her eyes.

"Kamala?" Gage asked as a second one did the same.

"It's how we say thank you." He held out his hand to the oldest and received the same honor.

"What do I—"

"Nothing. The more you acknowledge the thanks, the more you devalue the act. For this, do not speak of what happened to them ever again, or you'll insult them."

"Fair enough."

****

Bertram carried a box of stolen goods to the middle of the clearing and set it down next to a neat stack of cases.

"That's the last of it," he said, wiping his hand

across his brow. "The weather never gets better, does it? Just hotter and wetter. We'll have to swim back to base camp at this rate."

His eyes went over the line of equipment packs…his gaze stopped at the last missile tube strapped tight to Clyde's gear.

"Commodore Gage, sir?"

Gage looked up from a data slate where he was cataloging the contents of an open case.

"What is it?"

"Just a thought, but what about the G9? We can't leave it out there where another pirate could fix it up. Who knows what kind of trouble that would lead to?"

"All the pirates are dead," Clyde said.

Bertram elbowed him in the side and said, a bit too loudly, "Well, those poor ladies were under so much stress. Maybe they got their count wrong. There's one or two more in those woods. If we just leave that shuttle in its repairable state and…"

"What're you getting at, Bertram?" Gage asked without looking up.

"We've another mortar tube…" Bertram shrugged his shoulders, then gave Clyde a wide-eyed look.

"It makes perfect tactical sense, sir." Clyde perked up as Bertram's idea spread. "Leave nothing for the enemy. We blow up the G9 with the mortar. Perfect strategic…continuity…of operations. Yes."

Gage finally looked up. He shook his head slowly.

"Could use the fire to signal the incoming shuttle," Chief Eisen said. "Helpful, what with all the interference in the atmosphere. Doubt the civilians can make that hike back to the city. I'd rather not spend the night out here, listening to Bertram whine about drop bears."

"Master Chief Eisen," Gage said.

"Sir."

"Have the men destroy the pirate shuttle with our last mortar. I expect better aim this time."

"All right, lads, you heard the man. Time to blow shit up!" Bertram announced to the rest of the sailors. "In a most professional manner, of course."

CHAPTER 4

A man wearing an untucked shirt and stained pants relied on a wall to stay upright as he shambled down the sidewalk.

"You tell her I hope she's happy with him!" he slurred at a passing couple. He took a sip from a metal flask and lost his grip on the wall. His shoulder thumped against the faux-brick exterior, but he didn't spill a drop of his drink.

"They *deserve* each other!" He tilted his head back for another swig, then sank to the ground and kicked his legs out.

"Always knew he had an eye for her…bastard." His chin sank to his chest, then his head lolled from side to side. Bleary eyes stared across the street to a two-story townhouse nestled between a robot services emporium and a clothing store.

"All right, your little act got an emergency services response," came through the drunk's earpiece.

"No activity from the target location," the drunk mumbled. "Surveillance still have all four suspects inside?"

A bird flit overhead and landed on a windowsill two stories above the drunk's head. He waited as the artfully disguised drone examined the townhouse.

"All four still there. Heat maps of their bodies consistent with everyone who's been in and out of that house for the last two days...You sure about this, Tolan? Bunch of well-behaved nobodies in that house, and this is a nice neighborhood. We could have them all picked up by uniforms the next time they go to work."

Tolan sniffed at the alcohol soaked into his clothes, then took a sip from his tea-filled flask.

"One is always in the house ready to destroy any and all evidence. This is a state security matter, not local police. Your input was received and ignored. Deliver the crawfish on my mark," Tolan said and then slumped against a garbage can.

"You get to go back to the ivory tower after this. I get to clean up your mess, thank you very much. Drone in the air. Squad car with your assault team on the way."

A teenage boy walked in front of Tolan and did a double take.

"Hey, mister. You OK?" He reached for Tolan's shoulder.

"Piss off!" Tolan made a lazy swipe that missed by a mile. "That bitch locked me out of my own house. She wants freedom to-to-to live her own life…so I'm going to live my life out here with the only thing I can trust." He took a drink.

"That sounds…rough. Maybe you have a friend I could call?"

A delivery quad-copter buzzed overhead and hovered over a lockbox two doors down. It slid a package the size of a cinder block into the box and zipped away. The top of the lockbox stayed open.

"Don't need a good smarayman right now. Beat it." Tolan squirmed away from the teenager.

"There's a church around the corner. Pastor Smith is a good listener. Let me help you up…" He reached for Tolan's wrist.

A police cruiser rounded the corner. In the target house, someone peeked around the edge of the curtains.

Tolan grabbed the teenager and looked him in the eye with a stone-cold sober expression.

"Son. You need to leave. Right. Now."

"What the—what's going on here?"

Six darts rose out of the open lockbox with a high-pitched whine. The crawfish drones flew across the street and broke through windows on the first and second floor of the townhouse.

A bright flash of light erupted from the home, like a bolt of lightning had been born and died within its confines. The afterimage seared across Tolan's eyes, blinding him.

Through a tinnitus roar in his ears, he heard the meddlesome teen crying in shock. Tolan blinked hard…then saw the police cruiser driving right for them. He grabbed the kid by the shirt and shoved him into the street. Tolan got his feet under him and jumped up, cleared the hood of the cruiser by inches, then took the windshield against his thigh. The impact sent him rolling over the cruiser and spilled him onto the sidewalk.

Tolan used the momentum and stopped on his hands and feet. He looked up at the townhouse, which was completely dark. Every building and light source was without power. The faux-bird drone lay in the street, wings broken from a bad landing.

"Control, was that an EMP?" Tolan reached behind his back and drew two sidearms, one with a much larger barrel than the other.

The lack of response from the command center

was all the answer Tolan needed. He felt sick to his stomach as he realized the suspects inside the house were using this confusion to either escape or destroy any trace of their crimes.

He aimed the wide-barreled pistol at the doorframe and fired three times. Each shot of breach gel stuck to the frame and the doorknob, changing color from black to red as the chemical goo reacted to the air.

Tolan raced over to the teenager sprawled in the middle of the road and put himself between the coming explosion and the teen.

A sharp crack blew the door off its hinges and sent it barreling through the house with a crack of breaking wood. Tolan tossed the breach gun aside and ran through the smoking entrance, his other pistol held high and ready.

The door-turned-projectile had torn gouges along the walls before crashing into the kitchen and leaving a sizable dent in the refrigerator. Tolan stopped in the doorway as a rancid smell assaulted his senses. The scent of burning BBQ and burning copper filled his nose and stung his eyes.

There, lying over the threshold to the living room, an arm stretched into the hallway. The flesh was burnt black, and white tips of bone jutted from the remains of fingers. Tendrils of black smoke rose from the arm and pooled against the ceiling.

Tolan squared the corner to the living room and choked down bile. One body sat on a couch, a data slate still gripped over its lap. Two more lay on the floor. All were burnt beyond recognition, jaws frozen open, white teeth bared in silent screams.

A grunt and shuffle of boots against a wooden floor came from the front room.

Tolan turned away from the horrific scene and sidestepped to the open door leading to the living room.

A man lay on the floor, a crawfish drone sticking out from his back. The drone's pincers sent jolts of electricity into the prone man, sending his limbs into spasms with each shock. His face twitched constantly and a line of drool stretched from his lips to the floor.

The crawfish drones were designed to incapacitate and restrain suspects, not torture them. Tolan slipped a set of cuffs from his belt and approached the last living suspect. The electromagnetic pulse must have damaged the crawfish. As an agent in the King's service, he was skilled in many intelligence and combat disciplines. Removing a malfunctioning and electrified drone was not in his repertoire.

He touched the cuffs to the suspect's wrist and got a nasty shock up his arm.

Tolan cursed and shook his half-numb hand. He waited until the crawfish finished a jolt, then snapped the restraint over one wrist. He tried to bring the man's wrists together and got another shock.

"To hell with it." Tolan kicked the crawfish off the man and dropped a knee onto his neck. The man uttered a guttural phrase and tried to get up. Tolan brought the man's wrists together and the restraints locked in place.

"Shemalge! Shemalge!"

"Shut up." Tolan rammed an elbow into the back of his head with enough force to bounce his forehead off the floor. The man went slack, unconscious. The agent took another set of cuffs from his belt and fastened them to the man's ankles. He ran a metal wire to the handcuffs and the restraints tightened, bringing the suspect's feet off the floor and hog-tying him into place.

"Central, one in custody." Tolan tapped at his earpiece but got nothing but intermittent static.

"Mister?" came from the doorway.

Tolan rolled his eyes and looked up at the teenager, who stood slack-jawed, pointing a finger outside.

"The…the police in the cruiser are hurt. They crashed into the Murphy's house. No air bags or crash foam," he said. "What…" He twisted around to look at the three burnt bodies. "I mean…what happened?"

"What's your name, kid?"

"James Seaver."

Tolan felt the left half of his face tingle...the first sign of a more serious issue. One he couldn't have anyone witness.

"James, did you see anything?"

"Well, you were drunk—pretending to be drunk, then—"

"James," Tolan's grip on his pistol went white in frustration, "did you *see* anything?"

"No, sir!"

Tolan sighed in relief as the kid started to get it. The sound of sirens filled the air.

"And I didn't see you either. Let's keep it that way. Get out of here." Tolan got to his feet.

James took a tentative step back, his head twisting from the bound man to the three smoldering bodies.

"Move!"

The teen bolted from the house and then down

the street.

Tolan went to the front doorway and found a cracked mirror bolted to the wall. The left side of his face had gone slack, like he'd survived a stroke, and the color on that half had bled away to alabaster white.

"Not now…please not now." Tolan pressed a hand over his stricken half and concentrated on a mental image of his face as it should be. Taking a metal cigarette case from his pocket and flicking it open, he plucked a thin cigarette from within and pressed one end against his throat. A tiny hidden needle injected a drug that sent a shiver through his body.

He took his hand away from his face and found his reflection as it should be. An itch formed in the back of his mind, a desire that would grow worse in the coming hours.

Tolan went back to the bound man. He'd regained consciousness and stared at Tolan with hatred.

"What's your name?" Tolan asked. "What the hell

happened to your friends?"

The prisoner sneered at Tolan and turned his face away.

"Fine. You'll talk eventually, buddy. How hard that'll be is up to you." Tolan kept his pistol trained on the man as a half-dozen police cruisers and ambulances arrived.

CHAPTER 5

The armory felt like home. The hand-carved wooden pillars against the eight corners ran to the center of the ceiling where a painted fresco of the Genevan Alps' Oath Keeper Peak seemed to look down on Salis. The faint smell of ozone in the air and the round exercise platform made her anxious. She'd trained for years in a dojo just like this, all in preparation for this moment.

Salis, in the middle of a scan ring, clenched muscle groups in response to prompts from a wire diagram of her body floating in the air in front of her. She wore only the barest of undergarments that were surely scandalous by Albion standards. The Genevan had little concerns for modesty between each other.

Royce, his body covered in matte bronze armor that appeared little more than a skin suit, stood beside a Genevan woman as her fingers danced over a holo screen.

"This is your first gestalt?" the stern-faced woman asked.

"Correct." Salis raised a hand and spread the fingers wide, then touched each digit to her palm. The woman, who'd introduced herself as Chiara, had a thick scar from the middle of her forehead to the base of her chin that skirted around her nose and split her lips. To repair such a maim was almost trivial for a surgeon, but a Genevan did not hide wounds earned in the line of duty.

The scan ring powered down and Salis' heart began pounding.

A panel opened on a wall, and an upright, clear coffin slid out and floated toward Salis. A suit of bronze armor sized for a man larger than Salis floated within. The armor's visor was modelled after helms from Earth's medieval past. Salis stared into the darkness beneath the thin wire mesh over the eye sockets.

"This gestalt has served us for eighty-seven years," Royce said. "Through your bond, House Ticino will know your quality."

"I serve to honor my house, my charge, and the gestalt," Salis continued the ritual words older than all the cities on Geneva.

"How long will you honor your oaths?"

"Until my last dying breath."

The empty armor raised its helm and looked at Salis. A chill ran down the base of her skull and through the neuro-wires stretched through her body. She gasped as the gestalt's presence flowed through her. She lifted a hand and the armor mirrored the gesture. Salis pressed her hand to the coffin in tune with the armor.

The lid slid aside and the bronze metal touched her flesh. She felt a vibration through her fingers as the armor separated and flowed over her hand. Bronze squares and individual links of chain mail ran up her arm as the armor broke apart and reassembled over Salis' body.

She clenched her jaw, feeling the gestalt's touch pass over her shoulder and across her chest and back. The armor formed a ring around the base of her neck...then rose into a helm that covered her head, cutting her off from the world.

+Morgaten+ The gestalt whispered its name to her mind.

Salis. She focused her mind on the word. Communicating with the gestalt would take some practice, but the crude artificial intelligence would become a seamless extension of her body and mind in time.

Her surroundings returned as the gestalt closed around her legs. She lifted a foot as the last of the mail and squares slithered down a calf. She looked at her now-armored hands and squeezed them into fists. Her body felt...larger, almost as if it didn't fit anymore.

"The seal isn't perfect," Chiara said. "Andrin's

pathways are still embedded in the gestalt, but they've nearly faded out. Give it a few more days and the dislocation will ease."

Salis sent a desire to the gestalt and a square slid over an eye. The armor projected a perfect holo for her to "see" through the square and fed her system information.

"Why are some data feeds blocked? I can't locate the royal family…local data feeds only…I'm not even connected to the palace's security network," she said.

"King Frederick hasn't accepted you into his household yet," Royce said. "The gestalt will unlock full functionality once you've sworn yourself to the throne. King's orders."

Royce stepped onto the round sparring mat and gave Chiara a quick glance.

The woman nodded.

The metal ring around the base of Royce's neck stretched up and formed into a helm. Pale blue flashed from the eye lenses and the captain of the King's Guard snapped a punch at Salis' face.

The blade of her hand hit Royce's wrist with a snap of metal on metal. Her gestalt flooded her body with adrenaline as she ducked a hook kick aimed at her temple. She launched a flurry of punches at Royce, her fists moving faster than she'd ever thought possible as her new armor acted in concert with her body.

Salis' knuckles missed Royce's jaw by a hair. The captain drove a knee toward her stomach. Her armor solidified before the blow landed, dispersing the force of the impact across her midsection. He slid his foot behind her leg and tripped her up with an almost casual bump from his shoulder.

Salis rolled with the momentum, dodging a stomp that cracked the dojo mat. Salis stopped, one knee on the mat, and saw Royce charging toward her. She jumped straight up, kicking the tip of her foot toward her attacker. The satisfying impact of her foot to Royce's chin didn't happen as she flipped backwards and landed on her feet.

She looked up and saw a fist an instant before it crashed into the bridge of her nose. Her gestalt braced armor against her neck and saved her from a blow that would have killed a normal person. Her vision swam as the blow knocked her onto her backside. Her left arm swung across her face without her even thinking of it and deflected a kick away from her throat.

Salis swept a leg into Royce's ankle hard enough to trip him up and send him to the ground. She dove on top of him, pummeling his head with hammer blows that managed to either glance off his helmet or strike the floor as he evaded her attacks.

Royce lowered a hand to his waist, leaving his neck exposed. Salis locked a hand in place. The armor on her fingertips lengthened into knife points and she readied a blow that would rip into the thin armor over Royce's jugular.

A flash of steel came up with the captain's hand, a knife driving straight for her heart.

Salis angled her locked hand toward her weapon, but her armor fought against her, trying to carry out the original attack on Royce's exposed neck. Her striking arm jerked to a halt.

Royce reached up and tapped a code into the base of Salis' helm. Her armor lost all power and pulled her to the mat with its tremendous weight. Salis lay on her side, shame burning through her heart. For a fighter to disengage another's gestalt in a fight was a humiliation, no matter how more experienced the opponent.

Royce got to his feet, then dropped the knife in front of her face. The blade was nothing more than a dull lump of metal, no threat to her armor.

"You had a killing blow, yet I beat you. Why?" Royce asked.

"My gestalt…it knew the blade wasn't a threat, but I didn't. We acted against each other." Salis raised a heavy arm and slammed a fist to the mat.

"Your gestalt is older, wiser. You must learn to

trust it." Royce motioned to Chiara and Salis' armor came back online.

"Marginal combat effectiveness from her," the woman said. "Let me put her through the paces with robots and a few hours on the firing range."

Royce grabbed Salis by the forearm and hauled her onto her feet. He rapped the back of his knuckles against her collarbone, an old Geneva way of thanking another for a good fight. Salis withdrew her helmet with a thought, her cheeks red with embarrassment.

"I'm taking her to the armory for a sidearm and shield. We have a matter of honor to attend to," he said.

"She doesn't need to know about—"

"She does. The King will question her before he accepts her oath. There is no hiding what happened."

Chiara shook her head.

"What's happened?" Salis asked.

"Come. I'll explain on the way."

****

Tolan watched a screen of the man in the interrogation room, his hands shackled to a table, his ankles similarly bound to a chair bolted to the floor. Tolan tugged at his lips as the man mumbled a word over and over again.

"Any hit on that word 'shemalge'?" Tolan asked over his shoulder.

Director Ormond, chief of the Albion Intelligence Ministry, shook his head.

"Linguists at the university can't place it," Ormond said. "After all those years running around with the freaks in wild space, I half-expected you to know what he's been saying."

"Wild space is full of religious fanatics, techno-arcanists, pirates, and lots of normal men and women that just want to be left the hell alone," Tolan said. "I didn't meet any 'freaks.'"

"I get that you had to go native to accomplish

your mission, but you're in civilization again. Time to remember who you were and what Albion values. You've got a mountain of vacation time and back pay waiting for you. I expect you to make the most of it once this...situation is resolved."

"I'll relax the minute Ja'war is executed for his crimes. When is his trial?"

Ormond clicked his tongue. "About that. More than half the nations involved in the last war lost senior diplomats in the attack on Westminster Station. There's a pretty long list of political bodies that want their hands on Ja'war."

"We have a mountain of evidence pinning the attack on him. A recorded confession. Drag him in front of a magistrate and send him to the gallows. I volunteer as hangman."

"But who hired him?" Ormond tossed his hands up in frustration. "Albion fought in the war. We pushed for it to end as soon as the shooting started. There were plenty of losers when the armistice was finally agreed to. The biggest brains in human space think one of the nations that lost territory and ships wanted the war to keep going so they could recover what they lost—that's why someone hired Ja'war to hit the negotiations. If we just execute him before anyone else has the chance to get their hands on him, it'll look like Albion has something to hide."

"I could have killed him on Scarrus. But instead I brought him back for justice. Justice, boss. Not to be a pawn in a blame game for a war that ended two decades ago." Tolan abandoned his normal poker face of impartiality and let his anger show on his face and through his words while speaking with his commander and longtime mentor.

"You went through a lot to catch him." Ormond put a hand on Tolan's shoulder. "Lost good people along the way. Bringing him back was the right thing to do, even though it's caused an enormous pain in my ass. The wounds from the war are still fresh for some. The Indus and Cathay are at each other's throats over neutral-zone violations. We flub Ja'war's situation and that may be all the excuse they need to start shooting."

"Shemalge," came over the speakers from the interrogation room.

Tolan picked up a data slate and swiped a finger over the surface. A bio scan of the man came up. Pictures from a deep cell scan popped up and down the man's back. Silver filigree laced through his spinal cord.

"This tech," Ormond said, "was badly damaged when the crawfish sent the initial shock pulse through his system. Whatever EMP ripped through the house damaged him even further. Doesn't conform to any known augments or neurological therapy. It isn't a stretch to connect the implants to whatever burnt the other three into a crisp."

"We have positive ID on the dead?" Tolan asked.

"No biometric markers survived the…crisping.

Can't even get DNA. Techs say they've never seen anything like it. We swept the house and got hits on four individuals. One body had a woman's frame and a build similar to the initial subject in the investigation; got a DNA match for her too from a bedroom."

"That's not a hundred percent, but enough to work on." Tolan pressed his hands into a steeple and tapped his fingers together as he watched the prisoner on the screen.

"Bunch of nobodies," Ormond said. "No connection to any critical security systems. I've got my squirrels building out their social networks now. The only other lead we had is exhausted. The King is convinced the four were here to spring Ja'war out of prison. He wants to know who sent them here."

"Yes, that would be most illuminating. Any law firms with connections to off-world powers come sniffing around to provide counsel?"

"None. Not even the usual ambulance chasers."

"Odd…" Tolan stood up and pulled his skin taut over his temples.

"We'll get you to a surgeon who'll—"

"Later, boss. We'll worry about that later." Tolan looked in a mirror and concentrated on the face he'd worn when he'd run into the prisoner's home. His features morphed: a bigger nose, darker skin, and a suitable five o'clock shadow. He thinned his lips slightly, then stepped out of the observation room.

The armed guards outside the interrogation room nodded to Tolan.

"Instructions?" one asked.

"Don't come in unless he breaks his restraints." Tolan put his palm to a sensor on the doorframe and the reinforced panel slid aside.

The prisoner didn't acknowledge Tolan as he entered and sat down.

Tolan ran the fingertips of one hand across the table, noting the unacceptable amount of dust his touch accumulated. The room hadn't seen use in some time. Albion hadn't had a real threat since the last war ended so long ago. Peace had broken out across settled space. The only reason Albion had an oversized navy was for regular forays against pirates in wild space. Complacency was evident everywhere he looked in the palace. Tolan could accept that he was overly paranoid, a survival trait he'd cleaved to while undercover in the near-anarchy of worlds where Ja'war had been in hiding.

The man across from him was an enigma. His implants didn't conform to anything in known space…and his rather dull lifestyle was at odds with the mystery of him and his dead roommates. There was one thing that Tolan knew better than any intelligence agent on this side of the galaxy, and that was Ja'war the Black.

"Darren Polonius." Tolan said the man's name and tapped out a quick beat on the table. "Sous chef at a steak house on Exeter's spaceport. Before that you were a galley mate on the trader *St. Barts*." Tolan paused, watching

Polonius' reaction to the ship's name. The man kept his head down.

"The ship had an interesting trade route, came awfully close to wild space several times during the years you were aboard. Bet you met some interesting characters while you were out there," Tolan said. "They say a man can have anything he wants in wild space, so long as he's willing to pay the price. That how you got your implants?"

Polonius chuckled.

There's something, Tolan thought.

"You know the penalty for undocumented augmentation? Ten years on a prison asteroid breaking out ore with a gravity pick. Immediate removal of the implants. Just need a writ from a judge for that, no trial or jury. You want to tell me about what's woven into your spine before the docs get ahold of you? They won't be careful—they're shielded from malpractice suits while carrying out a judicial order. Ten years in jail is rough. It's even worse if you're a quadriplegic."

Polonius looked up. One of his eyes twitched and the pupil dilated slowly.

"Maybe you liked wild space during your time on the *St. Barts*. Maybe I could get you back out there, help find a doctor that can fix you up, but I need you to cooperate."

The prisoner's face went slack. His mouth opened and closed, like he was trying to remember how to speak.

"Malarai Shemalge," Polonius said.

"What's that?"

"There's a slicer on Tokara." The words rasped out of Polonius' throat. "Malarai Shemalge can fix me."

"Tokara…that's a planet in wild space, right? Big place, I'm sure. You want to give me some more information on this Malarai…" Tolan paused as Polonius stiffened at the word, "…this Malarai person."

"Malarai Shemalge," the prisoner spat, struggling against his restraints for the first time.

"Where does he or she work? If your health takes

a bad turn, we can have him here in a few days. Help me out."

"Clinic on the Shigewa River, couple miles north of Naha City. Make sure you ask for the right Malarai Shemalge. She has a gene twin that does womb edits. Not what I need," Polonius said. "You know her name?"

"I've got it." Tolan stood up, noting the twinge of frustration across Polonius' face. "You want something to drink? You sound parched."

Tolan backed out of the room and returned to the observation lounge where Ormond was waiting for him.

"You got us a lead. Well done," the intelligence director said.

"He lied to me." Tolan clasped his hands behind his back and began pacing across the small room. "I was on Tokara running down a lead on Ja'war the same time our subject was bouncing around the *St. Barts*. Couple years before that, the Shigewa River flooded out the entire valley when a glacier broke loose from an ice shelf. A wall of water spread Naha City across the ocean floor. Tens of thousands dead. Tragedy."

"If this guy is a spy for a major power, he's not a good one," Ormond said. "Even if we didn't have someone with your firsthand knowledge of wild space, it would take…twelve, maybe fourteen days to get a courier ship to and from Tokara and confirm that he's lying to us."

"He bought himself time. If I go back in there, I bet his slagged augments will start giving him fits. Two weeks…a lot can happen. Still, there's something bothering me. I got to know most every ethically challenged flesh sculptor in wild space while I was making—" Tolan gestured to his face. "—this work. None ever used tech like what Polonius has wrapped around his spine. Whatever suicide switch he and the others have, I don't think it's wild-space tech."

"That kind of augment violates more parts of the Vitruvian Accords than I can think of off the top of my head," Ormond said. "Any intelligence agency that got caught using that would put their parent government in a heap of trouble with the League. Too much risk, not enough reward, especially when the old standbys of a poisoned tooth or subdermal toxin can still kill a compromised spy."

"He may not be an agent of a foreign power." Tolan tugged at his bottom lip. "His story and travel don't fit with being part of a wild-space group either."

"Why don't you go ask Ja'war about him?"

"Ja'war worked alone. Always. His clients never met him face-to-face." Tolan laughed derisively. "Which is what made catching him so damn difficult. He has no idea who this guy—or his barbequed friends—are. I already know the answer; no point in asking Ja'war."

"So what am I supposed to tell the King?"

"We don't know." Tolan shrugged. "Not yet, at least. In the meantime, we should put the navy and internal security on high alert."

"The whale passage festival starts tomorrow, you know that? There are eighty-seven slip transport ships loading and unloading freight from orbit. You expect me to go to the King, tell him to make things miserable for tourists, dignitaries, and every last potential complainer that has his ear? He'll ask me why and I'll have to do this…" Ormond raised his palms and shrugged his shoulders almost up to his ears.

"There's something more to this situation than just Ja'war being in our custody. We got this lead from that Genevan who developed a guilty conscious. There's a deeper connection we haven't found yet. Tell the King that people don't just burst into flames when the police knock on the door. Better safe than sorry."

Ormond shook his head. "You've been out in the field way too long, Tolan. The galaxy is at peace. The King won't turn the system upside down just because a few events don't fit the normal mode. I'll see him tonight, pass on what we've learned. He may want an audience to congratulate you for capturing Ja'war. I'll encourage it, despite how the Genevan will react to your augmentations, so long as you keep the conspiracies down here."

"I like being paranoid; keeps me alive," Tolan said.

"I need more than that to convince the King," Ormond said and left the room.

CHAPTER 6

Gage waited as Kamala led the four rescued Siam down the shuttle ramp and to a waiting team of Albion medical personnel. This landing pad of the Lopburi spaceport held field hospital quick emplacement tents and a constant in and out of medical ships ferrying injured Siam to ships in orbit.

"Master Chief, deliver the recovered property to Siam law enforcement, then return the men to their normal duties," Gage said.

"Aye aye, but they're from a cannon crew on the *Orion*. Colonel Horton's already pulled down every sailor that's not vital to keeping a ship in orbit. They'll be back clearing debris or installing solar plants soon as their warm bodies are ready. Least we'll stay busy this deployment—tends to keep the men out of trouble. Was a pleasure, Commodore," the Chief said. He turned back to the other sailors and set them to unloading the crates recovered from the pirate landing site.

"Back to the ship, sir?" Bertram asked. "Showers. Food served with proper silverware. No carnivorous bears overhead."

"The Admiral expects my report," Gage said as he wiped ash off a forearm screen and grimaced as it synched with the local data network. E-mail alerts, missed calls, and texts scrolled up the screen. "Gone for eight hours…missed two days of work. Sartorius is in the command center."

Gage locked his helmet to his lower back and went down the ramp, with Bertram following a few steps behind.

A gust of hot wind blew across the landing pad. The heavy scent of ozone from idling shuttle engines gave way to something else as the air settled. Death. A massive pile of debris at one edge of the pad, bulldozed aside by the Albion pathfinder teams and engineers to clear the spaceport for landers, still held the remains of Siam that died in the tsunami. Colonel Horton had directed his crews to focus on rescue operations for those still trapped in collapsed buildings or beneath the wave-born destruction, not the dead.

Gage didn't fault the man for the decision. The smell was a small price to pay for saving lives. Gage veered into rows of open cargo containers, sidestepping robots moving from container to container as they amassed requisition orders for later delivery.

"Sir, where are you—watch my foot, you blasted thing—" Bertram kicked at and missed a robot as it zipped past him. "—going? The automation master will be most cross if he catches us in here futzing with his minions' algorithms."

Gage ducked into a cargo container that had been

ignored by the robot swarm. Inside were small toys, children's video projector cubes, and a box full of shrink-wrapped packages. He tossed a pair to Bertram, then stuffed one into a hip pouch.

"Hungry, sir?"

"Thinking ahead." Gage hurried out of the container and toward a domed prefabricated building with many smaller tents attached to the outside.

"I used to think about opening a restaurant on Siam once my enlistment was up," Bertram said. "Albion comfort food: Scotch eggs, Strammer Max, bacon cheeseburgers, fried just about anything. Proper beer, not the piss they drink. Give those rich well-born on safari a taste of home after a taking a turn in the bush or going after those puma things in the mountains. At a premium price, naturally."

"'Used to think?'"

"Whole planet's been knocked down to the Stone Age. Wasn't a single operating power plant when we arrived. What's the estimate on the death toll? Fifty percent? Then there's the nuclear winter that's coming. The Siam might be better off if we relocated them all to Coventry or one of the other colonies."

"I doubt they'll ever leave. The local religion is a mix of Buddhism and Animism. Their family spirits are in the land…more so after this," Gage said. "They'll fight on. We can mitigate the atmosphere changes with particulate kites. There's time to stop the worst of it. Not like Earth after Mount Edziza erupted and sent the whole planet into a new Ice Age."

"Siam's lucky they've got neighbors like us. What did Earth have? Couple colonies on Mars full of skinny ingrates that could barely grow enough food to feed themselves—not billions starving on the home world."

"If it weren't for the Mars colonies keeping the fire of civilization and technology alive, you and I would probably be hunting caribou on the Dakota ice shelf with spears," Gage said.

"Let a man have his grumbles, sir. Costs nothing to poke fun at those Martian degenerates in their iron caves."

Gage entered the central tent and stopped beneath a mechanical arm tipped with nozzles and camera diodes. A technician behind a glass wall gave his dirty uniform a once-over, then shrugged. The arm emitted a harmless laser line the width of a pencil and scanned him from head to toe. A spritz of antiseptic fog hissed over his hands and the bottom of his feet.

"Cholera and typhoid cases popped up around the east refugee camps," the tech said. "Do use proper sanitation facilities and wash your hands regularly." A green light blinked over a doorway.

Inside the main room, work areas were divided into neat wedges around a raised platform. Printed signs hung from the back of each wedge, marking the area for medical, construction, sanitation, mortuary, and other segments of the Albion relief effort. On the platform,

Gage found Admiral Sartorius, Colonel Horton, and several Siam civilians and naval officers.

He traded greetings as he made his way up the stairs. Bertram stayed back, chatting with the steward of the *Concordia*'s captain.

Admiral Sartorius stood straight-backed with his hands clasped behind him, his neatly cropped beard and receding hairline of ivory-white hair almost gleaming beneath the light of the tall holo tank on the platform. He made no reaction to Horton's next words.

"My team of engineers finally found the fault with the geo-thermal power lines along the Sepon River; they're demolished," said Colonel Horton, who looked like he hadn't slept in days. "Aftershocks from the seismic event of the asteroid's landing pulverized the transfer stations at nodes alpha through epsilon. We're looking at a complete rebuild before we can get power from the plant to the outlying cities. Time frame is months, and that's after we get proper excavators from Albion."

"So much for the quick fix," Sartorius said. "What about the orbital solar collectors?"

"Computer models give the collectors sixty hours of functionality before micro-strikes disable them," a naval officer said. "Even then, with all the particulates in the atmosphere, we'd lose half the redirected energy to dispersion."

"Then we'll rely on ground solar arrays until a fusion plant arrives with the next convoy from Albion." Sartorius' eyes glanced at Gage. The Admiral gave him a slight nod.

"Shipboard foundries can produce...ninety ground arrays a day," Colonel Horton said. "Which means they aren't making water purifiers or prefab housing units."

"The housing units can wait," said a Siam woman with wire-rimmed glasses and salt-and pepper hair. "Monsoon season is weeks away, and with the disturbance to the atmosphere, it might not happen at all. We need the

114

power stations for water treatment and sanitation."

President Hu had inherited her post after the last President—and the nineteen officials in line of succession ahead of her—had died in the tsunami. Two weeks ago, she was the vice minister for fisheries; now she was in charge of the entire planet. For everything she'd been through, Gage was impressed she'd held up so well.

"How long until the tent cities in the Sepon valley are ready?" Sartorius asked.

"Ten thousand beds will be ready tomorrow morning," Horton said. "Thirty thousand in the next forty-eight hours; that's assuming the drones keep to the schedule. The crap in the atmosphere is causing malfunctions more often than we're used to."

"There are several hundred thousand people sleeping in what remains of this city or beneath open skies, Colonel. We need to get them someplace more manageable. The ships are on minimal manning as it is. If more sailors can make a difference, we can reduce to prize crews and transfer them down here to work."

"We scared away three pirate ships when we arrived," said Captain Norris of the *Concordia*. "There have been several slip translations detected since then, more vultures circling. If they realize we're down to skeleton crews, they might get bold."

"Your point is taken, Captain. Draw up completion timelines for each manpower course of action and present it to me after mess," Sartorius said.

"Of course." Norris clacked his heels together.

"I'll leave you to your duties." The Admiral walked down the steps and Gage fell in beside him. A pair of armed Marines, Bertram, and Jeneck, the Admiral's steward, followed.

"Commodore, glad to see you back in one muddy piece," the Admiral said as he walked down the gap between wedges to a doorway along the outer wall. Sailors rose to their feet and snapped to attention as he passed. "Successful trip?"

"Four civilians rescued. Wyverns are here, likely leftovers from our initial arrival. They were in a shuttle that could have broken orbit. Must not have a friendly ship anchored to one of the outer planets or anywhere else in the system, else they would have left a long time ago given the amount of stolen goods we recovered," Gage said.

"Good assessment." Sartorius nodded. "Think you'll hear the call to adventure again while you're down here?" The Admiral looked at Gage with a slight smile.

"There was no one else available to help when Mr. Kamala came over the emergency frequency," Gage said. "I doubt we'll have such an incident again. My apologies for leaving your side."

Sartorius chuckled as they exited out the opposite side of the main chamber. A two-story wall of chain-linked fence ran around the spaceport's perimeter. Siam lined up along the wall, waiting for the daily handout of emergency ration packs from an open cargo container with a many-armed robot in the middle. The robot snatched up the

117

bright yellow plastic packs from drone truck beds, each containing dried food, water purification tablets, and foil blankets that could be used to weatherproof damaged houses or to keep warm.

The robot passed packets through holes in the fence, giving one to each person in line and clicking a picture to ensure only one ration went out per capita per day, and kept up a regular pace.

Armed Marines stood nearby, their presence more to dissuade anyone from attacking the robot and food stores than crowd control.

The Siam formed an orderly line, obeying shouted instructions from men and women with torn bits of cloth around their foreheads. After a few difficult days, the Siam realized that the Albion were here to stay and that they'd brought enough food for the survivors. Knowing that they had a meal each day coupled with their slowly improving quality of life had done wonders to restore public order. How the line monitors in headbands came to be, or who they even worked for, was a mystery Gage didn't care to solve. Albion didn't need to address every issue on the planet; they just needed the dying to stop.

The Admiral's clean clothes and chest full of medals earned stares from the Siam, but any that asked questions of him were quickly shouted down by those in headbands. Sartorius stopped by the fence and smiled at a little girl clutching her mother's skirt. He tapped a pocket, then looked at Gage.

Gage opened the packet he'd taken from the cargo container and handed the Admiral a wrapped hard candy. Sartorius pressed it through the fence and the girl snatched it away. Gage passed candy to the Admiral as he went down the line, smiling at children and giving them treats.

Gage's data slate beeped with more e-mails and text messages.

"Sir, status reports from Executive Officer Kelly. She says—"

"Anything important?" Sartorius passed two pieces each to a pair of children with no parents around them.

"Not particularly," Gage said.

"My officers are all capable and well trained. Let me know if anything is bleeding, on fire, or about to enter either of those conditions. Otherwise, keep quiet and let me finish this important duty," Sartorius said.

"Aye aye." Gage held a hand out to Bertram and his steward handed over a fresh bag of candy.

****

Admiral Sartorius and President Hu walked toward a waiting naval shuttle; Gage and the Siam's assistants followed several yards behind as the two spoke.

"I'll dispatch a courier back to Albion within hours," Sartorius said. "If you need to update the logistics request, send it to Commodore Gage. We can expect the next convoy in five or six days, slip stream dependent."

"Your generosity and empathy speak well of your world," Hu said. "While we will have the worst damage under control soon, the climate effects from the mine's explosion will plague us for generations."

Sartorius stopped and looked toward the setting sun. Spectacular bands of red and orange painted the sky, rising far higher than the sunsets Gage remembered from Albion. A flurry of meteors zipped across the sky.

"Terra-forming engineers could stave off the worst of it," the Admiral said, "but such efforts are costly. Very costly."

Hu swallowed hard and said nothing.

"Time to return to the *Orion*," Sartorius said, continuing on to the waiting shuttle. He put one foot on the ramp, then turned back to Hu. "Do send on anything else you may need. Farewell, Madame President."

"And you, Admiral." Hu pressed her palms together over her chest and bowed slightly.

Gage followed his commanding officer but

stopped when Hu tugged on his arm.

"Ma'am?" Gage whipped out a stylus from his sleeve and put the tip to a data slate, ready to record.

Hu took his hand with the stylus still held between his fingers and pressed his knuckles to her forehead.

"Kamala told me what you did for us. You are a good man." She let his hand go and walked off before Gage could reply.

He hurried up the ramp and found the Admiral already strapped into his plush leather seat embroidered with his name and a flag with the 11th Fleet's colors. Gage sat across from the Admiral and readied for the flight back into orbit as the rest of the Admiral's travelling entourage filed into seats in the back of the cargo bay.

"Tell me, Thomas, how long until President Hu formally requests protectorate status?" Sartorius asked.

"I'm sorry…a protectorate? Siam has been fiercely independent since it was first founded. Neutral through all the wars, fending off the larger pirate gangs. That it would all change now…"

"Siam was neutral because they were never worth fighting over." Sartorius took a glass of ice water from a steward's tray. "The only core-world slip connection they have is with Albion. Any of the other powers that had eyes on this place would have to go through us. This world is pretty, and that's about all."

"So we're here for more than just humanitarian reasons…"

"We would've come to stop the suffering no matter what; that's King Randolph for you. But the cost and effort to stop a full-blown nuclear winter…we're looking at a significant commitment. Very significant."

The ramp closed with a snap and cool, dry air flooded around them. Sighs of relief went up from the seats behind Gage and the Admiral.

"Siam sits on the edge of wild space," Gage said. "They've nexus with a dozen other systems, most under pirate control. There have been rumors that the last few presidents allowed transit for marauder squadrons into the core worlds, but they were just rumors."

"Rumors? Hardly." Sartorius drained his cup as the shuttle's engines kicked on. "President Lin—rest his soul—paid tribute to Harlequins, Totenkopf, and Triad bosses to keep them off his planet *and* let them come and go as they pleased. The raids on Tribeca and Cannes were both traced back through here. Every disaster is also an opportunity. Now we have a chance to cut off a compliant avenue of attack for the pirates."

"Why didn't we do anything before now?" Gage asked.

"You're a smart man. You tell me."

Gage pressed his lips into a thin line as he considered his response. "The Second Reach War started when the Reich took over a half-terra-formed world the Biafra Empire claimed. Ten years of war between the core worlds and billions dead later, we have the Accords. Well, we almost have the Accords. The terrorist attack at the ratification convention kept everything in limbo."

"The Accords are in effect in practice, if not law," Sartorius said. "Claiming sovereignty over new worlds is now a very bureaucratic process—which might explain why new colonies are few and far between these days."

"We couldn't put any real pressure on Siam to stop the pirates because we had no leverage," Gage said. "A little tourism, minor trade; nothing compared to what they had with wild space. If we send over a fleet to stop the pirates from using this place as a launching point for rough slip transit to the core…the other powers would step in."

"Exactly. The Accords are unwieldy, slow and a mess of fat bureaucrats doing little more than forwarding e-mails around to each other, but they keep everyone honest. A unilateral move by Albion would give the Reich—or some other state that's itching to flex their military muscles—an excuse to fight. It's been too long since we've had a proper war. Too many in power have forgotten what it's like to see ships burning in space...cities bombarded from orbit."

"But if Siam petitions to become part of Albion space, then there's no violation of the Accords." Gage ran his hand over his restraints as the shuttle rumbled into the air. "That doesn't mean there won't be any complaints. If the pirates can't come through here, then they'll find another unaligned border world. It shifts the problem to someone else."

"You're thinking ahead. Good. No doubt we'll launch more anti-pirate expeditions into wild space to make others happy. Interstellar politics can be a zero-sum game."

"You think President Hu knows what the long game is? She might tell us to leave if the choice is between our help and annexation versus going it alone."

Sartorius looked out a porthole to the devastation stretching from the shoreline and through Lopburi City.

"If she tells us to leave tomorrow, how many of

her people will die? If she tells us to leave a year from now, before the terra-formers can sift out all the dirt in the atmosphere, how many will die? We're not the Quantou Dynasty or the Caliphate that would kick them off world or enslave them. They can keep their religion, their language, their culture, even their silly voting customs. We need their skies. Do our ulterior motives bother you?"

"We serve at the King's command. My opinions are irrelevant."

"No one doubts your loyalty, son, but you didn't answer my question."

Darkness passed over the portholes as the shuttle ascended through the upper atmosphere.

"Siam is in a difficult position," Gage said. "The disaster is of their own making. No core world would ever mine an asteroid that size so close to an inhabited world for exactly the reasons we're here. Our aid will save lives, but accepting our help is almost Pyrrhic for their sovereignty. I see the humanity in helping them. I see the benefit of incorporating them into Albion's fold, but I fear they will resent it. A choice between your children dying from disease or starvation against any other option that promises life isn't much of a decision. I see the logic—the value—in what comes later. King Randolph is a wise man."

"For almost twenty generations, the royalty of Albion have been trained since birth to make such wise decisions," Sartorius said. "I'm glad the last King chose Randolph as his successor. Could you imagine if we went by straight succession? We'd have King Christopher, that fop. Last I heard he's on Beverly Station, leading some sort of variety show. Twenty minutes to the *Orion*, enough time for a ten-minute nap." The Admiral tucked his head against the side of his seat and closed his eyes.

"Yes, sir." Gage took his data slate from a pocket and skimmed through e-mail, looking for anything vital to pass on to the Admiral once he woke up. He looked out across Siam, through the haze of shields as they deflected micro-meteors.

He'd marched into the jungle to save the civilians for no other reason than to help the weak, the suffering. Did Albion's eventual goal detract from what he'd done? He stared at the star field and passing shuttles as their ship entered hard vacuum.

Those girls didn't seem to care about why they were saved from pirates, only that they wouldn't be sold into slavery, he thought. *If Albion's motivations extend beyond altruism, does it even matter? Lives will be saved. A planet pulled back from the brink of disaster. Security and safety for the Siam.*

Gage scrolled through an ever-growing list of messages, debating what Sartorius had shared. He could accept doing the right thing for questionable motives, but he still didn't feel good about it.

CHAPTER 7

A crowd of citizens flowed by a double door recessed into the castle's outer wall on their way to a pier extending into the bay. Enormous screens floated over the packed harbor area where people thronged around food vendors and open-air stalls. Each screen showed the same image, a small set of steps at the far end of the pier surrounded by armed Albion soldiers and a pair of Genevans.

Salis stood beside the castle access door, scanning the passersby. Another Genevan named Lucan was on the other side of the doorway. For the past half hour, the crowd had slowly contracted around the pier, which had been full since before Salis took her post.

"Underwater sensors have the whales en route," Lucan said over their suit-to-suit network. "King will move soon."

In the crowd, a man wearing a red and white jersey blinked on Salis' faceplate.

"Got a biometric trip," she said. "Elevated heartrate, neural action consistent with aggression."

"Need a face for the database," Lucan said.

Her gestalt nudged her attention toward a bar stall. The man in the jersey walked close to it, and she picked up his reflection from a tip jar. She snipped his face from her HUD with the barest movement of her fingers and sent the image to Lucan.

"Known narcotics user," the other bodyguard said. "His bio's in line with a recent hit of ersatz cocaine. I'll send it to the locals for action. Not our responsibility. Good technique with the reflection grab. Your gestalt teach it to you?"

"Yes, how'd you know?"

"Andrin liked that trick. The personalities of previous wearers fade from the armor in time, but some things stick with the gestalt, almost like instinct. You must be synching well if the gestalt is sharing this with you."

"I don't have much of a frame of reference." The armor pressed onto her shoulders, almost as if the gestalt within was sad. Salis decided to change the topic away from the absent Genevan and keep the gestalt focused on the job at hand. "I'm a bit surprised that we're being ignored by the Albians. Few pictures taken from the crowd. No nuisance or harassment. I trained for much worse."

"We're exempt from local laws by contract, but it's illegal to impede us in our duties. If anyone tries to take their picture with us or address us for any reason other than official business, we send up their bio reading. Offender receives a fine in the mail. Noncitizens get a levy when they leave the planet. Keeps things running smoothly."

"I'm anxious to get access to the local networks. I can't say I feel entirely useful right now."

"King Randolph has his quirks. Doesn't want to put his full trust into someone until he's looked them in the eyes."

"Such as things are," Salis said, paraphrasing an old Genevan saying for accepting fate.

"Principal moving." Lucan raised his head to the right and a hovercraft flew over the outer wall. A cheer rose from the crowd, starting at the very edge where the hovercraft flew over and spreading down to the tip of the pier.

The craft stopped near the steps and Captain Royce jumped out of a hatch. After he quickly swept the area, a ramp lowered from the hovercraft. The crowd cheered even louder as Prince Jarred, Prince Nathaniel, and Princess Daphne, all adults in their thirties, descended, all waving and smiling. Salis felt a chill from her gestalt as a rumble rose through the crowd.

King Randolph came halfway down the ramp, a wide smile showing within his salt-and-pepper beard. His crown was little more than a circlet atop his thinning hair. He was healthy-looking and broad-shouldered, and Salis found some comfort in knowing she'd swear an oath to defend a man that at least cared enough to take care of himself.

Queen Calista came behind him, dressed in a shimmering silk gown that would have driven the finest fashion lords of the haute couture of Reuilly or Gangnam green with envy. She led a small boy by the hand, who was positively wide-eyed at the throng of people along the pier. The hovercraft rose straight up, where it remained ready to return at the barest hint of danger.

"Quite the age disparity between the children," Salis said.

"Prince Aidan was a surprise," Lucan said.

"Which is in line to inherit the throne?"

"Albion doesn't do succession by age. The King or Queen creates a secret list the day they take the crown. Only royal blood can be on the list, and the sovereign can change it any time they choose. There are expulsions from the royal family from time to time for lack of interest in leading or for conduct, but by and large, the family is deeply vested in leading Albion well," Lucan's head snapped up as a camera drone the size of the palm of his hand rose from the crowd.

A mechanical falcon dove from the battlements over their heads and snatched the drone from the air with a crack of breaking polymers.

"Tourists," Lucan muttered.

"Who's seen the list?"

"Royce, the King and Queen. There's a copy in the deep vaults in case of a catastrophe," Lucan said, quickly crossing himself. "The sovereign abdicates well before they're especially elderly or infirm—tradition. Only twice has Albion lost a king suddenly, both times in war."

The King stepped up to a microphone and all the screens hanging in the air switched to a close-up.

"New Exeter…" Randolph's words boomed

across the crowd and they answered him with a prolonged cheer. "The whales have graced us once again. It was here, in that first season after our ancestors made landfall and settled the city, that Good King Nathaniel the First met the whales and they bestowed their blessing."

Laughter from the crowd.

"Nathaniel got drenched by a whale spout," Lucan said. "The Queen declared it a sign of good fortune and everyone went along with the idea."

"You can't be serious."

"That's why there are so many people on the pier. The wetter you get from the whales, the more good fortune you'll have through the next year."

"And I thought the Cathay were superstitious."

"I was on the pier five years ago, got hit by those beasts. Went home on leave and the missus and I finally conceived. I'll not question it."

King Randolph continued with an almost rote recitation of the prism whale festival. Royce stepped close and whispered into his ear.

"Our cameras tell me the whales are nearly here," Randolph said. "I sent them an exact itinerary, but they think they can ignore their king."

"Same joke every year," Lucan said.

Queen Calista hoisted Aidan onto her hip and the boy began waving his arms wildly.

Around the pier, pale white whales the size of a city bus broke through the surface. Their bodies shimmered, then changed color, like they were made of fractured rainbows.

King Randolph went up the steps and Royce attached a safety line to his belt with a single swift motion. The King spread his arms wide.

"King ever fallen in?" Salis asked.

"Once, before our House was hired. Right before we were hired, actually. Now we'll see if the whales will spout. The wetter the King gets, the longer the holiday."

There was a long, unfortunate pause, then one

whale let off the barest puff of a spout and all the whales sank back beneath the water. Groans of disappointment rippled through the crowd.

Randolph came down the steps and went back to the microphone, his face long.

The Queen came over and gave him a pat on the chest, back, and shoulders. She leaned over to the microphone and said, "I find the King to be rather dry."

"Alas," Randolph said, putting his arm around Calista's waist, "this means work for us all on Monday."

The crowd grumbled, but Salis didn't make out a single boo.

The Queen whispered into Randolph's ear. He frowned, then began nodding with enthusiasm. Salis felt an electricity build in the air.

"The Queen, in her excellent wisdom," Randolph said, "asked me to bestow a boon on you all for your patience, and I agree with my wife…because I am a wise king. I hereby suspend tax on all food and drink for the rest of the weekend. Celebrate responsibly. May the whales grant us even more fortune next year!"

The royal family waved to the crowd as a decent cheer rose around them. The hovercraft returned, and Royce ushered them back on in short order.

"Is that tax excessive?" Salis asked.

"Up to twenty percent on liquor," Lucan said. "Be glad we're not local law enforcement. They're in for a hell of a weekend."

"Small favors."

CHAPTER 8

Gage straightened out his dress uniform top in front of a mirror just outside the Admiral's wardroom. Every medal gleamed and ribbon rows were laser-straight over his chest. The black cloth with gold trim was devoid of the slightest wrinkle or speck of dust. Gage wondered, not for the first time, how Bertram could take such exceptional care of his officer's uniform but be something of a slob himself.

Gage brushed a finger over a fan of scabbed-over scratches near his temple. While preparing for this mess, he'd come across several minor injuries from his time in the jungle. He wore every combat award he'd ever earned, but he wasn't one to flaunt that he'd just come from a life-and-death encounter with pirates.

He pressed his palm to a slate on the doorframe and the entrance slid open with a hiss. The smell of tobacco-scented mist wafted over him as he entered the waiting room where almost two dozen officers chatted with each other.

Most lounged around the carved wood furniture or perused the shelves packed with data slates. A group clustered around a sim table as two teams played Fleet Strike, a tactical simulation with dozens of tiny holo ships pounding away at each other. Admiral Sartorius encouraged officers of similar rank to debate tactics and the issues of the day for an hour before the infrequent formal dinners aboard the *Orion*. He believed that without access to a rugby or football pitch, the officers needed a venue to spark comradery and competition.

Every ship's executive officer in the fleet was here while the Captains and the Admiral entertained themselves in the main dining room. No one was quite sure what they did in there, but guesses ranged from dirty jokes to arcane rituals to determine the next to receive an admiral's star.

"A nip, sir?" A steward had come over, holding a silver tray with several glass snifters, each containing a finger of brandy. The steward's eyes lingered over Gage's ribbons as the commodore picked up a glass. Gage was used to the extra attention. Very few officers in the fleet had a St. Michael's medal for destroying an enemy ship in combat, or a Blood Stripe down the side of their legs for being wounded.

"Thomas, heard you had a dustup down there," said Commander Michael Barlow, executive officer on the *Concordia*.

"Couple Wyverns left behind decided to raid an outlying town. Local guide led us to them. Pirates aren't a problem anymore." Gage took a sip of his brandy.

"You look no worse for wear. Trust you didn't go in with just you and some safari man. Isn't there some dreadful kind of cave bears or something out in those jungles?"

"Took a gunnery crew sent down to work the supply yard. No injuries. Civilians are safe. Can't ask for a better outcome. And they're drop bears…they're horrifying."

"I'll stay up here with the risk of explosive decompression and the freezing grasp of the void, thank you," Barlow said, finishing his drink. "Daresay the crowd's been waiting for you to arrive. You're the only one getting any excitement this trip. We're supposed to be out on maneuvers in the Cygnus Phi sector, not carting supplies back and forth like an armed-to-the-teeth logistics corps squadron."

"Bad luck—or good, if you ask the Siam—that we were about to weigh anchor for slip space when word of the disaster came through. Arriving so fast with a few cargo ships loaded down with supplies saved lives," Gage said.

"Yes, lovely all that, but up here, we're dreadfully bored."

"You could volunteer to come to the surface. A chief would find something meaningful for you to do."

"Ghastly. I'm an officer. I supervise and direct. I don't actually get my hands dirty. Chiefs get all bothered when we try to do more than expected."

"I say, Commodore Gage," a commander called out from the holo table. Arlyss of the *Renown* waved him over.

"Oh, not this twat," Barlow mumbled. "He's been rehearsing this for some time. Be careful."

"If he's not going to shoot me in the face and wear my rank insignia for a trophy, I say he's not the worst man I've come across lately." Gage walked up to the holo table and raised his drink slightly in salute.

"Ladies, gentlemen," he said.

Arlyss tapped his ring against the holo controls as he brought up a simulation. He, like almost all the officers present, wore a Sanquay class ring. The elite officer training school took in only the most well-connected noble-born officer cadets; every admiral in Albion's history wore one of those oversized gold rings.

Gage's thumb rubbed against the back of his class ring, one earned from Portsmouth, a school known best for not being Sanquay.

"We've had a lively debate about you, Gage." Arlyss tapped two fingers against a screen and the holo changed to a single desert world with two ship icons breaking out of orbit.

Gage's chest tightened as the worst day of his life came up for all to see.

"The *Starchaser's* encounter with the Harlequin pirate ship *Robbins* over Volera II…" Arlyss said, "…where you were the gunnery officer serving under Lieutenant Commander Darrens."

"I know. I was there," Gage said with a restrained smile.

"Certainly, but I and our comrades weren't." Arlyss sent the holo into action and the time sped up greatly. The *Starchaser*, Gage's destroyer, closed on the much larger *Robbins*, trading cannon shots and torpedoes that flared out between the two ships as point defense turrets and counter missiles sparred.

"The *Starchaser* was certainly faster than the pirate ship, but they had something of a head start before you engaged in pursuit," Arlyss said. "What I don't understand is why the *Starchaser* did…this."

The holo slowed with a tap from Arlyss. The Albion ship's fire ceased and it veered to port as the maneuver thrusters flared like miniature suns. A pirate torpedo exploded off the prow, sending a storm of metal spikes into the hull.

The deck shaking beneath his feet, the shouts of alarm, and the thick smell of blood played through Gage's mind.

"Now, those of us who went to Sanquay know better than to maneuver into the path of an active torpedo," Arlyss said. "Could you explain why this happened? I would have kept up the pursuit. The lance cannon would have entered effective range two minutes after this…event, ending the engagement in your favor."

"And why do you think the *Robbins* would have been there two minutes later?" Gage asked.

"The slip nexus to Firenze was at least ten minutes away, eight if the *Robbins* captain would risk a rough passage," Arlyss said with a slight roll of his eyes. "The Harlequins have a significant presence there. Of course they'd—"

"Volera II is a significant trade world in that part of wild space," Gage said. "We had an away team investigating stolen goods from a merchant ship attacked by the *Robbins*. Seems the Harlequins had changed the ship's hull and electromagnetic signature after the attack, which is why we didn't pick them up during our arrival. I was dirtside with the team when we encountered the Harlequins with stolen goods. After a brief firefight, the pirates retreated to orbit and led us to their ship. We recovered intelligence telling us that the Harlequins had a buyer for items stolen off the merchant ship that weren't on Volera II...but Deschanel."

Gage swiped his fingertips down the holo tank and called up a menu. A moment later, a slip transit point appeared just ahead of the pirate ship.

"They weren't running for Firenze," Gage said. "I had both the gunnery and sensor feeds coming into my station and saw the fluctuations in *Robbins'* slip drive as she readied for transit. I made the decision to maneuver for a spine cannon shot. At the time, I didn't believe there was a risk from that torpedo." He tapped the exploding weapon in the tank and a screen full of telemetry data popped up next to it. "The *Starchaser*'s electronic warfare systems read that torpedo as defeated. Seems the Harlequins put in a secondary proximity fuse that wasn't tied to the guidance computers—an illegal modification in the core worlds, but pirates..." He shook his head. "Four sailors died in that explosion."

"Why did you have both gunnery and sensor feeds?" one of the onlookers asked. "Trying to manage both while in combat is insane."

"Because Ensign Foche was dead," Gage said. "Gravely injured on the ground by a pirate murder-construct. She died before we could get her back to sick bay. Commander Darrens was off the bridge at the time I ordered the maneuver. He'd lost suit integrity during an earlier hit on the bridge."

Gage twisted an imaginary dial in the holo tank and the replay continued. The *Robbins* streaked forward just as the *Starchaser*'s lance fired. The beam clipped the pirate ship's hull and sent it into a barrel roll, hurtling forward at a much greater velocity than the Albion ship as the slip bubble failed.

"Remarkable construction," Gage said. "I doubt even one of our warships could survive a mis-jump like that. But they had enough distance to evacuate their crew into a smaller slip-capable ship and make it to Deschanel before we could catch up."

He twisted the dial again and the *Robbins* leapt forward. The ship exploded just as the *Starchaser* entered weapon range.

"Seeing her scuttled was a victory. Shame you couldn't catch the crew," Barlow said, "though you did hurt their pride enough for them to declare a vendetta. What's the price on your head now? Five thousand grams of gold?"

"Seven," Gage said. "Seems the Harlequin pirate master that lost the *Robbins*—goes by the name of Loussan—has come to a higher position since this incident and upped the bounty."

"This is why you're forbidden from returning to wild space?" Arlyss asked with a huff.

"I'm most eager to return," Gage said, "but the admiralty thinks it would be better for me to go in something larger than a destroyer. Seems the Harlequins are well known for honoring their bounties. So,

Commander Arlyss, how would you have handled this encounter? Four sailors lost their lives. If you have a way to stop the *Robbins* while paying less of a price, I'd be glad to learn."

The assembled officers all looked to Arlyss.

"Well…well, first I'd…" he stuttered as he wound the recording back to the initial salvo, "…if they really were going for Deschanel, then we could…" His face grew red as a mechanical clock on the wall ticked through the silence.

Jeneck came through a sliding door and stomped a foot against the deck as she braced at attention.

"Dinner is served," she announced.

Officers pulled away from the holo tank and quickly formed a line by rank. While Albion naval officers might hold the same rank on their uniforms, the order of merit on each promotion list let every officer know exactly where they stood above or below their peers. The custom was a holdover from the old wet navy days of America and the United Kingdom, one the navy had no intention of changing.

There were some exceptions. As the fleet admiral's aide, Gage outranked everyone in the room and it was his duty to see everyone seated.

"I dare say that didn't go as Arlyss planned," Barlow said to Gage. "You know he was supposed to be Sartorius' man on this cruise, until you got penciled in at the last second."

"I didn't know that." Gage smiled at Arlyss as he shot him a dirty look before entering the mess. "Makes some sense."

"Well, you're one of those Portsmouth barbarians," Barlow said, wagging his Sanquay-ring-laden finger at him. "Arlyss and his fellow snobs weren't your friends yesterday. Today didn't make things any better. Tomorrow doesn't look good either."

"Barlow," Gage said drolly, "how will I ever survive?"

****

Sartorius drank the last of his brandy and set the glass on a nightstand next to his reclining chair. Albion flag-grade officers had wide latitude in the furnishings for their private quarters. Of all the officers Gage had ever served with, the Admiral's love for the beat-up chair was one of the odder foibles.

Gage sat on a couch across from the Admiral, the top and bottom buttons of his dress uniform undone for comfort. He swiped across a data slate and frowned slightly.

"Captain Simpson had a personnel transfer request for your signature," Gage said.

"Ha! Who's irked him this time?" The Admiral kicked off his shoes and flexed his toes.

"Commander Price, the *Orion's* executive officer. Simpson believes, and I quote, 'Her mental faculties and decision-making capabilities are best suited to shore duty where she cannot endanger sailors or equipment. Further, should she ever—'"

"That's enough." Sartorius waved a dismissive hand at Gage. "Simpson has never met another officer that lives up to his own glorious example. He went through five different bridge crews while he was on battle cruisers. He's never written a single positive officer evaluation during his entire career. The Ministry of Personnel automatically deletes his eval letters when they come in. But I didn't say that to you."

"Say what, sir?"

"Yes, precisely. Simpson's family may have bought their lordship and greased the wheels to get him this command, but he'll go no further. I'll have a word with him about Price. What's next?"

"Another brandy, Admiral?" A blond woman in her early twenties with curly blond hair pulled into a bun stuck her head into the room.

"No, Jeneck, I've had quite enough. I'm about to

tuck in. See you in the morning."

"As you like." She gave Gage a slightly unprofessional smile and disappeared.

"That one's trouble," Sartorius said. "I had my last steward, Smithy, with me for twenty years. Knew me so well he could have led the 11th in an attack on a Reich's fortress world and won the day. Then he comes down with some terrible malady weeks ago. Can't wait to get him back."

"Jeneck seems competent. Her tea is outstanding."

"No sailor will get through the steward's course by burning the leaves. She's just too much of a distraction. I'm loyal to my dear Gracie to a fault, but if anyone sees me with a young and pretty sailor like Jeneck, there are assumptions." The Admiral wagged a finger in the air. "Assumptions. Gracie will have my hide once she sees Jeneck."

"I will testify to your good behavior, sir."

"You've never been married. You don't know

women, my boy."

"My time in the King's service has kept me away from social circles."

"Best that you don't have a lady at home waiting for you. Spending most of any year in the void is no way to be a husband…or a father. How was the conversation in the wardroom before the mess?"

"The usual minutia," Gage said. "Nothing of consequence."

"That the simulation of the Volera II incident came up was of no consequence? Let me guess: Arlyss tried to trip you up."

"An official court of inquiry can find no fault in my decisions, but everyone seems to have an opinion on the incident."

"Opinions are like…" The Admiral reached for his glass and sneered at the melting ice cubes. "Bother…You're much like your father, you know that? He and I were at the Battle of Urien. Different ships, different part of the line, but I remember how he took command of his squadron when the *Baron Franks* was lost. Shame we lost him. Glad you chose to follow in his footsteps."

"I never met him," Gage said. "Just had the pictures of him and Mother. All the stories of him and then-Crown Prince Randolph coming up through the service together."

"The first commoner to ever command a ship of the line," Sartorius said. "Quite the scandal back in the day. Then King Randolph put out a decree that anyone who opposed the change to naval tradition should bring their concerns directly to him…no one complained after that. After your mother passed, there were those of us in the navy that kept an eye out for you."

"I'd rather earn my own keep than rely on the goodwill my father earned."

"Don't be so defensive. You're an excellent officer with successful commands from corvettes to battle cruisers. That you don't come from nobility might have kept the best opportunities from you. You're my aide and a commodore because you're damn good at your job. Imagine if every officer in the navy had to fight as hard as you to climb the ladder. We'd be that much stronger for it." Sartorius grimaced and stretched out his right leg. "Damn, I hate getting old. What's next?"

Gage swiped again. "Loss report from the *Ajax*. Three void-proof containers knocked into a decaying orbit by a meteorite."

"Blast it. Go to the bridge and have Simpson raise the orbital stockyard another five miles. Don't come back unless there's something worth waking me up for."

"Yes, Admiral." Gage stood up and buttoned his uniform. Sartorius was snoring by the time Gage made it to the door.

****

Gage felt the tension on the *Orion*'s bridge as soon

as he walked in. Crewmen stared intently at the holo screens around their work pods, heads bent and shoulders slumped as Captain Simpson glared at his executive officer. Both stood on the command dais in the center of the bridge, elevated three feet off the deck. Through the holo tank in the middle of the dais, Gage saw Simpson's face was red, his hands on his hips and a lock of hair plastered to his forehead.

"This report is thirty minutes overdue, Price," the Captain said as he rapped a data slate against the holo tank. "Late reports delay decisions. Late decisions impact timetables. Disrupted timetables cause operational friction and friction is what destroys solid planning."

"I'm well aware, sir," Price said, standing at rigid attention, "but the last detritus scan was fouled by the loss of the *Ajax*'s cargo pods and a high confidence—"

"You think I don't know how detritus scans work to protect our ships from bits of space junk and the mess the exploded asteroid mine left behind? I've been in His

159

Majesty's Navy for twenty-five years and you think I need to be told this?"

"No, sir, you obviously know the protocol for an orbital radar survey." Price lifted her chin slightly and Gage suppressed a grin. The bait had been set.

"Correct. With our satellite coverage and the pause in operations after the *Ajax* reported the strike and the calculation delay, you should have had this to me…"

Simpson looked down at the data pad, then snapped his gaze up at Price. He turned to the holo tank and tapped furiously on a control panel.

"Even if this was done on time, when did you think to inform me of the new data?" Simpson asked.

"I sent you a text message and a runner to your quarters. Your steward said you were indisposed…in the lavatory."

Someone snickered from a workspace behind Gage. Sailors always kept an ear to officer discussions, pleasant or otherwise, while pretending to focus on their other duties. Scuttlebutt would no doubt distort this encounter into something more comical and profane by the time it reached the lower decks.

"Thank you, XO." Simpson waved a dismissive hand at her.

Gage stepped aside from the small curved staircase leading up to the command dais as Price came down the steps. She looked at him and mouthed, "Not now."

Gage nodded slightly and took the steps two at a time.

"Captain," Gage said politely, "Admiral Sartorius sends his regards."

Simpson's mouth tugged into a brief sneer at the sight of the commodore.

"Mr. Gage." The *Orion*'s master used the more proper form of address for the Admiral's aide. While Gage was a commodore, technically outranking the Captain, Gage's position was brevet, not fully endorsed by the admiralty or the King. If he was summoned back to Albion, he'd revert to being a commander, one on the verge of pinning on a captain's eagle. Despite his rank, Gage lacked any command authority on the *Orion* and the only orders Simpson followed came from Sartorius. The Albion tradition of frocking an aide to one rank higher than the fleet's senior-most ship captain kept an air of authority when the aide acted in the Admiral's stead.

"Well, don't keep me in suspense," Simpson said.

"The Admiral wants the logistics park altitude increased another five miles."

Simpson gestured in the holo tank and Siam appeared in the bottom. The cargo ships AMS *Helga's Fury* and *Mukhlos* sat in high orbit directly over Lopburi. The spine haulers vessels by themselves were little more than engines connected to a long reinforced keel and a square command section where the ship's drones and crew lived. Spreading out along either side of the spine were hundreds of cargo containers in a lattice of connecting spars.

The cargo ships arrived with the containers wrapped around the spine and unfurled when the ships took up anchor. With each cargo pod exposed to vacuum, the swarm of drones had easy access to whatever was requisitioned from the relief effort. Watching the drones flit from container to container, then to a waiting shuttle for transport to the planet, always impressed Gage. The sheer precision of the math behind the efficiency of so many moving parts resembled an angry beehive.

"As the Admiral wishes," Simpson said through a clenched jaw. "I must realign the screen force to…"

"I can assist." Gage traced a circle in the holo tank and a screen of the entire star system appeared in front of him. "Always something to keep operations from moving smoothly, eh?"

Simpson muttered.

Gage looked over the patrol schedule of the two destroyer squadrons scanning the outer planets for any remaining pirates and made no changes. He called up status reports on the three battle cruisers and five frigates arrayed in a loose hemisphere over the supply park and the *Haephestus*, the fleet's repair ship. The ship's systems read green, but the personnel numbers were blinking red.

"Has the Admiral mentioned when I can have my sailors back from the surface?" Simpson asked. "Digging around the mud is something for Marines or soldiers to play at. Keeping my crew on double shifts will lead to fatigue and preventable accidents before too long."

"The situation on the ground is tenuous, Captain. But those still buried in the rubble will likely die of thirst or exposure in the next few days. I'm sure we can cut back rescue efforts once the mission shifts to recovery," Gage said.

"Command should have sent a Marine division, not our fleet…yes, pirates…" Simpson rolled his eyes.

Gage prepared new anchor coordinates for the warships, then sent them to Simpson's cue for approval.

Simpson huffed at Gage's changes…then made

miniscule adjustments.

Gage stepped back from the holo tank and looked through the windows surrounding the bridge's forward half. The *Orion* was one of the older battleships still in Albion's service, but her banks of plasma cannons and recessed torpedo tubes along her hull were as deadly as anything in settled space. The hull stretched for slightly longer than a mile, ending with forward launch bays. Starlight glinted off the white and red armor plating as the ship adjusted her position above Siam.

Commanding warships was a vastly different experience than serving as an admiral's aide. Gage felt a pang of guilt that he wasn't somewhere else in the Albion fleet on a bridge leading sailors as a master of a vessel, but every officer that wanted to advance beyond commander was required to have senior staff experience.

Gage's thumb brushed against his Portsmouth ring. The chance of him becoming captain of a ship like the *Orion* was slim to none. He'd come further than any other common-born officer in Albion history, and a great man once told him that only his ambition and ability would hold back his career.

Why the then-Crown Prince Randolph had made such a promise to Gage was something of a mystery to him. Randolph had come to see him just after Gage's mother passed away and spent the afternoon with the grieving teenager, sharing stories of Gage's father. When Gage had mentioned he wished to follow in his father's footsteps, the Crown Prince promised to cover the rest of Gage's schooling and see that the young man had a fair shot at entering the academy and then the navy.

That Gage's father had died fighting alongside the Crown Prince at the Battle of Urien wasn't a secret, but Randolph had insisted Gage keep their meeting and the promise of help between the two of them. Being a common-born officer was difficult enough; for his peers and superiors to suspect that Randolph had his thumb on the scale for Gage would have made his career almost impossible.

Gage broke out of his reverie and found Simpson glaring at him. Competition between Albion noble families was almost a blood sport, one they didn't want the royals interfering with. Intrigue at court within the naval hierarchy was one such game, one Gage had no chance of winning if the King's influence was known.

"By your leave, Captain," Gage said politely.

Simpson shooed him away with a wave of his hand.

CHAPTER 9

The solitary confinement cell had nothing more than a concrete slab for a bed and recessed lighting that never shut off. The only door was perfectly flush with the wall. A screen flickered with a continuous newsfeed on mute. The only choices allotted to the prisoner were which of several channels to watch and volume controls.

Thorvald sat on the edge of the slab, wearing a sleeveless gray tunic and pants that did nothing to fight the cold air. His rested his hands over his knees, watching as his fingers twitched of their own accord. They'd stripped his gestalt from him, which he knew would happen when he turned himself in. After so many years being joined to that armor, his body hadn't been able to adjust to the loss.

His gestalt had felt so confused, almost frightened, when Royce separated Thorvald from the armor. He hoped Chiara had reset the AI, let it forget him and prepare for the next bodyguard who would take his place on Albion. But the House lords on Geneva would tear his gestalt apart, looking for signs of Thorvald's treachery in order to improve the rest of the House's armor.

Thorvald knew the gestalts were simple AI; they felt nothing beyond base emotions and could be set to complete impartiality if needed. Still, his gestalt would suffer for his choices.

Two knocks echoed through the cell. Thorvald stood up and pressed his nose to the far wall, then interlaced his fingers behind his head. Why were the guards here? His last meal of nutrition yeast and room-temperature water sat untouched on the edge of the bed, delivered less than two hours ago.

He felt a gust of air as the cell door slid open.

"Turn around," Royce said.

Thorvald kept his hands behind his head and followed the instruction.

The Captain wore his armor beneath his formal Albion uniform, his collar rank pins and a blue and yellow stripe down the side of his trousers setting him apart from any regular Albion officer. A young woman the prisoner didn't recognize watched Thorvald from behind Royce. She stood with her feet slightly wider than shoulder-width apart, fists at her waist, ready to attack.

"At ease." Royce crossed his arms over his chest and slowly shook his head. "Why did you do it, Thorvald? Do you know how much damage you've caused?"

"I told you why," the prisoner said. "My reasons haven't changed. And what damage? I came to you with the breach. I showed you where it was and how to repair it."

"*After* you used it to compromise the castle's

170

systems." Royce's lips tugged into a snarl. "You put the royal family's safety at risk for something so trivial as…Fifteen years, Thorvald. Fifteen years we've served side by side on Albion and then you broke your oath to the King, to our House, to your fellows. I can't comprehend how, or why, you abandoned everything you were."

"Beneath it all I was only human. No amount of training or conditioning could take that away from me."

"Which is why you're going back to Geneva under Constable Guard. The King has decided to let our House figure out exactly why you betrayed us. Had you not saved His Majesty's life on Firenze all those years back, you'd be due for the gallows. We can only hope the King extends our contract when the terms end. If he doesn't, our entire House will lose honor in the eyes of the other lords. It will take centuries to recover from that."

Thorvald felt the icy sheen of fear blossom in his heart. He would have preferred the hangman's noose than to go back to Geneva and have his failure laid bare to the House.

"You promised…you promised…" Thorvald cleared his throat and regained some composure, "that I could see her if I cooperated fully. I've answered every question of yours and the intelligence section. They were just here, asking about—"

"Yes. Their consensus is that you're either telling the whole and complete truth or you're a better spy than any of them. I believe the former. You were an excellent bodyguard, a great fighter, but never a liar. I can't let you see her, Thorvald. She's dead."

Thorvald's lips moved, but no sound came out until he stammered, "What? How?"

"Some sort of failsafe against capture, done of her own choice before she even heard our demand to surrender. Cooperate with our lords and I'll see that you get the final report."

Royce picked up a set of overalls and shoes from

172

behind the wall and tossed them onto the bed slab.

"You're leaving Albion. My recommendation to the House is that you be stripped of your augmentations, full forfeiture of pay and benefits, your name expunged from the honor rolls, and a burn notice be sent to the other Houses. Get dressed. There's a civilian liner in orbit and a pair of Constables at the spaceport who'll deliver you home."

Thorvald looked at the rumpled clothes, the sum total of his service and self-worth now reduced to that of a common criminal. His gestalt was gone. She was gone— his deepest fear that she was merely using him now an ugly fact. Despite hoping for some manner of salvation by cooperating with the investigation…even his pride was reduced to nothing.

"My gestalt," Thorvald said, looking at Royce with pleading eyes, "let me take it back. Set a restraining bolt or keep the AI locked away. I won't be a threat to anyone, but at least let me—"

"No!" Royce's armor crept up to the base of his neck in response to the man's anger. "You threw away your dignity. I won't let you carry a shred of honor back with you. The House will send their own ship for your gestalt. Now. Get. Dressed."

Thorvald picked up the jumpsuit and nodded slowly. At least Royce would let him walk out on his own two feet.

****

Thorvald shuffled down an access hallway, his wrists cuffed together and shackled to chains that ran from his ankles to his waist. He knew the route Royce and the new bodyguard were taking him down; Thorvald had used it himself several times to transfer prisoners around the palace. He never thought he'd be the one under guard.

A doorway to the castle's central square lay a few dozen yards ahead. Thorvald eyed a descending stairwell between them and the door.

"Royce," Thorvald said, motioning to the stairs

with his chin, "let's take tunnel 9C to the subway."

"The prisoner will not speak." Salis tapped the butt of her shock stick against his lower back. A warning. The next time would hurt.

Royce stopped and half-turned to Thorvald.

"It's nearly shift change. The square will be full of loyal and trustworthy men and women going about their duties. Why shouldn't they see you in chains? Why should I give you that courtesy?" Royce asked.

"You've kept…what I've done quiet, right? That's protocol for a breach. Gives you and the intelligence ministry time to fix the issues and arrest anyone else involved before word gets out. The castle still has full confidence in us, our House. If they see me in chains, it begs questions. It seeds doubt."

"And it is all your doing," Salis snapped. The snap-hiss of her shock baton activating echoed down the hallway.

"You ask this for the good of the company."

Royce glanced at Salis and she turned off the shock baton. "We'll take the tunnel, but not for your sake."

The Captain touched a fingertip to the base of his ear.

"Control. Route deviation. I'll be out of comms for thirteen minutes while in the maintenance tunnels. Royce, out."

Royce led them to the stairwell. Wet, musty air wafted up wrought-iron steps from the maintenance tunnels running beneath the castle. He touched the edge of a foot-thick metal door recessed into the walls.

"Electromagnetic shielding," Royce said to Salis. "Seismic sensors. Hard lines for communications. Don't be caught down here during an alert unless you really like the dark. I'll take you through the entire complex once the King takes your oath."

Thorvald had to take the steps one at a time. The metal cuffs bit at his ankles as he descended into the half-lit, bare rock tunnel.

CHAPTER 10

Commander Kellogg of the Albion Orbital Corps ran his hand through a holo plot, double-checking that the ore freighter *Cayuga* would keep its required standoff from incoming and outgoing passenger traffic through the slip nexus.

"Franks," Kellogg said to the OC sailor in the first ring of workstations circling Kellogg's raised platform in the center of the control room.

"Sir."

"Have *Cayuga* adjust speed to put another five miles between it and the *Yinjing* at close passage," Kellogg said.

"Aye aye." Franks touched the *Cayuga*'s plot on his holo screen and tapped out a message. "*Cayuga*'s captain will certainly reply back that minimum safe distance is assured. Why are you trying to slow me down when I have this cargo of etcetera, etcetera?"

"*Yinjing* is full of tourists ogling the view. The *Cayuga* is three kilometers from stem to stern, built like a brick shithouse and moving at high velocity. If they see her barreling right toward them, even at minimum safe distance, they'll about lose their minds in terror. Then we'll get bitchy messages from the Tourism Bureau and the *Yinjing*'s captain, followed by very stern looks from Admiral Bancroft."

"*Cayuga* decelerating," Franks said as a text message popped up in the holo screen. "Want me to read what her captain thinks about the request?"

"Nope." Kellogg took a sip of tea. "Orbital Corps requires swift and complete compliance with all instructions, not anyone's happiness."

"Commander Kellogg?" A technician on the second ring of workstations stood up and waved to Kellogg. The watch commander set his tea down on a railing, debating if he should let his Master Chief loose on the sailor for breaching protocol or go see exactly what the pressing issue was. He scanned around the command center and didn't see the Chief.

Kellogg sighed and left his tea behind as he took the few steps to the lower level and went to the astrogation section of the control room.

"It's Plyman, correct?" Kellogg looked over the holos around the junior sailor's workstation.

"Yes, sir." Plyman touched a holo and expanded a screen showing the entire Albion system. Three bright points of data floated near Albion and its two moons. "These are the slip nexus points around the planet."

"As watch officer aboard the throne world's orbital command platform, I'm familiar with them." Kellogg tapped a finger against the back of Plyman's chair.

"The Ashtekar particle feed defaults to the three nexus points connecting to out-system nexus, which you know." Plyman shifted in his seat and ran his fingers over a menu. "But I accidently triggered a wide sweep during my calibration check…and found this."

An amorphous point popped over the northern pole, between the aurora playing across the upper atmosphere and the star fort high above New Exeter.

"That can't be right," Kellogg said, straightening up and frowning. "No slip nexus can form that deep inside a gravity well…what's the particle count?"

"Over thirty-seven thousand. Which would mean a mass load on the slip greater than the Home Fleet and—"

"Where's the other terminus?"

"Some system way beyond wild space, even beyond the Veil."

"Now I know there's something wrong with the sensors. No slip can stretch that far and nothing goes through the Veil." Kellogg put his hands on his hips. "Reset the primary system and go to backups."

"That's the thing, sir," Plyman said. "I already did that. This is the backup feed."

"Admiral Bancroft is going to lose his mind," Kellogg mumbled as he hurried back to his platform. "Comms, get me Fort Coronado on the line and someone find the Master Chief."

"Commodore Travis on screen three," a sailor called out.

"That was fast," Kellogg said.

"Fort Coronado called us."

Kellogg touched a blinking icon and it flipped over to reveal a rather pale-looking Commodore Travis.

"OC, you picked up this anomaly over the North Pole?" Travis asked.

"I was just about to ask you about it." Kellogg felt his stomach clench. "I'll kick this up to Bancroft."

"I'm raising my fort's combat status," Travis said

and cut his feed.

Kellogg felt eyes on him as the bridge crew's attention drew toward him. The watch commander ran his hand through his hair and composed himself with a shake of his head. He tapped in a code to connect to the Admiral's direct line. An icon turned over and over as he waited for Bancroft to answer. Kellogg glanced at a clock and did the math to adjust for the Admiral's time zone. He winced as Bancroft picked up, his face puffy and eyes red. Bancroft squeezed one eye shut and rubbed a knuckle against his nose.

"Kellogg?"

"Sir, we've picked up an anomaly of some sort. It seems there's a massive slip nexus over the North Pole. Fort Coronado confirms the readings," Kellogg said firmly.

"That's impossible." Bancroft sat up and squinted at data feeds as Kellogg dragged and dropped more information onto his screen. "We've done nearly four hundred years of slip line cartography in and around the system. A new nexus doesn't just pop out of nowhere...especially where it's theoretically...the other terminus is *where*?"

The Admiral swiped across his screen and glared at Kellogg.

"Wake up one of the professors from Cotgrave and see what they think. Ready a Pharos buoy and a tender in case they want to do something more academic than shoot a monkey into this anomaly of yours." Bancroft looked over his shoulder to the first rays of dawn breaking through his window.

"Yes, Admiral. Right away. My apologies for waking you with this—"

"Unscheduled slip translation!" Franks shouted as his workstation went berserk with warnings and a swarm of new holo screens. Kellogg swept Bancroft's panel aside and pulled up a mirror of Franks' station.

A starship larger than the Home Fleet's flagship

Excelsior coasted away from the slip nexus over the North Pole. The ship was a flattened dome with silver lines extending from a small ring at the top to the edges, like lines of longitude. The surface was polished obsidian, reflecting the stars and the distant swirl of the Veil. A single point of light flickered within a crystal the size of a building at the apex, set into a metal base within the silver ring.

"What the hell is that?" A chill of fear spread through Kellogg's chest as he fumbled to press his palm to a reader on his station. A panel popped open with three red switches. Kellogg held a trembling hand over the system-wide alarm, a trigger that hadn't been touched since the First Reach War over two centuries ago.

More ships came through the nexus, obsidian cubes linked from point to point with energy cannons or open docks on each face, massive engine cones glowing star bright as dozens of ships overtook the dome. He heard Bancroft yelling at him, panicked yells from his crew…and Kellogg stayed frozen in shock.

"The dome ship is launching drop pods…on track for New Exeter!" Franks yelled.

The crystal over the dome ship flared to life and an azure beam launched toward Fort Coronado. The weapon slammed against the ventral armor with enough force to kick the entire station out of its anchorage. Two of the docking arms cracked open, spilling air and flame into the void. The beam bored through the fort and erupted through the command superstructure. Fort Coronado canted to the side, exposing the burning wound running through the entire station.

Someone grabbed Kellogg by the wrist and pressed his fingers to the alert switches. Green lights blinked as the system read his biometrics. Kellogg snapped out of his shock and clicked each trigger. Plyman let go of the watch commander and backed away from the screens, his face pale.

"What the hell is going on up there?" Bancroft

screamed through his screen.

"Missile track!" came from the floor.

Icons traced away from the dome ship, dashed lines connecting the missiles to their projected targets. One was seconds away from the city of Kingston and Admiral Bancroft.

"Sir," Kellogg looked the Admiral in the eye, "you need to get to your—"

A bright flash of light overwhelmed Bancroft and his feed cut out.

Kellogg opened a system-wide emergency channel.

"All Albion forces, this is Orbital Command. We are under attack from an unknown hostile force. They're coming through a nexus over the North—"

"Energy weapon from the dome ship aiming toward us!"

"This is not a drill! God save the King!"

The beam annihilated Kellogg and the entire

bridge an instant later.

****

Ensign Nick "Freak Show" Wyman considered alert sortie duty as nothing more than another haze junior Albion pilots had to endure. While every combat-rated pilot was eligible for the six-hour stint in a cockpit—in vac suit with no bathroom breaks—that only the junior-most pilots got assigned to the rotating duty during the holiday weekend didn't escape his attention. Rank had its privileges, and as a rookie pilot with fewer than a hundred hours of rated time, he knew he'd be stuck with the worst alert sortie duty shifts until he got promoted or more junior pilots arrived.

Wyman shifted in his cockpit and felt a trickle of sweat run down his back. His tall, solid frame was better suited for the rugby pitch, not a Typhoon fighter. Not for the first time, he wished he'd put in for bomber training instead of the air supremacy pilot track.

He double-tapped his gloved thumb and forefinger together, advancing the page of a trashy mystery novel projected across the inside of his canopy. The squadron commander expected alert pilots to engage in "professional reading," but what would the old man do if he caught Wyman nose deep in the long-ago adventures of some detective in Las Vegas? Assign him to alert sortie duty in the middle of the prism whale festival?

Red lights began spinning around the open bay doors to the *Excelsior*'s flight deck. Wyman's head popped up, his eyes darting from one warning light to the next.

"Briar?" Wyman put his helmet on and activated the seal. Air puffed into his helmet as his flight suit locked itself off from the atmosphere in the cockpit. He looked over at the other alert fighter where the pilot sat with her helmet already on.

"Briar!" he yelled into the channel he shared with his wingman. Her head snapped up as if startled.

"I wasn't sleeping!" Her hands flew around her

cockpit, bringing the entire fighter online and ready to launch.

Wyman keyed the vision tracking systems and double-checked the laser cannons beneath his fighter's nose and missiles mounted on the wings.

"Alert flights, all decks, this is Commander Matthews," came through Wyman's helmet and he heard an edge of fear in the woman's voice. "Some sort of unauthorized slip arrival around the pole. Orbital command and Fort Coronado are off-line. Nothing's coming off the nets. Admiral Laughlin's mobilizing the entire Home Fleet. Launch and make for the site of the incursion and get us some goddamn idea of what's going on. Drummer has in-flight command."

Wyman activated the Typhoon's thrusters. He raised both his hands and, with his thumbs pointed out, double-tapped the base of his fists together to signal for a crewman to pull the chocks away from his fighter's front landing gear.

"Freak, what the hell's going on?" asked Ensign Betty "Rosy" Ivor.

"Hell if I know, but it looks like we're going to fly face-first into whatever it is. Engines to power. You ready to burn?"

"Two seconds behind you. Go go go."

A shudder passed through Wyman's fighter as thrusters lifted it off the deck. He eased his Typhoon through the force field and gunned his ion engines. The acceleration pulse pressed him against his seat as his body dumped adrenaline into his system and his heart pounded. He couldn't tell if his body was reacting to the fear in the back of his mind or the excitement of his first combat sortie.

"All ships, tiered wedge formation on my wing," Drummer said over the radio. A hollow diamond pinged at the edge of Wyman's vision and he banked his fighter to the side. A half-dozen other fighters were already in echelon around Drummer. Wyman brought his craft a hundred yards behind and below Drummer and became the point of the next wedge forming beneath the first.

"Just keep it together, Rosy," Ivor said to herself over the private channel to Wyman. "This is a joke. Some crazy training exercise that ass Bancroft came up with because he hasn't got laid in the last fifty yea—"

"Hot mike, Rosy." Wyman heard a gasp from his wingman before the channel clicked off.

Wyman linked his fighter's speed and heading to match Drummer's, then looked over both shoulders as four more Typhoons joined his formation. Something flashed in the distance, just at the upper edge of the atmosphere.

"To answer what most of you're thinking," Drummer said, "I don't know what's going on either. Nothing's coming out of Fort Coronado or New Exeter, not even open-wave radio."

"Freak, you think it's the Reich? Maybe some sort of pirate raid out of wild space?" Ivor asked him.

"It would take the Reich ten years to get here without using nexus points. We'd have heard if some massive fleet was bouncing its way toward us through Cathay or Indus space. Pirates have never done anything *this* bold." He rubbed his thumb against the switch over his laser cannon trigger.

"Maybe it's aliens?"

"A thousand years of space exploration and no one's ever found a trace of intelligent life. You think they'd show up during the prism whale festival?"

"You're not making this any easier for me, you dick."

Wyman's eyes traced up the coastline against the Siar Ocean…and stopped at a bright spot shining within the darkening twilight.

"My God, is that Brighton? Is it on fire?" Wyman pinched his fingers over the spot and pulled his fingers apart to make his canopy zoom in. A carpet of smoke spread to the east of the city, pulled along by evening winds. The neat grid of Brighton laid out on either side of the Sheffield River was aflame. A ripple of explosions stitched along the undamaged neighborhoods. Then another. A diamond-shaped ship the size of a city block hovered over the devastation.

"Drummer," Wyman said through the squadron's channel, "Brighton's being bombed. Permission to take my tier and—"

"Denied," Drummer snapped. "Home Fleet is vectoring in everything it has toward the capital. We're to observe and report before we engage any hostiles. I…Christ, my sister lives in Brighton. Prep a half-burn to ion engines. That'll get us within line of sight to Exeter."

The Typhoons' engines carried a fixed amount of charge for acceleration and maneuvers. They could burn them to almost empty and reach Albion's main city in minutes, but they'd be almost dead in space with nothing but their carried momentum until the engines recharged. Drummer's order could put him and the rest of the pilots

193

at risk if they ran into the middle of a prolonged dogfight.

"Burn on my mark. Three…two…one…mark."

Wyman opened the ion throttle. His acceleration suit clenched around his body, preventing his blood from draining away from his organs where he needed it.

More brief pinpricks of light flared and died on the horizon like fireflies on a summer night as the squadron raced toward New Exeter. The engine burn ended, jerking Wyman against his restraints. The squadron, stretched out of formation by the burn, settled back into place.

Wyman's world almost fell away as he saw the armada massed over the planet's capital. Dozens on top of dozens of linked diamond ships held high anchor over the massive dome ship hovering over New Exeter. A cloudbank lit with diffuse light from fires on the ground below broke around the mothership.

Hunks of Fort Coronado fell through the atmosphere, leaving comet trails of fire in their wake.

"Oh…kay…" Wyman flipped the safety latch off his cannon trigger.

A dozen of the invader ships angled toward Wyman's squadron and flew toward them. Hatches on the linked sections slid down and fighters spat into the void, accelerating faster than Wyman could have ever pushed his Typhoon.

"New mission," said Drummer as he wagged his wings and then pulled his fighter up into a climb. The rest of the alert squadron followed. "We're to screen Home Fleet. The *Excelsior*'s on her way. Command wants us to hold them off until she and her escorts are in attack formation. Keep to your wingman and good hunting."

The squadron angled over and dove toward the incoming swarm of enemy fighters, each an elongated spear tip contrasted against the devastation below.

"Freak Show, you're awful quiet over there," Ivor half-whispered as she flew level with his wing.

"They'll cross the engagement envelope in ninety

seconds." Wyman waited as Drummer and his flight marked their targets on the leading enemy fighters, then singled out his own glinting ship to engage.

"It's OK to be scared—you can tell me," Ivor said.

"I'm not scared. I'm terrified."

"Thank God; me too."

"Just stay close to me and remember your training. Same as popping pirates in the sims. Wait for Drummer to fire, then light these bastards up." He shunted more energy from his power plant to weapons. Even at full power, if he missed, the cannon bolts should burn out in the atmosphere or hit the ocean.

A voice waveform from muted channels came up on his HUD. The same patter repeated itself several times before Wyman added the frequency to his speakers.

"We are the Daegon," came the words without a hint of accent. *"You will be ruled. Surrender or die. We are the Daegon. You will—"*

"Briar, you ever heard of a Daegon?" Wyman asked.

"Nope. Their ships don't look like anything in the targeting database either."

Why the enemy chose to come in over New Exeter suddenly dawned on Wyman. The city—all those civilians, the royal family—they were all at risk during a battle overhead. The Home Fleet would have to fight with one hand tied behind their back or risk significant collateral damage. Given what he'd already seen on Brighton, he gathered that the enemy didn't share such a concern.

The sharp edge on an incoming fighter glowed bright blue, then a blast of energy as thick as a missile lanced out of the leading tip. Wyman slid his fighter to the right, losing his aim on his marked target as the blue beam cut through the void just over his cockpit.

"Making friends already," Ivor said as she let off a burst from her cannons, her flurry of red bolts joining the weight of fire from the rest of the squadron in a hailstorm of directed energy.

Wyman picked out a fighter that accelerated out of the line of fire and angled toward the Albion fighters. Its maneuver slowed as its edges burned bright. Wyman fired and landed two hits against the gleaming hull. The first slapped the pointed nose down toward the planet, and the second shattered a side and blew out the engine block. The crippled ship spiraled toward the ocean below.

"Splash one bandit!" Wyman locked his cannons on another enemy fighter. "Watch for when they're about to fire. I think—"

The entire enemy squadron let off a phalanx of solid energy. Three Typhoons exploded as the beams blasted through them while another pair careened into the beams and were ripped apart. Wyman slowed his fighter and tried to steer it away from a burning line. His canopy nicked it, leaving a slash through the composite glass before he pulled away. The HUD on his helmet flickered as it tried to adjust for the loss of data from his damaged fighter.

"Freak! Down!"

Wyman heard Ivor's warning and slammed his control stick forward. A spear tip flashed overhead. Wyman activated the thrusters on the rear of his fighter and spun it into a backwards roll. A Typhoon came into view, pursued by an enemy fighter, its edges alight. Wyman opened fire, sending out a fan of bolts. The enemy ship blew the Typhoon into burning fragments a half-second before one of Wyman's shots struck and broke its nose off.

Wyman's spin took the damaged enemy out of view. He twisted his ship around and sped back toward the dogfight.

"Briar?" Wyman put another shot into the wobbling fighter he'd shot and broke it in half.

"Got one on me." Ivor's words strained against g-forces. "To your four."

Wyman banked hard to the right…and found Ivor barreling right toward him. He brought his left wingtip up and could have sworn the two fighters swapped paint as they passed. He opened up with his cannons and blew her pursuer into bits. Wyman tried to skirt the expanding cloud of wreckage and felt pieces slap off the bottom of his fighter as if he was in a metal shack during a hailstorm.

His fighter chugged forward as his engines malfunctioned. Warning icons popped up in his HUD, all yellow.

"Freak? You OK?" Ivor asked.

"Still kicking." He pulled into a loop and found Ivor. They accelerated back to the dogfight where only six other Typhoons remained, outnumbered two to one.

"Going for lock." Wyman slipped his thumb onto the top of his control stick and tagged an enemy fighter. He clicked the trigger on top of the control stick, activated the Shrike missile mounted to his wingtip, and felt a thrill when a lock tone sounded through his earpiece. With another click, he launched the missile. The fighter shuddered as the missile sped away, propelled by a blazing point in its base.

Red icons popped up and his stick went sluggish.

"I've got a problem…losing main power." Wyman tapped at his battery control panel, which flickered on and off.

"Missile away!" Ivor shouted.

Wyman jerked his stick from side to side, bouncing him against the tight confines of his chair. His battery control panel popped off with a brief shower of sparks…but his flight controls returned to normal. He shrugged his shoulders and looked back to the dogfight.

Ivor's missile streaked toward its target and exploded when a pencil-thin beam struck out from a spear tip.

"Same thing happened to yours," she said.

"Then we'll do this with guns." Wyman increased his speed ever so slightly, unsure what the strain would do to his damaged ship.

"Alert flight, this is Excelsior *actual,"* came over the radio. *"Clear the field."*

Wyman twisted around and saw the *Excelsior,* two battleships, and a host of cruisers and destroyers cresting over the horizon.

"Roger, *Excelsior,*" Drummer said. "Don't think these bogies are about to let us—"

A pale white column of energy struck out from an enemy capital ship, blinding Wyman as it passed.

Wyman felt his restraints cut against his chest and waist as his fighter spun out of control. The afterimage of the monstrous enemy attack burned against his eyes, a solid beam that jumped around each time he blinked.

Shouts filled his ears, a wild panic of voices that Wyman ignored as he struggled to do something— anything—that would get his world back under control.

"Atmosphere. Atmosphere," came through his helmet as his fighter's on-board computer warned him of the loss of altitude. Wyman flailed around and grabbed onto his control stick with both hands. He swung the stick to the side and felt his momentum shift in response. At least something was working.

"Emergency heat shield active. Orbital return course non-optimal," his computer said, which was a polite way of saying the fighter—and he—would burn to a crisp if he didn't get his ship under control immediately.

He squeezed his eyes shut and then opened them to find some peripheral vision had returned. He swung his fighter around, pointing the nose into the direction of his fall as flames licked up the side of his cockpit.

"Freak, you OK over there?" Ivor asked. "I'm just behind you with—"

"Dandy," a strained man's voice said. "Drummer, the rest are all off my scope."

"Heat shields are back to optimal. My feet are a little singed, but it's not bad," Wyman said.

"I don't think we can power out of this descent,"

Ivor said. "The *Excelsior*'s going to need us."

Wyman looked up. The flagship of Home Fleet charged toward the unnamed enemy. An ugly black scar ran across her port side. Cannon fire traced across the gap between fleets. Attacks from the Albion ships impacted the enemy ships, pounding against energy shields.

A pair of enemy ships fired, their beams converging on an Albion cruiser. Her shields lit up into a cocoon around the ship, struggling to dissipate the assault. A third beam broke through the cruiser's energy shields and bored into her hull just above the engines. All three beams converged into a single point within the ship and blew it into smoldering fragments.

"Eight hundred people on that ship," Wyman whispered.

Torpedoes streaked toward the enemy ships, trailing comet tails in their wake. Beams from fighters ravaged the incoming barrage, but three made it to the leading enemy ship. The forward cube exploded into a momentary sun. The explosion rippled up the ship's keel, peppering the other ships in her formation with a storm of debris.

The shields on another enemy ship failed and the Albion bombardment broke it into three pieces.

Wyman banged his first against his canopy in excitement as the tide seemed to turn. Then he remembered the gash in the glass as wisps of air snaked into his cockpit. He rapped knuckles against flickering control panels, then took a hard look at the black and yellow chevrons over his eject lever.

"Rosy, Dandy…you remember what we're supposed to do during an atmo reentry if we don't have cabin pressure under control?"

"Don't eject," Rosy said. "You'll make it to the ground, but you'll do it in many burnt pieces."

"If your suit still has integrity, you'll be OK," Dandy said. "Vent your cabin anyway. Less risk of an explosive decompression when you…my God."

"What?" He looked up and saw the star field over the Albion fleet shimmering.

Enemy ships burst from the nexus point and decelerated to a complete stop. Wyman watched in horror as the ships opened fire on the *Excelsior* and her battle group, joining their fire from the ships to the flagship's fore.

Half a dozen beams smashed against the *Excelsior*'s shields. The forward emitters buckled and a single beam speared through the ship's bridge and out her belly. The *Excelsior* canted to the side, then rolled over, succumbing to Albion's gravity.

Wyman had to look away as two more ships exploded into fireballs.

"Shit, shit, shit," said Ivor. "What do we do now?"

"There's…an unmanned landing pad outside Reading." Wyman swiped a map screen and found a solid icon over the town. "It's still online. We set down, rearm, and recharge, and then we get back in this fight."

Brief shadows formed in his cockpit as another ship exploded overhead. He looked toward New Exeter, where the massive dome ship hovered high above the city.

"We're not out of this fight yet," Wyman said.

CHAPTER 11

Thorvald followed Royce through a dank tunnel, marching through the same ankle-deep puddle as the Captain. Gestalt armor trivialized all but the most hazardous of environmental concerns. Royce had no worry about the discomfort of wet socks like Thorvald, but the prisoner kept on as if he was in his armor. He hadn't complained once as the air shifted from freezing cold to the heat and humidity of a sauna as they passed through the machinery that serviced the castle.

"If the King wishes," Thorvald said, "I will renounce my oath to him or another of the royal family before I leave. My protocols are still active in the system and if he's worried that—"

"The King and the family are involved in matters of state," Royce snapped. "That you'll be under Marshal guard the entire trip to Geneva is enough of a guarantee for me and the King. You're no longer worth the family's time."

"As he wills." Thorvald's head dipped a bit lower.

"These tunnels aren't in my protocols," Salis said. "The risk of an infiltration is too high for this to be off my gestalt."

"Access is restricted to robots and a few others. Gene scanners throughout," Royce said, motioning to a featureless plate on a wall tucked against the ceiling. "You'll have it all once the King accepts your service. You still need to memorize the layout."

"I have been," Salis said.

A slight smile tugged at Thorvald's lips. He was starting to like her.

The puddles on the floor rippled in tune with a

slight rumble. Royce held up a fist and the other Genevans halted.

"Earthquake?" Salis asked.

Deep booms echoed through the tunnel and the floor heaved up, slamming Thorvald against the wall.

"We're under attack." Royce gave Thorvald a look of disgust as his armor slid a helm up his neck and over his face.

"I don't know anything about this!" Thorvald used his shoulder to wipe blood away from a gash on his cheek.

"To the King!" Royce took off down the tunnel, Salis close behind.

Thorvald hurried after them, his gait hampered by the restraints on his ankles. A crack split the ceiling as another hit shook the castle. A fog of dust billowed out from the connecting tunnel just as the two guards rounded the corner.

He found Salis and Royce digging through a

partially collapsed stairwell. Thorvald dodged a rock the size of his head and hurried to their side.

"Let me help!" Thorvald shook his arms against the restraints.

Salis gave him a quick look, then used her armor to haul a boulder that must have weighed half a ton off the stairwell.

"Useless without armor." She stepped aside as Royce broke a rock in two with a knife-hand strike and let the hunks tumble past her.

"There…we can climb out." Royce looked up as rays of light played through thick dust and reflected off his armor. A distant strike sent pebbles cascading down the stairwell.

"Him?" Salis asked. "He'll die down here."

"For the King until my last dying breath," Thorvald said. "You know I'm still loyal!"

Royce touched his forearm and Thorvald's restraints fell to the ground.

"Then I expect you find your breath up there and die with honor." Royce bent at the knees and waist, then leaped up. Salis climbed after him.

Thorvald grabbed a handhold and hauled himself up, testing each new grip and foothold as he went higher. A doorway beckoned above, where Royce was braced against the rocks. The Captain beat at the door with his foot, kicking out an exit.

Thorvald fought back a cough as loose dust fell around him and ignored the jagged rocks biting into his skin and ripping his jumpsuit. He wiggled through a gap just as the Captain climbed through his ersatz exit.

The sounds of blaster fire and panicked shouts came from beyond the door.

Thorvald's pants caught on a rock before he could get his legs through the gap. He kicked at it and accomplished nothing.

"Help me," he said, holding a hand out to Salis. She followed Royce without even a look at Thorvald. He grunted, ripped his pants leg free, and crawled to the opening.

What should have been the castle's outer wall was a wreck of blasted masonry spreading into a haze of dust. He looked up at the blinking lights on the underside of the massive domed ship hovering over the castle. Dueling fighters and energy bolts cut through the air above as smoke mixed with the haze of pulverized stone.

Royce and Salis knelt next to a still-standing segment of the outer wall. The Captain touched his fingers to one ear, his head shaking. A fighter shaped like a spear tip roared overhead and sent a blast into the top of the air defense tower, which exploded into flames, blowing armor plating and bricks into the air.

Thorvald jumped aside as a flaming hunk of twisted metal slammed into one of the gigantic marble bricks. Shards of rock pelted his body, sending a flare of pain over his right arm and his face. He struggled to his knees and pulled a flake the size of a coin out of his flesh just above his elbow.

The hard rain lessened. Thorvald looked up and saw a flaming bit of debris falling toward Royce and Salis.

Thorvald shouted a warning.

The mangled remains of the tower's main gun hit a dozen yards from the two Genevans and bounced straight toward Salis. Royce shoved her aside just as the debris took a wild bounce off the ground. It struck Royce in the face and sent him flying.

The Captain rolled like a rag doll over the field of broken bricks before coming to a stop, his back bent over at a sharp angle.

"Royce!" Thorvald ran to his still form. The armor was intact…but the Captain's neck was bent at a horrid angle. Thorvald reached for his old friend but didn't touch him. There was nothing he could do.

The Captain was dead.

Salis ran over. The armor pulled away from her face and she looked over the dead man, her lips moving in shock.

Blue laser bolts shot overhead. Shouts in an unknown language echoed off the broken walls.

Thorvald pressed his hands together and touched his fingertips to the bridge of his nose in prayer.

"Be at peace…and forgive me," Thorvald said as he pressed his hand to Royce's chest.

"What do you think you're doing?" Salis drew her pistol and knelt behind a broken brick the size of a small ground car.

"The gestalt is still alive. I'm taking his armor." A chill went up Thorvald's arm as the armor's spirit felt the connection to another Genevan.

"Are you insane?" Salis asked. "It takes weeks for a gestalt to recover from the trauma of a separation. If you take up his mantle now, it'll drive you and the gestalt insane."

"Do you know how to find the King? Any of the royal family?" Thorvald winced as the thin armor plates flowed off Royce's chest and up his arm.

Salis peeked over her cover and then looked around. Her silence was all the answer Thorvald needed.

+Traitor!+ thundered in Thorvald's ears and the armor pulled back.

"We are sworn to the King." Thorvald pressed his other hand to Royce's faceplate. "You cannot save them if you stay with Royce. I feel your grief, your pain, but your duty does not end with his death!"

Thorvald pulled up a memory from the day Prince Aidan was born, remembering the feeling of holding the baby and repeating his sworn oath to the tiny boy. The emotions of that moment flowed into Royce's gestalt.

+I hate you.+ The gestalt swept over Thorvald's arms, shredding his uniform and covering his body. The armor sent a spike of pain through his neuro-wires. Thorvald gripped his head and fell to his knees, screaming as he tried to pry the armor away. One hand went to the ground as he fought to control his breathing.

Blue energy bolts snapped overhead. Two more struck Salis' cover, blowing fist-sized holes into the rock.

"Nobis regiray!" came from the haze. Three Daegon warriors in deep-blue armor, each carrying a rifle tipped with a serrated bayonet, charged at Salis.

She leveled her pistol and fired a three-round burst into the leading Daegon's chest. An energy shield flared against the first two hits and failed with a loud pop as the third bolt broke through. It struck his collarbone and twisted the warrior halfway around.

One of his companions jumped onto the broken block and lunged at her with his bayonet. Salis grabbed the weapon by the barrel and swung it and the warrior into the ground. She raised a foot and slammed her heel into the warrior's head, caving in the helmet. She backed up, putting distance between her and Thorvald, who'd remained out of view behind the brick. She took another shot at the warrior with no shield and hit the third when he jumped in front of his companion.

The warrior aimed at her and fired, hitting the ground as she sidestepped far faster than an unarmored fighter could have ever moved. The Daegon thrust his bayonet at her, glancing a blow off her shoulder. He twisted the blade to the side and ripped it across her chest. The blade drew sparks as it passed but didn't break the armor.

Salis struck the warrior with a cross to the jaw and then slammed an open hand against his face. Her gauntlets squeezed, breaking cracks across his visor and eliciting a weak scream. Salis jabbed the muzzle of her pistol through his shield and shot him in the throat. The bolt exploded out of his spine and she tossed him aside.

Thorvald tried to rise, but his new armor clung to him like a blanket soaked in lead.

A bolt flashed over his head and struck Salis in the knee. Her shield took the brunt of the hit, but the impact knocked her to the ground.

The last warrior walked past Thorvald, his rifle at

218

his shoulder, and aimed at Salis' head.

"If we don't move, we're going to fail!" Thorvald pulsed the words from his mind to the gestalt…and his armor loosened. He tackled the warrior just before he fired, sending the bolt straight into the air.

Thorvald punched straight at the Daegon's faceplate, but the warrior caught the punch with an open hand. Thorvald tried to focus more strength into the blow, but the Daegon's hold stayed true. The warrior brought his other fist back and spikes popped up from the knuckles. The spikes glowed red hot and the warrior drove his fist into Thorvald's stomach.

Feeling like he'd been stabbed, Thorvald fell on top of the warrior, pinning his spiked fist between their bodies. Thorvald's hand closed over a rock. He reared back and slammed it into the warrior's head. The warrior released Thorvald's other hand and the Genevan gripped his weapon with both hands and slammed it into the warrior's face. Blood spurt onto Thorvald's helmet. The

Daegon flailed against Thorvald as the Genevan rammed the rock home again.

Thorvald's enemy went slack. His faceplate broke apart and sloughed to the side. Beneath the broken glass was a human face…one with deep purple skin. Metal wires embedded in his temple ran down his jaw and neck. The Genevan Houses took great pride in knowing every potential culture across settled space to better understand potential threats, but this Daegon was unlike anything he'd ever seen.

Warmth ran over Thorvald's body as the gestalt and his nervous system blended together. After decades of use, some gestalts developed distinct personalities. This one, Thorvald realized, enjoyed killing.

"Are you OK?" Salis asked.

"It's still…fighting me…but…" Thorvald fought to his feet, then looked down at his gauntlets and worked his hands open and closed. Data flowed through his faceplate.

"The King is alive. He's with the rest of the company at Angelo Tower. Queen Calista and Aidan are with him." Thorvald looked down at Royce, the dead man's half-open gaze staring at Thorvald.

He reached to him and closed his eyes.

"To my last dying breath," Thorvald said and then ran off into the smoke and fire.

CHAPTER 12

Keeping her back to a wall, Salis slid toward a corner, holding her pistol perpendicular to the wall and sweeping the muzzle around the turn. The cameras in the weapon sent video to her armor.

"Clear." She cut the corner, weapon still leveled and ready. Thorvald, holding a broken metal rod as a weapon, followed.

Dead Albion and Daegon soldiers littered the hallway, most of the former still in their parade uniforms. Broken glass from the ceiling littered the floor. Blast scoring on the walls and floors smoldered, igniting into small fires on the bloodstained carpet and large paintings of Albion royalty and other notables.

A thrum filled the air and Salis went flush with the wall as one hand went over Thorvald's chest. Overhead, a Daegon lander floated by.

Thorvald slapped her hand away.

"You think I need your protection?" he asked.

"I think you need a weapon and you're something of a liability until that happens." Salis moved a blaster carbine away from a dead soldier with her foot, then kicked it to Thorvald.

He scooped up the weapon and shook his head.

"Capacitor's fried." Flipping the weapon around, he held it like a club, set the curtain rod down gently, and pulled another carbine out from under a body. Half the weapon crumbled to the ground.

"That one's smashed…overloaded…what happened here?" Salis asked.

"These Daegon are thorough. Every one of our

dead have been stabbed through the heart, every weapon rendered useless…"

"Who are they? Some new pirate kingdom from wild space?" Salis saw a dead Albion soldier gripping a Daegon rifle. Stepping over a dead blue-armored warrior, she reached for the weapon.

"No!"

Salis pulled her hand back, then glared at Thorvald.

"Look at his hands and neck," Thorvald said.

Lightning bolts of scorched flesh ran up the corpse's exposed skin, unique injuries compared to the smoldering blast wounds and torn flesh of the other Albion dead.

"These Daegon booby-trap their weapons," Salis said, "and destroy ours."

"Pirates pillage, attack for slaves. They're here to conquer. There's no one like them in wild space." Thorvald flicked a lever on the damaged weapon in his hand and removed the damaged upper section. He tossed it aside and found another rifle with an intact receiver but a mangled magazine and handle. He pulled that weapon apart and cobbled together a banged-up whole weapon. He slapped in a magazine and the weapon cycled a bullet into the chamber.

A ray of light swept through the broken roof and moved across the floor. The Genevans jumped aside and went flush against the wall. The hum of repulse engines grew in the air as the Daegon lander descended.

Thorvald watched the pool of light as it lingered over Albion bodies…then shrank down to nothing. The whine of engines died away as the lander ascended.

"We're close to the main—"

As the bang of a rocket launcher crashed through the walls, the flash of an explosion burst through the broken roof and the Daegon lander's engines changed pitch. A silhouette crossed over the broken glass and a hulking form came down in a shower of clear shards.

A Daegon warrior landed in a crouch. His armor was black lacquer, and even in a crouch, he was almost as tall as the other warriors Thorvald had fought. The Daegon held a hammer in one hand, the head of which snapped with raw electricity and whirring servos. The other hand carried a wide-barreled gun with a drum magazine. Additional plates of armor were bolted to his front.

Salis levelled her pistol and shot the Daegon in the temple. The bullet bounced off with a spark, barely nudging the helmet.

The enormous warrior snapped his head toward Salis, his faceplate molded into a screaming demon. Light burned in his eye sockets as he stood to his full height, towering over both Genevans.

The warrior swung his hammer at Salis, far faster than Thorvald thought something that size could move. She leapt aside and the hammer hit the wall with a thunderclap. Dust filled the air as the energy field surrounding the weapon discharged and blew out a section of the wall as if it had been hit by a wrecking ball.

Thorvald ran toward the opposite wall, jumped onto it, then sprang away and onto the giant warrior's back. He wrapped an arm around the Daegon's thick neck and jammed his heels against the warrior's lower back. Thorvald switched his grip to latch on to the enormous helmet with both hands, then heaved upwards.

For all the strength his armor and his gestalt could lend, he managed to tilt the Daegon backwards, not rip the helmet clean away like he'd intended.

The warrior remained perfectly calm. He let his hammer slide down his grip several inches, then used the additional reach to strike at Thorvald. The Genevan let go and fell back, tendrils of electricity reaching from the hammer to his chest as the blow nearly hit its mark.

Thorvald's back slammed against the ground and the Daegon raised a foot to stamp the life out of the bodyguard. Thorvald rolled to the side, and the warrior's heel cracked the floor right where Thorvald's head had been a moment earlier. The Genevan bumped against the wall and found himself boxed in by the warrior.

Salis unloaded her pistol into the warrior's back, with no effect.

The warrior reversed the grip on his hammer, then raised the weapon over his head.

The crack of a rocket launcher slapped Thorvald against the wall with a wave of overpressure and the hallway exploded into fire and shattered masonry. Thorvald found himself buried beneath bricks and the remnants of King Archibald II's portrait. He dug himself out, thankful for his armor, which protected him from the explosion that would have killed anyone protected by anything less than Genevan craftsmanship.

The Daegon lay on his side, arm locked in mid-swing, a massive hole in his chest. Thorvald could see straight through the warrior from the entrance wound in his back. There was no blood, no viscera…nothing at all inside the armor.

"Royce?" a man asked. "No…who's in his armor?"

A Genevan guard stood in the gap blown open by the Daegon's hammer, a smoking rocket launcher on his shoulder. Albion soldiers clustered behind him, their uniforms torn and dirty.

"Thorvald. He fell, Lucan." Thorvald stepped around the fallen Daegon. "I took up his gestalt to—"

"Fight now. Explain later." Lucan took a battle rifle off his back and tossed it to Thorvald. "Enemy troops have the King pinned down near the St. Angelo redoubt. Come on."

****

Tolan stumbled into the Intelligence Ministry control room as another explosion rocked the palace. Screens along the walls were alive with attacking fighters, explosions in orbit and panicked newscasters trying to make sense of the sudden onslaught.

A holo table in the center of the room, holding Albion and near space, roiled with red enemy icons that far outnumbered the green of the planet's forces in orbit.

Director Ormond gripped the table edge, fear in his eyes.

"Tolan, who are they? You spent years in wild space. Tell me what we're dealing with," Ormond said. He tapped icons in the holo, pulling up a live feed of the linked diamond cruisers and the domed ship holding over New Exeter.

"I…I've never seen anything like this before. Wild-space fleets are full of dregs, decades old and bought off the black market." Tolan shook his head.

"Bring the prisoner," Ormond said over his shoulder to a guard. The woman hurried away.

The director reached into the holo and zoomed away from the planet. Civilian ships streamed away from Albion toward the half-dozen nexus points to nearby stars.

Tight red formations of enemy ships advanced on the same paths and at faster speeds.

"They've brought more ships than the entire Reich fleet," Ormond said. "Hell of a lot more than what we have…and we're spread out over a half-dozen systems." The old man turned his gaze to Tolan.

"We can't win," Tolan said. "The star forts are gone. *Excelsior* and her battle group are destroyed…They have ground troops here, Brighton, Herford."

"None of their ships are on course to Siam." Ormond rapped his knuckles against the table edge. "I want you to take your ship there and find Admiral Sartorius. Tell them not to return home. Get to Cathay, Indus, anywhere. By this time tomorrow, they will be the last of our military. The colony worlds won't last long."

"But what about the King? He may—"

Ormond grabbed a fistful of Tolan's shirt and yanked him closer. The fear was gone from the director's eyes; his features were set, determined.

"You think I'm *asking* you to do this? Albion will need hope to survive. So long as Sartorius and the 11th are still fighting, we have a chance." Ormond let the spy go.

"Sir?" The guard pushed a bound Polonius up to the table, the bottom half of his face covered by a black gag that kept his jaw shut.

"These are your people, aren't they?" Ormond asked. "What do you want? Why won't they speak with us?"

Polonius looked over the holo, then chuckled within his gag.

"You have an answer for me?" Ormond's hand went to a pistol on his belt.

The prisoner nodded. The guard touched a fingertip to the gag and it fell slack around Polonius' neck.

"You will be ruled," he said with a sneer.

"Give me an answer or you'll find out just what Albion does to spies." Ormond drew his pistol.

Polonius stared daggers at the director and

laughed through clenched teeth. Veins popped out over his forehead and temples.

"Sir…" Tolan reached for the flex-blade flush against his belt.

Polonius grunted and his hands ripped through the cuffs with a snap of breaking metal. He lunged for Ormond.

Tolan snatched the flex-blade off his belt and flicked it to snap it into a rigid knife. He threw it at Polonius and impaled the man through his left eye. Polonius fell to the floor face-first, the impact driving the blade out the back of his skull. His corpse twitched and kicked for a moment, then went still.

Ormond backed into a workstation, pistol trained on the body. The flat-footed guard stood over the body, fumbling for a new set of cuffs.

"That's not possible!" the guard said. "Those cuffs are rated against augmented prisoners and…is it getting hot in here?"

"Get away from him!" Tolan tackled Ormond to the ground.

Polonius' body erupted into jade flames. A wave of heat singed Tolan's back and a smell of scorched meat and copper filled the air.

Tolan rolled off of Ormond. All that remained of Polonius was a blackened skeleton and lumps of caramelized flesh. The guard slapped flames off his boots and pants.

"Tolan, you have your orders." Ormond got to his feet and raised a hand to assure the others in the command center that he was unharmed.

"What about you and the rest of the directorate?"

"We have contingency plans for an occupation…but nothing like this. The directorate will frag the castle's records, then we'll lead the resistance. Get out of here. God's speed, Tolan."

"Yes, sir." Tolan backed out of a door, his eyes on the blackened corpse and the fearful faces of his fellow intelligence operatives that he was about to leave behind.

****

Thorvald, Salis, and Lucan ran down a hallway leading to the Angelo Tower, the castle's fortified bunker. Holding a battle rifle in his hands felt good, like he was finally useful, and it was a welcome change from Royce's gestalt. The armor's spirit seethed in the back of Thorvald's mind, pulling away from Thorvald's consciousness like a child that did not want to be held.

The sound of blaster fire echoed up the hallway.

"That's not coming from the St. Angelo," Lucan said. "That's the royal gardens."

"I hear blaster pistols—several." Salis gave her handgun a brief shake. "Must be ours."

Thorvald skidded to a halt and peeked around a corner. The blast door to the gardens was shut, but a wide circle had been cut through it; the center of the reinforced metal door lay flat against the floor where it fell.

In the gardens beyond the broken doorway, blaster fire crisscrossed between the trees and bushes imported from Earth. Red-armored Daegon fired over and around the fallen trunk of an oak bearing the carved names of royal children. Yellow bolts from Genevan and Albion weapons struck hunks of bark and splintered wood from the invaders' cover.

Thorvald shouldered his rifle and swung around the corner. He ran for the blast door, firing off quick bursts into the Daegon. He shot down three before they realized they were being flanked and turned their attention to Thorvald. The Genevan slid forward, red bolts cracking over his head as his feet hit the wall and his momentum carried him upright. He stuck his rifle around the portal edge and blind-fired the rest of the weapon's battery on full auto. The rattle shook his arms, but his augmented strength kept the weapon aimed at the enemy.

The weapon ran empty and he pulled it back. Lucan and Salis charged through the opening, weapons blazing.

Thorvald grabbed the edge of the opening and swung into the garden. A Daegon leaned against a tree, one arm pressed against a smoldering wound on his stomach. The Genevan grabbed his empty rifle by the barrel and swung the weapon like a club. The butt connected with the invader's head, snapping it aside with a crack of broken armor.

Thorvald grabbed the falling Daegon by the wrists and used his grip to swing the bayonet-tipped rifle up, impaling a warrior charging the Genevan from behind. Thorvald landed a hook to the dying Daegon and sent him to the ground. He whirled around, reloading the battery in his rifle as he searched for the enemy.

Salis and Lucan stood surrounded by dead red-armored troops, their weapons smoking.

"Royce!" came from a circle of boulders in the center of the gardens.

Thorvald ran over—he'd correct whoever called

to him later.

A half-dozen Albion soldiers formed a perimeter around a sunken fire pit ringed by several curved benches. Two Genevan guards lay dead inside the circle, their armor leaking blood, mangled by blaster fire. Blue-armored bodies littered the gardens as small fires burned through flowerbeds and tree bark. The smell of sap and smoke crept through Thorvald's faceplate. A man with gray-black hair holding an ornate pistol kneeled next to a woman in white lace and silk. She lay face down, blood staining her left side and seeping into the dark soil.

King Randolph III looked up from the dead Queen Calista to Thorvald. His eyes were half-dilated and his skin pale. Thorvald's gestalt sent a chill of panic down his spine as its sensors scanned the King. The King was wounded, bleeding from several cuts to his legs and back. Second-degree burns on his neck from a near blaster miss oozed blood.

The wail of a crying child came from inside a

rough protective circle formed by a pair of dead soldiers, the bodies propped on their sides. Salis reached down and lifted up a filthy little boy, the three-year-old Prince Aidan. She turned, keeping the child from seeing his dead mother, and pressed a thumb to the boy's neck. A tiny dose of tranquilizer stopped his cries. Salis cradled Aidan in an arm and her armor shifted into a cocoon around him.

"Sire," Thorvald said, grabbing the King by the shoulders to steady him, "we have to get you out of here—"

"No, Royce, they've been after me since the first attack." The King's words were slurred; he was going into shock. "Calista…they killed her…you must take Aidan."

Thorvald's armor mixed together a concoction of stimulants, blood coagulators, and anti-shock medication. When the drug injection was ready, his right gauntlet squeezed against his forearm. He pressed his palm against the side of the King's neck and took in more biometric readings as the drugs transferred with a hiss.

"I'm not Roy—"

"You take him!" Randolph poked Thorvald in the chest weakly, then pointed to a boulder. "Old tunnel. Grandfather built them."

"Lucan, under there. Should be a passage to the catacombs." Thorvald held the King steady as the other Genevan gripped the rock that was taller than he was and shifted it aside with a grunt. He swept dirt off a hatch with his foot, then lifted it up. The hatchway was just big enough for a single person.

Red bolts snapped overhead, fired by a pack of Daegon at the breached door. Thorvald put his body between the King and the attackers. Lucan joined the soldiers taking cover around the rocks and firing on the Daegon.

"Royce…" said the King, putting a bloody hand on the side of Thorvald's face, "I can't go any further. You will save my sons—"

A sealed door on the other side of the gardens

buckled against an impact.

"We will buy you time." The King tried to shove Thorvald toward the open hatch. "Go!"

+Obey!+ Thorvald's gestalt shouted into his mind.

"Yes…sire." The Genevan pointed at Salis, still holding Prince Aidan, then to the hatch. "Lucan, can you—"

"Get going. There's no one else that can move the boulder over the hatch," Lucan said.

Salis stepped onto the ladder leading into the dark below, moving quickly and ably even with just one arm available.

"Don't tell me where you're going," Lucan said. "Just get the Prince to safety."

Thorvald got onto the ladder and climbed down, stopping when his head was clear of the hatch. He looked up at Lucan and saw energy bolts from Daegon weapons zipping through the air from more than one direction.

"I'll remember you to the House," Thorvald said, giving an old Genevan farewell offered when death was close.

"Tell my wife and daughters I died well," Lucan said and slammed the hatch. The moan of the boulder moving over metal drowned out the sound of blaster fire as Thorvald, Salis, and the sleeping Prince descended into darkness.

****

Lucan took a rifle from a dead soldier and checked the charge—eight shots left. King Randolph leaned against the same boulder Lucan used for cover. The King held the dead Queen's hand, his breathing strained, uneven. Lucan's gestalt sent him a readout of the King's condition. Broken ribs had pierced his left lung with bone fragments. He'd last for several more painful hours before succumbing to his wounds.

Another thunderclap bent the doorway to the gardens. Lucan knew the King's injuries were almost irrelevant. The enemy would break through in minutes.

"Lucan…Royce'll protect my boys. He will." The King gently put his wife's hand down and raised his pistol.

Lucan aimed his rifle over the boulder. The pathway Thorvald and Salis used to escape with the Prince was just beneath the rock. The longer he kept the Daegon away, the better chance they had to reach someplace safe. He wouldn't tell the King who was in Royce's armor. Genevans believed it was better to die with hope in one's heart.

"Aim for the neck of the big one," Lucan said to the remaining soldiers. The King grunted and tried to get up, but Lucan pushed him back down. "Stay there, My Lord. We'll get you out of here soon as we can."

The doors buckled beneath a blow that split the air loud enough to pop Lucan's eardrums. A siege warrior ducked beneath the doorway and charged forward. Daegon came behind him, roaring war cries and with bayonets levelled at the Albion soldiers.

Lucan took careful aim, timed the hammer-wielding giant's steps, and fired. His shot smashed through a glowing eye lens. The shot rattled inside the helmet, batting the warrior's head from side to side. The giant pitched forward and dug a shallow trench through the garden's soil before coming to a stop. The Daegon continued their charge.

"For the King!" shouted a soldier next to Lucan as he fired on the invaders.

"For Albion!" King Randolph hauled himself to his feet and shot a Daegon in the forehead.

Lucan fired his last shot, then grabbed the rifle by the red-hot barrel and raised it over his head. That the Daegon weren't firing as they charged meant only one thing to him—they wanted the King alive.

The Genevan swung the rifle down and onto the hands of a charging warrior. The butt hit with a satisfying crack of armor and bone, deflecting the serrated bayonet to the side. Lucan shoulder-checked the warrior, knocking

244

him into the legs of two Daegon behind him. A warrior stumbled forward and into Lucan's reverse stroke. The blow crushed the warrior's throat.

Lucan grabbed the dying warrior and jerked him into the path of a lunging bayonet. The blade stabbed through his back and out his chest. The Daegon holding the impaled rifle held on as the weight of his fellow dragged him forward.

The Genevan grabbed the invader by the front of his faceplate and rammed his head into the boulder with a crunch. Lucan whirled around and parried a bayonet strike, sending the blade bouncing off the rock. Lucan backhanded the attacker, then kicked him in the crotch so hard his feet left the ground.

A blow pitched Lucan forward, and his personal shield fogged with static across his face. He looked up and saw a rifle pointed directly at his head, then the weapon swung aside…straight at the King.

"No!" Lucan slapped the rifle aside and the bolt

struck the boulder in a shower of sparks and fragments. He scrambled back, shielding the King where he lay against the rock.

Daegon formed a half-circle around Lucan and the King, jabbing at the Genevan with their bayonets like dogs baiting a bear. Other soldiers removed weapons from wounded and dead Albion soldiers. The invaders stabbed each soldier in the base of the neck before moving on to the next.

A Daegon warrior a head taller than the others pushed through the throng around Lucan. This one had four yellow lines angled up the left side of his helmet and a red cape clasped to his pauldrons. One of his hands rested on the pommel of a gladius sheathed on his belt; the other held an ornate pistol.

"Give him to me," came from speakers on the warrior's throat. "You've earned your life. Go back to Geneva and herald our arrival."

"Never." Lucan shook his head.

The leader said something in his own language and the other Daegon cheered. He handed the pistol over to a warrior, then put both hands on the side of his helmet. It came loose with a hiss of air. His skin was a deep purple, his face otherwise perfectly human. Thin cables ran from the back of his head down the side of his neck. Golden irises looked at Lucan with a hint of disdain.

"I am Tiberian. I will have your name for a wager," the leader said.

"Save yourself," the King said. "There's nothing you can do for me now."

"My Lord, I ask you not to insult me," Lucan whispered.

"I am Tiberian," he repeated, pounding his fists against his chest. "Beat me and you both shall go free. My charge demands the King or my life. Name yourself or they will end this."

A Daegon warrior gave his rifle a quick shake.

The Genevan stood up, hands hung loosely at his

waist.

"Lucan."

"A word without a face is nothing," Tiberian said.

Lucan's armor pulled back from his head, adding another layer to his shoulders.

"Lucan. Let the King live. He can't fight anymore. His people will never forgive you for his murder."

"No…I can…" the King said weakly. Blood trickled from his mouth, staining his beard and shirt. He coughed and tried to grasp the pistol lying in the dirt next to him. A Daegon stabbed the tip of his bayonet through the trigger guard and dragged the weapon away.

"He's dying," Lucan said.

"Then you'd better kill me quick." Tiberian's cape fell to the ground. He grabbed his gladius and lunged forward, sweeping the blade toward Lucan's throat.

Lucan reared back, caught almost flat-footed by the Daegon's speed. He used the momentum to bring a foot back, then ducked under a stab to his throat. The

Genevan swung his foot around low to the ground and caught Tiberian's ankle with his kick. The blow rang with metal on metal, but the Daegon stayed on his feet.

Tiberian flicked the gladius toward Lucan's face. His armor scrambled up his throat and intercepted the cutting edge. The Daegon laughed briefly, then stepped away, the sword held in high guard, the tip waving in the air.

Lucan popped to his feet and raised his arms into a boxer's stance. His gestalt retreated from his face…and whispered to him.

+I am stronger than his edge.+ The brief contact against his armor was enough to gauge the sword's capability.

Tiberian whipped the blade around and slashed at Lucan's neck. The Genevan kept his feet planted and let the gladius strike his forearm. The blade twisted at the impact and bounced up. Lucan drove his armored fist into Tiberian's mouth, but a flash of an energy shield deflected

249

Lucan's punch. A cloud of white particles hid Tiberian's face from view and Lucan snapped a kick into the man's knee. The cloud flashed down and almost stopped his blow.

The kick buckled Tiberian's knee, sending him stumbling to the side. Lucan charged after him, trying to wrestle him to the ground. The Daegon planted a foot and then jumped straight up. He hooked a kick around and hit Lucan just below his eye.

Light exploded across Lucan's visage and his whole world went sideways. He hit the ground hard. Part of his mind demanded he roll, raise his arms in defense, but his body refused to answer. Blood seeped off his shattered cheekbone and dribbled into his mouth.

+Up. Up!+ came from his gestalt.

Tiberian stepped over the Genevan, reversing his grip on the sword and raising it over his head. He drove the tip through Lucan's chest, pinning him to the ground. Blood spurted out of the Genevan's mouth. He grabbed the blade and tried to pull it free.

"Enough sport," Tiberian said as he stood up and pointed to the King. "The time of false kings is over. Your people will see this and they will learn. They will be ruled."

A pair of Daegon dragged the King to Tiberian. He slammed a hand around Randolph's throat, then lifted him into the air.

"*Nobis regiray!*" Tiberian snapped the King's neck with a twist of his wrist, then tossed the body beside Lucan. Daegon cheered and raised their weapons high. Tiberian looked across the bodies on the ground, stopping at the Queen. He picked up a dinosaur doll made of cloth, half-soaked with blood.

He barked a question, and his warriors answered him with silence.

Tiberian went to Lucan and grabbed the impaled blade by the handle.

"Where is the child?" He brandished the doll over Lucan's face. Lucan's lungs were too full of blood to laugh, but he managed a weak smile.

Lucan raised a hand as the light faded away. It fell across Randolph's chest as he joined the King in death.

CHAPTER 13

Thorvald jogged down the dank tunnel, his rifle swaying across his body as his sabatons splashed through puddles of water. Light from overloaded, half-functioning lights flickered against roughhewn walls, casting irregular shadows.

"Are you sure this is the way?" Salis asked from behind him.

"I know where we are. Another two hundred yards and we'll find the exit path."

"You said that the last two times."

"Did I know both ways were caved in? No.

Neither did you. Now, unless you…" Thorvald's gestalt sent him a pulse, jostling his arm toward a tunnel on their left.

"Someone's coming," Thorvald whispered and raised his weapon. His armor amplified the sound of footfalls from around the corner.

"Leather shoes…running but carrying something, judging by the uneven steps…one person," Salis sent on a closed channel. "Not Daegon."

"Not the time to take risks." Thorvald and Salis pressed their backs to the wall just to the side of the dark tunnel where the runner approached. Thorvald took one hand off his rifle.

A man in dirty overalls ran into the hallway. He managed one step before Thorvald grabbed him by the collar, slammed him against the wall, and slapped a pistol out of the man's hand. Thorvald pressed his elbow into his throat.

Tolan let off a croak.

"I don't know you," Thorvald said through his faceplate. His gestalt sent a chill down his spine, trying to warn him of danger, but the only thing around was the disarmed man pinned to the wall.

"How about...now?" Tolan's visage shifted to thinner lips, pointed nose, and skin tone that was a few shades lighter.

"Faceless!" Salis raised her pistol and twisted her body away from Tolan to protect the Prince shielded against her chest.

"He's with intelligence," Thorvald said, lessening the pressure on the man's neck.

"And you aren't Royce. He's two inches taller." Tolan's eye twitched and Thorvald felt pressure against his sternum where Tolan held a vibro-knife point against the joins in his armor. The blade was unpowered, but a flick of a finger and a twist of the wrist would plunge the blade into his heart, armor or no armor.

Thorvald retracted his armor away from his face.

"You…" Tolan's lips pulled into a half-sneer. "Bet if I had a chance to dig deeper into your little friend, we'd figure out your part in this disaster. Patsy or traitor? Why don't you just tell me now?"

The blade powered up with a whine.

"What's he talking about?" Salis asked.

"You were assigned to wild space," Thorvald said. "I saw your mission reports. Ship. You have an off-the-books ship. Where is it?"

Tolan let out a low growl as the muscles in his knife arm readied to strike.

"Salis. Show him."

"If he's hostile, we can't risk it," she said.

Thorvald felt the blade's pressure lessen as Tolan's eyes darted to Salis.

"Show him."

Salis retracted armor from Prince Aidan's cocoon, enough that Tolan could see the boy's face.

"The King ordered us to keep him safe,"

Thorvald said.

Tolan pulled the knife away and slid it into a sheath on the small of his back.

"You were going for the Reading tunnel?" Tolan asked. "Useless. The city is burning. What isn't on fire is full of Daegon troops. Come with me. I'm going to Siam to find Admiral Sartorius."

+Go!+ The gestalt's order hit Thorvald like a punch.

"That's not an Albion world," Salis said. "Get us to Cardiff or—"

"Under attack and the Daegon have all the nexus points blockaded," Tolan snapped. "I can make it to Siam in two days if I make a good entry into the slip. Now are you coming or not?"

"Aidan's best chance is off world," Thorvald said to Salis.

She closed the cocoon and motioned down the tunnel with her pistol.

Tolan picked his pack out of a puddle and ran off; the Genevans followed close behind.

"How did he get a knife on you?" Salis asked through the suit-to-suit comms as they ran.

"I don't know this gestalt. It's like a hand-shy dog...nothing about this is right. It'll take time to sync."

"What was the Faceless talking about with you? Why are we even trusting someone who'd mutilate themselves like that? That augmentation is forbidden on every core world. Even the Mechanix won't go that far."

"Save it. If I become a danger to Aidan, my gestalt will kill me. Worry about getting the Prince out of here first."

Tolan looked up at a brass plate on the wall and slowed to a stop. He tapped a rock jutting from the wall, then another, then another.

"What the hell are you doing?" Salis asked.

"She new here?" Tolan looked to his left, then snapped his hand onto a rock on his right. The wall sank back several inches, then slid to the side. Lights flickered on, revealing a hangar housing a single dingy freighter with a decent share of dents and scorch marks from poor thermal shielding.

"You're kidding," Salis said.

"Tell us you're kidding," Thorvald said.

"The *Joaquim* has plenty under the hood where it counts. You try flying around wild space in something shiny. See how long you last before scavs rip you—and your ship—open and sell the parts to the highest bidder," Tolan said. He took a data slate from a pocket and tapped out a command. The cargo ramp lowered with an ugly creak, catching several times before it hit the ground.

"Now how about you two not look this lovely gift horse in the—"

An energy blast shattered a rock over the hidden entrance. Daegon warriors raced out of the distant darkness down the tunnel.

"Get in! Get in!" Tolan slapped a red button on a control panel inside the hangar as the Genevans ran past.

Energy blasts smacked the doors and slipped through the closing gap before the door shut with a pneumatic hiss. Tolan tapped a code onto the panel and the hangar doors slid aside slowly.

The setting suns over the East Ocean cast red and ochre bands across the sky. The crash of waves sent spray into the air and onto the *Joaquim*'s nose.

"Of course this happens at high tide." Tolan aimed his pistol at the control panel, waited until the doors were clear of the freighter's wingtips, then fired twice.

Thorvald stopped on the cargo ramp as Salis continued into the ship.

"Are you coming or not?" Thorvald asked.

"You know how to fly this thing, meathead?" Tolan sprinted up the ramp and tossed his pack onto an acceleration couch where Salis was strapping in a groggy-looking Aidan.

"No." Thorvald raised the ramp as Tolan opened the bridge door with a spin of the lock.

The spy jumped into the helm station and slapped controls. The engines came to life with a chug and a brief squeal of metal.

"That's not a good sound," Tolan muttered.

"When was the last time you had this thing serviced?" Thorvald asked as he buckled himself into the astrogation station.

"Right before I ran like a bat out of hell from Scarrus with the most wanted man in the galaxy chained up in the cargo hold. Did I mention getting shot at by the most wanted man in the galaxy's buddies before I hit slip space? Or was it before I dropped off that shipment of spliced panthers on Orosis?" Tolan cocked his head to the side in thought. Shrugging, he fed power to the thrusters. "You know how to do a pre-flight check?" Tolan asked.

"No…"

"No big deal. That part's boring. Pull the grav buoy data for Siam."

"Ugh…"

"How about you get on the ship's nose and pretend you're a hood ornament? At least then you wouldn't be taking up space on my bridge." Tolan flicked a comm switch. "Hang on back there, other Genevan and Prince Aidan. This'll be ugly."

Tolan brought the ship off the deck and roared out over the waves.

****

Wyman ducked beneath his fighter and quickly surveyed the damage. The bottom of his Typhoon had ugly black streaks peppered by silver shards of metal. He frowned and touched one of the shiny bits, which was cool against his fingertips. The metal must have come from the enemy fighter he'd destroyed…but it wasn't like any kind of material he'd ever seen used in spacecraft. He flicked it with his fingers and knocked it loose. It fell to the tarmac with a slight *tink*.

"Ensign Wyman." A robot with a telescoping

body and several arms rolled over to the side of his fighter, then rose out of view. "The replacement of your canopy will take one hundred eighty-seven seconds. All facility units are in use. Connect battery cables to your unit to shorten your time at this station."

"Right. Got it." Wyman slid open the armor panel on his battery casing and electricity arced out of the housing and struck his finger. When he jumped back, he banged his head against the bottom of the fighter. Shaking his numbed hand, he rubbed the back of his head.

There, impaled in the battery, was a tiny bit of shiny metal.

"Service, you think you can get that out?" Wyman scooted away from the casing as it gave off an angry buzz.

A mechanical arm bent under the fighter and extended to the battery. A lens looked over the damage, then four rubber-tipped fingers sprang out of the arm. It plucked the metal out and dropped it to the ground. The lens clicked several times, then the arm retracted to the robot.

"Attach the power cables," the robot said. A section of the tarmac popped open, revealing a bright yellow cable head.

"You're sure?"

"This facility's central programming will not allow me to recommend an action that could be detrimental to the health and well-being of Albion citizens or allied military personnel." The robot dropped the gouged canopy to the ground with a crack as a mule-bot rolled over with a new canopy.

"Not the most dangerous thing that's happened to me today," Wyman muttered as he grabbed the power cable by a pair of handles on the neck and jammed it into the battery. Green lights blinked on the cable and the housing. Wyman scurried out from beneath the fighter and found Ivor leaning against her fighter, her head buried in her hands.

A distant thunderclap rolled through the air. The

sky over New Exeter glowed, a mock sunrise to the setting suns in the west. Fireballs crisscrossed high above, the final moments of the blasted remains of the Home Fleet and enemy ships.

The rearm/recharge pad was a simple clearing butting against the small town of Reading. The faux-grass covering had rolled up next to the tree line once the three fighters signaled their approach. The automated facility kept its service robots and some munitions buried in a low hill a few yards away in the woods. Queen Diana had insisted on such facilities across most of the populated areas after the First Reach War when the Reich had landed a corps of soldiers outside New Exeter and laid siege to the city. The war ended before Albion had a chance to launch a counterattack, but that another power had touched down with near impunity had changed the royal family's outlook on planetary defense. Generations had grumbled at the expense and higher taxes, and right now, Wyman was thankful he had a place to get his Typhoon back into the fight.

Robots worked on the third fighter, swapping a burnt-out cannon and fixing missiles to the wingtips.

"Where's Dandy?" Wyman asked.

The sound of projectile vomiting came from the woods.

"Who the hell are they?" Ivor asked, looking to the sky. "No demands, no warning. They're just here to kill us?"

"I got a feeling they'd have nuked the entire planet by now if they just wanted to kill us. Their ships don't match anything I've ever seen…we just need to hold them off. Buy time for 9th and 5th Fleets on Cardiff to get back. The Cathay and Indus will send help, I'm sure of it."

She looked at a screen mounted on the back of her glove and shook her head. "Nothing on any network. We could have surrendered by now and wouldn't even know it."

Wyman grabbed her by the shoulder.

"Don't. To admit defeat is to dishonor the King. You remember the oath from the day we earned our wings?"

"'The navy's ships and sailors carry the weight of Albion on their shoulders. I will not falter. I will not fail in my duties.'" She nodded and stood up a bit straighter.

"Repairs are complete!" a robot announced as it backed away from Wyman's ship. The power cable detached on its own and retracted into the tarmac.

Dandy stumbled out of the high grass, his face deathly pale.

"You OK?" Ivor asked.

"One hundred percent. Let's get back up there," he said.

Wyman ran to his Typhoon and climbed up the robot to get into his cockpit.

"Your ship is rated at seventy-three percent combat efficiency," the robot said. "Please avoid any further damage."

"No promises," Wyman said as he slammed his helmet on and closed the canopy. His fighter powered up and he held his breath as some of the panels flickered…then stayed on.

"This is Rosy, almost green across the board."

"Dandy. Green enough."

"Stay on me. We're heading for New Exeter. Hug the coastline and keep your eyes open for anything else flying. We'll join up with any friendlies and engage any hostiles we can pick off."

Wyman sent power to his vectored thrusters and brought his fighter straight up. The Typhoon hovered in place as the engines realigned and sent the craft hurtling forward. Wyman crossed over the ocean a few minutes later and kept his ship low over the waves.

The domed mothership loomed over the distant city, its flat bottom alive with running lights. The crystal mounted on top glowed like one of Albion's moons. Brief flurries of exploding ships and energy bolts came and went around the ship.

"The big one doesn't seem that interested," Dandy said.

"Like it's just watching, no worries about being in a war zone," Ivor said.

"Doubt we could even scratch the paint with our guns…but look at this…" Wyman zoomed in on the underside of the ship where blocky shuttles took off from open bays. "Bet we'd get their attention if we sent a couple missiles in there to say hello."

"We don't have a chance in hell of getting that close," Dandy said.

"But they might. Whole wing of Typhoons coming in on our seven o'clock." Ivor sent the track for the incoming fighters to her wingmen.

"Either of you picking up their comms?" Wyman reached for his radio panel when he saw five of the spear-tip fighters swing around the crater wall surrounding the city.

"Contact! Straight ahead." He marked the lead as a target and keyed his missile sensors.

"We're better off joining—"

A civilian ship, barely larger than a ground-to-orbit shuttle, burst out of the crater wall just behind the enemy fighters. It angled its nose up, then suddenly dove for the ocean. The spear tips banked away from Wyman and made for the shuttle.

"What the hell?" Wyman's missile toned a lock, but he hesitated.

"Any Albion military, this is the Intelligence Ministry ship *Joaquim*. We need immediate air support! We have a bleed in our gamma relays. I repeat, a bleed in our gamma relays," came over several encrypted channels and in the clear.

Wyman fired his locked missile and opened his throttle. The enemy fighter's edges brightened as it prepared to fire, slowing as the missile streaked through its engines and sent the wreck crashing into the wave-pounded rocks around the crater. Two of the enemy fighters broke off their pursuit of the shuttle and looped back toward the Typhoons.

Mentioning "gamma relays" in any transmission was code for a member of the royal family in danger.

"*Joaquim*, this is Freak Show. I've got three fighters on the way." He dared a glance over his shoulder and saw the wing of Albion defenders spreading out to meet a wave of enemy ships coming off New Exeter. "We're all you've got for now."

Missiles leapt off Ivor and Dandy's wings. The diamond tips of the enemy fighters glowed as the four weapons closed the distance. Wyman targeted a fighter already painted by Ivor's missile and fired off his last Shrike.

Thin energy beams intercepted each of the initial missiles, forming a brief wall of smoke and fire between the two forces. Wyman's missile shot through the smoke and a massive fireball erupted on the other side as it hit home.

"Stole my kill," Ivor mumbled.

Wyman angled his fighter up and pushed his ion engines so hard his new canopy rattled on the hinges. The *Joaquim* was miles away, moving extremely fast for what looked like any other shuttle that plied Albion's skies during peacetime.

"Rosy, Dandy, handle the rest. I'm going for the bogie on the shuttle's tail," Wyman said. He let off a half-aimed shot that hit the water just ahead of the enemy fighter. His attempt to get the enemy's attention failed as it let off a blast that missed the *Joaquim* by a few feet.

"Anytime!" came from the shuttle.

"Shuttle, on my mark, I want you to pull up and cut your air speed," Wyman said.

"Do *what?*"

The enemy's edges glowed brighter.

"Mark!"

To Wyman's surprise, the shuttle did as instructed.

The pursuing fighter tried to match the maneuver and sent its shot wide. Wyman unleashed a torrent of wild shots that swarmed around the enemy. One connected, breaking through an edge and knocking the fighter around like a spinning top. It plunged into the sea.

The shuttle rolled over and flew back out over the open water.

An energy beam slashed across Wyman's nose cone and sent up a geyser of boiling water. He slammed his fighter to the side as steaming rain spattered against his canopy.

"One got away from us!" Ivor shouted.

Wyman leveled off and twisted from side to side, searching for the last enemy fighter.

His Typhoon kicked up as the enemy roared just beneath him, disrupting the airflow over his wings and sending him into a tail spin. He grabbed his thruster control and waited until he saw the darkening sky in front of him, then sent a burst of power through the engines, shooting him straight into the air. He throttled back once his wings regained lift and dove back toward the ocean.

Ivor was on the last enemy ship's tail, but she didn't fire—any miss would put the *Joaquim* in jeopardy.

A thin beam from the enemy hit the shuttle's right wing and almost knocked it into a barrel roll. A flare from Dandy's engines cast deep yellow light across the waves.

"Dandy, what're you—"

Dandy screamed and rammed the enemy ship. Both fighters vanished in a fireball, showering the area in metal fragments that splashed into the ocean.

"No chute; he didn't eject," Ivor said, stunned.

"Freak Show, was it?" came from the *Joaquim.* "Thanks for clearing the air. We need an escort to orbit. Can you break atmosphere?"

Wyman circled around the burning wreckage of Dandy's and the enemy's fighters, looking for any sign of life that was surely impossible.

"Freak Show?"

"On it, yeah…yeah." Wyman looked at his battery levels. "I can make orbit. Rosy?"

"Can do." She flew to the *Joaquim*'s wing and matched the shuttle's speed. "Ready when you are."

A flight path appeared on his HUD, leading to the starry sky above. He let his ship's computer handle the maneuver and settled against his cockpit's padding as the acceleration pressed him back. His mind went to the dying *Excelsior*, the loss of so many fighters, the burning cities.

Opening his eyes, he focused on his instruments, concentrating on the altimeter and the drain on his battery life—anything but the horrors he'd witnessed. His body lightened as gravity slipped away.

"Joaquim," Wyman said as the acceleration tapered off and normal breathing was possible, "we'll get you to a naval vessel. There should be another task force coming in from Sandov."

"This is Thorvald with the Genevan Guard," a new voice said from the shuttle. "We're taking the Crown

275

Prince to…Siam. No invading ships have translated through that nexus point yet."

"Crown Prince? Does that mean the King is…what about Sandov or even Cardiff?" Ivor asked.

"Both are under attack," Thorvald said. "The enemy, whoever it is, wasted no time before striking through our major nexus points. Siam is our best option. Come to a close formation. We're going to do a wide-field jump to bring your fighters with us."

Wyman swallowed hard.

"Hold on…there's no way a ship that small can expand a slip field to—"

"This isn't your standard shuttle, in case you haven't noticed," said the first voice from the *Joaquim*. "I made some extensive modifications to her over the years. The slip generator is the latest tech out of the Reich military development. They don't know we have it and would be most grumpy to learn as much."

Wyman settled on the shuttle's wing and looked

over the top at Ivor, who threw her hands up in confusion.

"This is crazy," Wyman said. "Our fighters can't survive in slip space for more than—"

"You stay here and you'll die," Tolan said. "I've done this before and it almost worked that time. Mag-lock your fighters to the hull once we're in slip space."

"We're not even near the—"

"You're starting to bore me, kid. I need to concentrate for a second so I don't smear your molecules over the next many light-years….Close enough. Activating in three…"

Wyman tucked his fighter closer to the shuttle as a milky-white bubble formed around them.

"Two…"

He'd done a slip transfer only once before in his life, tucked deep inside a void ship, and his stomach twisted into knots at the memory.

"One!"

A kaleidoscope of light swarmed over the bubble.

****

Wyman felt his fighter settle against the shuttle's upper hull and flicked on the mag locks in his landing gear. The electromagnets were designed as a last resort to save a fighter if its mothership was too damaged to recover void craft by locking on to the outside of its parent ship. While Wyman had practiced the maneuver many times, he'd never done it on such a small ship.

Or while moving.

Or while in slip space.

He balled his trembling hands into fists and refused to look at anything but his knees. The madness of slip space swirled around him, a riot of smeared light that danced like water reflecting off a pool over the protective bubble of true space around the three ships.

According to the navy's psychologists, his aversion to seeing raw slip space was quite normal and not a problem. Operating outside a ship's hull while underway in the gravity funnels between stars was extremely dangerous and not part of his job description. They assured him that he had nothing to ever worry about.

Wyman couldn't help but notice that none of those shrinks were there with him while he sat in his cockpit, almost too terrified to move.

"I'm locked in," Ivor said.

"Mmm-hmm," Wyman hummed.

"Well I'll be damned…that worked," Tolan said. "OK, now I need the two of you to get to the air lock on the back of the ship. Salis will let you in."

"You know what? I'm OK right here," Wyman said.

"It'll take us three days to reach Siam. How long will your life support last?" Tolan asked.

"Twelve hours," Ivor said. "It's not that bad, Freak. Kind of pretty actually."

"Nope! Just…bring me new air tanks. I won't get hungry. Three days of sitting right here…with my eyes closed."

"Wait a minute, are you afraid?" Tolan asked. "A fighter pilot scared of a little EVA? That's like a wet navy sailor that doesn't know how to swim."

"I've got him," Ivor said. "Get the air lock ready for us."

Wyman sat still, concentrating on each breath of recycled air that came through his suit. A knock on his canopy made him flinch.

"Freak, look at me," Ivor said.

Wyman shook his head.

"I know about the accident on the *Derringer*, know what you went through. But you're not there anymore; you're right here with me. I need you to unlock your canopy and get inside the nice, warm shuttle that's full of breathable air and…probably alcohol. Couldn't you go for drink after this shit of a day?"

Wyman turned his head to Ivor and opened one eye. She stood next to his cockpit, one hand gripping the emergency release that would have blown his canopy off his fighter. Madness swirled behind her and his stomach heaved.

He turned his head away and used one hand to unlock the canopy. She grabbed him by the hand and squeezed it.

"The docs said I wouldn't remember anything," Wyman said, his chin tucked against his chest. "But I do...I do."

He felt his restraints loosen and then he felt her grab him beneath his shoulder. She pulled at his bulk but failed to move him.

"I swear to God I don't know how you get your giant gorilla ass in the cockpit," Ivor said.

"Hey kids," Tolan said through their helmets, *"got a slight fluctuation in the slip drive. The bubble's going to shrink to standard size in the next few minutes if I don't figure out the issue. Long story short, get your asses in here before I reverse the polarity on the hull and jettison your fighters to save the* Joaquim. *Better get*

moving. Mr. and Mrs. Unfriendly will crush my skull if I put the
Crown Prince at risk."

"You hear that, Freak? You start moving or we die—we *both* die." Ivor shook his shoulder. "I'm not leaving you out here. Get. Out."

Wyman lurched out of the cockpit and fell onto the hull, gipping it with both hands.

"Progress, that's progress," Ivor said as she tried to lift him by the waist with a grunt.

"I don't want to look," Wyman said.

"You don't have to look. You just have to move." He got to his knees and gripped her wrist with both hands. Wyman took a halting step forward, then another.

Ivor led Wyman to the back of the shuttle. She peered over the edge and into the swirling abyss below. White light spilled out of the open air lock.

"OK, this part's going to be tricky," she said. "You need to climb down and swing into the airlock."

"What?" Wyman's eyes opened in shock, which

proved to be a mistake as he squeezed his eyes shut again and moaned in terror.

"Get him to the edge," a woman's voice said.

"About out of patience with you, Freak." Ivor swept her shin against Wyman's ankles, knocked him flat against the hull, and then pressed her hands against his shoulders and pushed him feet first toward the edge.

"Wait. Wait!" Wyman grabbed her by the forearms hard enough that she winced in pain.

A bronze armored hand reached over the edge and grabbed Wyman by the ankle.

He gave off a scream so shrill it could have come from a little girl. The hand yanked Wyman over the edge, who dragged Ivor along with him.

"Wait! Wait!" Ivor tried to dig her heels into the hull, but Wyman's grip held true. She flipped over the edge and got a close look at the energy wall that held the ship inside slip space. Touching the wall would send her into real space, and the physics of that transition would smear her every atom across a very long swath of interstellar space. She jerked away from certain death and slammed into a metal floor.

She stared at a pair of bronze boots, then looked up Salis's body to her masked face. The outer air-lock door shut and air flooded the chamber.

Wyman had an iron grip on Ivor's arms, his face tucked against the floor.

"Bridge, I've got them," Salis said. Her faceplate shifted away and she snorted.

"Finally," Tolan said. *"Bring them up when they're ready."*

"Freak, we're safe. Open your eyes and let go of me before you break my friggin' arms," Ivor said.

Wyman looked up, let her go, and sat against the bulkhead. He ripped his helmet off and wiped sweat-soaked hair away from his face.

"To hell with that," he said.

"You don't say." Ivor removed her helmet and

took a deep breath of chilly air.

"You're a Genevan?" Wyman asked Salis. "Who's here? What about the King?"

"I am Salis. Crown Prince Aidan is resting with Thorvald. The rest…"

Wyman saw the dents and scorch marks on her armor and got an idea of what happened.

Ivor raised a foot and kicked Wyman in the chest.

"What the hell, Wyman?" she asked. "Dogfights, bad orbitals in *and* out, and you lock up during something as simple as an EVA walk that we've done a hundred times in training?"

"We never did a slip space EVA. Did you see—" he pointed at the air-lock door "—that shit? There was an explosion when I was a kid…the docs said I was cured and good to join the navy…it all just fell apart when I was out there."

"Psycho conditioning can fail after enough physical stress," Salis said. "This isn't unusual."

"Not that unusual. You feel better, Wyman?" Ivor asked.

"A little, actually." Wyman shrugged.

Ivor sniffed the air and gave her wingman a disappointed look.

"Don't you judge me. Remember what happened to you after that night in Coventry City?" Wyman shifted his seat.

"It's called blackout drunk for a reason," Ivor said, standing up.

"I'll take you to the showers." Salis helped Wyman up and led them into the *Joaquim*.

****

Tiberian walked through a throng of Daegon warriors and into the hidden shuttle bay. The flash of laser fire still winked in the sky as the last of the Albion navy died to the Daegon guns. With the palace under his command, and the battle for the skies nearly over, Albion was all but defeated.

A warrior knelt before Tiberian and held up a stuffed doll.

"We found this here, master," the warrior said. "A vessel managed to escape orbit with the aid of two fighters."

Tiberian took King Randolph's crown from his belt, activated scanners in his gloves, and waved his fingertips over the crown and doll. DNA from both items showed they belonged to a father and son.

"Prince Aidan lives," Tiberian dropped the doll to the ground, "and he has escaped." He touched a golden box on a chain around his neck. The expectations of his command were simple. So long as the Albion royal family, any part of it, survived, he was a failure.

"The fleet tracked the ship's slip signature," the warrior said. "They didn't go far, to a backwater world called Siam."

"Bring my shuttle," Tiberian said. "The hunt continues."

CHAPTER 14

Wyman ducked his head and shoulders into the bridge. The sight of the light swirl around the ship's slip bubble made his stomach lurch, but the panic he'd felt outside the hull stayed away.

Tolan sat at the conn, eyes fixed on a holo pathway projected in front of him. His hands tightened and closed on the control stick as he gently adjusted the ship's course.

"You called?" Wyman asked.

"I know you're a fighter jock, but are you also rated for slip travel?" Tolan asked, keeping his gaze on the projections.

"I have instrument training and some sim time. Basic assessment stuff before I went down the single-pilot track. You need me to take over?"

Tolan's face twisted, as if something deep inside was giving him pain.

"The grav buoy's data was flawed. No doubt from the Daegon-created nexus points. We have a slip path to Siam, but we don't have a good enough read for the autopilot to make the whole trip. Should go easy once we're past Guernica's mass shadow. Have to have someone on the stick until then. Need you to—crap."

Tolan pulled the stick to the right, then back as the slip pathway changed.

"If we lose the groove, our effective speed gets cut to barely light speed," Tolan said. "It'll take hours to get back to best speed—hours the Daegon can use to overtake us. This day will get worse if we pop out of slip and into their welcoming committee instead of Admiral Sartorius' fleet."

"Yeah, I get that…how's this ship doing almost three hundred c? The navy's courier ships can't get over two fifty without flying apart."

"Daimler drive from the Reich factory on Far Carolina. Still in testing after an explosion destroyed the production factory. They don't know I have it and it'll stay that way, won't it?"

Wyman bit his lower lip in contemplation.

"Wait…what exactly are you? Some kind of a spy?"

The projection in front of Tolan straightened out and the man finally glanced over at the fighter pilot.

"I had a ship with no transponder hidden inside the Odin Wall term sporting stolen Reich tech and a half-dozen other tricks you haven't noticed yet that would let me smuggle Emperor Xin's favorite concubine off the Forbidden Continent on Lantau without anyone noticing. No, I'm not a spy."

"Well, since this is your ship, I guess that means

you're in charge."

"There are times I appreciate military narrow-mindedness. Sure, I'm in charge. Until the Genevans decide I'm about to put the Prince at risk and they crush my head like a grape. This smooth patch should last for a few more minutes. You ready to take the stick?" Tolan shifted uneasily.

"I can manage. Move."

Tolan struggled out of the seat and leaned against the astrogation station as Wyman took his spot. Tolan doubled over in pain, his hands pressed against his stomach.

"Controls are easy…slip groove looks steady…you OK?"

Tolan stood up, the fingers of one hand locked into claws.

"Adrenaline dump wore off. Nothing like hours of pants-shitting terror to upset the humors, right?" The spy rubbed his locked hand until the fingers flexed on their own.

Wyman's cheeks flushed in embarrassment.

"Send Ivor up here when she's out of the shower, please," Wyman said. "We'll work out shifts between the three of us. You got any food on this crate?"

"The galley is wherever you open a zip-pack. I think I've got a couple days' supply left over from my last stop on Wu-Gwai. You like chicken feet and fish stew?"

"What?"

"You get hungry enough and it'll taste great." Tolan pressed a knuckle against his temple. "I need to attend to some needs. Keep us on track. Prince Aidan's depending on you."

"You sure you're OK?"

"Worry about the ship. I'll worry about myself."

Tolan bumped against the doorway on his way out. He heard the Genevans talking to each other in his cabin and the sound of the sonic shower from the lavatory in the next compartment over.

He picked up his pack and went down the stairs to the cargo hold on stiff legs. The adrenaline in his system had tamped down the worst of his withdrawal, but now his body was making him pay for waiting so long between hits.

Tolan spun open the lock on a small compartment and tossed his pack to the floor. The room reeked of body odor and rotting food. He'd kept Ja'war chained to the walls in this makeshift brig during the long flight from Scarrus. Having anyone on Albion clean the off-the-books freighter hidden in the bowels of the castle would beg too many questions, questions neither Tolan nor Director Ormond wanted asked. So the room remained filthy.

He closed the door behind him as quietly as he could, then tore into his pack. Emergency medical bundles, data slates full of media, outfits from a half-dozen wild-space worlds all went flying.

"Where is it? Where?" Tolan turned the pack over and shook out the last bits of toiletries and spare power cells for his pistol. The silver case he needed wasn't there.

"No! No no no…" Tolan snatched up a set of grimy overalls and slapped at the pockets.

Thorvald cleared his throat.

Tolan spun around, clutching the overalls to his chest.

"I didn't…hear you come in," Tolan said.

Thorvald tapped a small metal case against his leg. Tolan looked at it and smacked his lips.

"That's mine. Give it back," the spy said.

"Amoricilia, street name 'bliss,' is illegal and dangerous." Thorvald tossed the case to Tolan, who sat back on his haunches and removed a small injector covered in a riot of colors. He pressed the tip against his neck and gasped.

Tolan fell back against the bulkhead and kicked his legs out.

"I had to do it…Mr. Thorvald. I spent years in wild space hunting Ja'war. You know what it's like looking

294

for a man with no face? No contacts? Like trying to catch smoke. So I went to a gene slicer and lost my old face…so that I could find Ja'war's. The surgeon wasn't as skilled as she claimed. There were some complications with my nervous system, and when you're on a backwater world chasing down terrorists and your skin starts turning into putty, you take whatever solution is at hand. The bliss got things back under control. The addiction was a little bonus."

"The Intelligence Ministry accepts that you're compromised by a narcotic?"

"Ooo…Mr. High and Mighty all the sudden. They sent me and my team to wild space expecting a result—that we bring Ja'war back for trial. Our methods were up to us. I brought that terrorist back to face justice. All that trouble to bring him back when I could've spaced him on a hundred different days. Now he's most certainly dead, if Ormond followed protocol or the Daegon didn't get to him first. As for my issues…my augmentations and the bliss go hand in hand until I can get to a full genome therapy clinic. There are two that could get me back to my old self. One's on Rajkot on the far side of Indus space. The other is a pile of burning rubble in New Exeter."

"The Prince could have come across your narcotics and harmed himself. Salis and I will keep an eye on you. If your addiction causes—"

"Piss. Off. You're very welcome for the use of my rust bucket to escape Albion. Clearly my health issue is more of a concern than a sky full of warships raining death everywhere. I'll be sure to make sure everyone we might need help from did all their homework in grade school and has only the purest of motivations. Oh, by the way, who's that new girl? Doesn't seem like she's on the up and up about exactly why you were about to get tossed off the planet."

Thorvald half-opened his mouth, then shut it.

"Yeah, that's what I thought." Tolan slipped the case full of bliss injectors into a pocket and let his head loll to the side. "Make you a deal, bucket head. You keep my problem hush-hush and I'll play dumb if anyone asks what got you in trouble. Fair?"

Thorvald stepped out of the cabin and grabbed the door.

"I'll be out in half an hour or three." Tolan let out a sigh as the drug smothered his nervous system. "Shut…the…"

Thorvald slammed the door.

****

Salis stood beside the cot where Prince Aidan slept. She kept her back to the boy, facing the only door into the compartment. She heard him breathing, the kick of his feet against the thin mattress, and the occasional whine.

Thorvald knocked twice on the door, above and below the handle to signal that he was coming in alone and without any duress. He carried in several freeze-dried packages of food and plastic bottles filled with juice.

"He'll be awake soon," Salis said. "He's too small for another dose of sedative, even if protocol allows for it."

"Two days to Siam at best speed," Thorvald said as he laid out the food on a nightstand bolted to the bulkhead. "We're all he has as far as support and comfort."

Salis lowered her chin to her chest.

"Once we arrive on Siam, we'll take him to Admiral Sartorius' ship. Where we go from there is up to him. Cathay space is a month away, Indus six weeks. You can book passage back to Geneva from any of the core worlds."

"What?" Salis cocked her head to the side. "What do you mean?"

"You aren't oath-sworn to Albion. By the contract with the royal family, you haven't taken Andrin's place on the roster. Our House lords expect you to bring your armor back to Geneva for another assignment. Sartorius knows he can't stop you if your gestalt isn't locked to

Albion."

"You think I'd just run back home after what we went through to save this child?"

"We're not of Albion. We are paid bodyguards. Our home is Geneva and if we are not oath-bound to a client, our loyalties are clear. You should go back home. The House needs to know that the rest of the garrison is lost. I will stay with Aidan until the contract ends or until my last dying breath."

"But I can…" She turned around and looked down at the sleeping child, his eyelids fluttering with nightmares. "He's the Crown Prince now, isn't he? I can take the oath before him. My gestalt will bind itself to him. Then I can stay."

"Who is making this decision? Your heart or your mind?"

Salis knelt down and reached to Aidan. Her armor pulled away from her hand and she set her palm against his forehead.

"Is it wrong to care? I take the oath, bind myself to him, does it matter if I wish to protect him out of…emotion instead of blind duty? All those years with King Randolph and it didn't tear you apart to leave him behind?"

"Of course it did." Thorvald's hands clenched. "Albion became my home. I would have stayed and fought had the Prince not needed me. This won't end well, Salis. The Daegon won't stop at Albion. This war will be worse than the Mechanix incursion, worse than both Reach Wars. If you bind yourself to Aidan, you'll stay at his side until the contract ends in five years. And then? You think he or what's left of Albion will have the money to hire us again?"

"A lot can happen in five years," Salis said. "If I stay on, the House will be paid for the remainder of the contract even if I die in service."

"You're young. You could go back and take on another full-term contract and earn even more."

"We can't take Aidan to Geneva. Our world takes no official side in any dispute. That most of our adults serve in mercenary battalions across the stars and we take weapons in lieu of payment has kept Geneva out of every war since the first colony ship landed centuries ago. Somehow I doubt these Daegon will respect our well-armed neutrality. If I leave the fight now, it'll find me again."

Aidan rubbed his eyes and sat up. He let out a panicked cry and hid beneath his blanket.

"Mommy! Papa!"

Salis' face broke with emotion for a moment…then returned to stone.

"Aidan? Do you remember me?" Thorvald grabbed a bottle of orange juice and knelt by the bed. "I have your favorite here."

Aidan lifted the blanket and stared wide-eyed at Thorvald. He buried himself in the blanket again.

"Mommy was red."

301

*"Does he even understand what happened? He's what,
three? I don't have children,"* Salis said in Genevan.

*"He's never been away from his mother for more than a few
hours,"* Thorvald said. "Aidan? Juice?"

A little hand reached out from beneath the
blankets and Thorvald stuck a small straw into the bottle
before he pressed it into the boy's palm.

"What are we supposed to do for him?"

"Shield him from danger…get him to a safe place."
Thorvald ripped open a packet labelled COOKIES.

Aidan lifted a corner of the blanket and tossed the
empty bottle to the floor.

"Mommy?"

Thorvald lifted the blanket. Aidan lay on his side,
his hands and knees tucked to his chest.

"My Prince, do you remember the exercises we
used to do?" Thorvald asked. "I'm going to be your big
brother. This is Salis. She'll be your big sister."

Aidan crawled across the bed and hugged

Thorvald around the neck. His armor slid away from his chest and lapped against the boy's sides. The gestalt would have formed a new cocoon, but Thorvald willed against it.

"I want Mommy."

"I know, little one. I know." Thorvald patted his hand against the back of Aidan's head. "I will keep you safe. I swear it."

"Thorvald," Salis said, "have your gestalt witness this."

The older Genevan stood up, still holding on to the child.

+Foolish,+ the gestalt said. +Morgaten knows this.+

Thorvald turned his body so Aidan could see Salis. She knelt on one knee, her head facing the ground.

"I am Fiona Salis of House Ticino. I offer my service to the royal family of Albion in accordance with the laws of Geneva and all binding contracts. For you, Prince Aidan, I will be your shield. Until my last dying breath."

"She's silly," Aidan said.

"If you wish to stay with us, just touch her on the head." Salis bent over and the Prince slapped her on the top of her head.

"I and my gestalt are one. We witness this oath and will record the deed for our House," Thorvald said. "It is done."

He felt Salis' gestalt sync with his own as his armor unlocked more functions for her. She would have constant location and biometric readings for Aidan now that the last restrictions were removed.

"The King did this with a good deal more pomp and circumstance," Thorvald said.

"I didn't think my first oath would be inside a tramp freighter that reeked of old socks…or that I would make it to a child," Salis said.

"Where's Mommy? Daddy?" Aidan asked.

Thorvald looked as Salis and raised an eyebrow.

Salis sighed and shook her head.

CHAPTER 15

The *Joaquim* came out of slip space, wobbling through the transition.

Tolan gripped his controls and fought to bring the ship under control.

"Woah, nelly." Tolan clicked thruster switches and the distant green world of Siam steadied. Wyman gripped the sides of the astrogation station and gave Ivor a nervous glance.

"I saw that," Tolan said. "You think I carry a pair of fighters through slip space every day? Speaking of, why don't you two get those barnacles off my beautiful baby?"

"Soon as you cut the deceleration so we don't go flying away once we're outside the inertial dampeners, sure," Briar said. "The inside of my fighter will smell a hell of a lot better than this crate."

"This is the thanks I get for letting you drink all my beer." Tolan tapped a screen. "Give me ten minutes to bleed acceleration. Go get changed."

"Finally." Wyman hauled himself out of the chair and pressed past Thorvald standing in the doorway, Briar close behind.

"What's next?" the Genevan asked.

"Well…" Tolan picked up a headset and held one speaker to his ear. He tapped it against his seat, tried it again, and then tossed it to the ground. "I'm not running my normal stealth suite and I've got a pair of Typhoons bolted to my roof like hunting trophies. Given the fleet's radar capabilities and the normal reaction times, we should—"

"Unidentified vessel, this is Albion ship HMS

Endymion. State the nature of your business here and explain why your transponders are off in violation of more safety regulations than I care to list," came over the bridge's speakers.

"In wild space, they call our navy the sticks," Tolan said.

"Sticks?"

"Up our asses." Tolan flicked a switch and said, "*Endymion*, this is the *Joaquim*. I need to speak to Admiral Sartorius aboard the *Orion*. Code baxter-seven-november-one-one."

There was a pause and a hiss of from the speakers.

"*Joaquim*, heave to and prepare to receive boarders."

"No, *Endymion*, I don't think you heard me right. Admiral Sartorius. Code—"

"Code Vermillion," Thorvald said, "authorization: bulldog three actual."

"Stand by," came from the *Endymion*.

"What's wrong with my code?" Tolan pulled a small notepad from his breast pocket and frowned at it.

"Expired three weeks ago," Thorvald said.

"I don't care what anyone says about you, Thorvald. You're OK."

"What? Who's been talking about me?"

"*Joaquim*, this is Admiral Sartorius. Switch to this cypher and connect via tight beam."

"Here we go." Tolan keyed in the code that popped up on his screen. The image shifted to the Admiral's ready room. Sartorius walked up to the camera a moment later.

"What is the meaning of this? You can't just show up and toss around a code vermillion without sending my bridge into a near panic over…why is a Genevan with you in that crate? If he's there, then that means a member of the royal family is too." Sartorius' face went pale as he put the pieces together.

"Admiral," Tolan said, "we have some god-awful

news. I think you're Albion's last remaining leader."

****

The Admiral closed the channel to the *Joaquim*. Albion occupied. The fleets destroyed. Colonies under attack. He'd served during the last few skirmishes of the Second Reach War…the very thought of something like this was impossible.

His wife had just finished the renovations on their retirement home outside Coventry. A cabin set deep in the pine forests surrounded by the squirrels and hummingbirds she so loved to feed…

He pushed the thought away and straightened his uniform. He was the master and commander of 11th Fleet. There was no time for worry or self-pity. Action would save Albion.

The news he'd just learned could shatter the fleet's morale if it spread through rumors that would layer on even more panic. Purpose would keep his sailors focused.

"All is well, Admiral?" Jeneck asked from behind

him.

The words startled Sartorius, but he played it off by turning and smiling.

"I didn't hear you come in," he said. Her demeanor was attentive and curious. She must not have overheard the conversation with the *Joaquim*. "All the captains will be arriving shortly. Prepare tea for the stateroom, then lay out my void uniform."

"At once." She nodded and slipped out of the room.

Sartorius turned back to the communications panel and tapped an icon to open a channel direct to every ship's captain.

"This is the Admiral. Set alert condition bravo. All ship masters and key staff to the *Orion* immediately." The fleet's ship roster scrolled up the screen. Individual ships went from amber to green as the captains acknowledged the order. Commander Gage's name stayed amber. The Admiral tapped Gage's spot and his location on Siam popped onto the screen. Gage's name blinked amber. The message was delivered but not acknowledged. He sent the order to Bertram to pass on and swiped the screen aside.

It would take some time for Gage to return to the *Orion*, time Sartorius didn't have to wait.

Sartorius opened another channel and Colonel Horton, wearing a construction helmet and covered in dust, looked up at the Admiral.

"Sir? We've got the power plant near Can Tho up and running. Should have the distribution lines—"

"Colonel. Prepare to evacuate but do it quietly. Leave all heavy equipment behind. Get personnel back to the ships as soon as possible."

"What? Sir, we're finally making some…" Horton stopped as Sartorius shook his head slowly. This wasn't up for discussion. "What do I tell the Siam?"

"Mandatory celebration for the prism whale arrival, or make something up. I'll deal with Hu later. Get moving."

Horton gave a salute and the channel closed.

The Admiral went to his desk and took out a small flask. He took a deep sip of vodka, then looked at the oil painting of Albion on his wall.

"God give me strength," he said and drank again.

CHAPTER 16

Dying buildings surrounded the field hospital. The suburbs of Lopburi City were far enough from the shore to survive the meteor-fueled tsunami, but fragments of rock ranging from the size of basketballs to small cars had pummeled the area. The many apartment buildings looked like they'd endured an artillery bombardment with half-collapsed floors and entire sides slouched against battered frames.

The field hospital had been set up overnight as recovery crews and their robots finished searching a nearby neighborhood.

Exhausted army engineers directed their platoons of multi-armed robots as they sifted through rubble, pinging the detritus with gentle sonar pulses meant not to disturb any voids that might still hold survivors.

Gage, wearing simple fatigues and a hard hat, stood off to the side of the field hospital, counting the many black body bags being piled up within a walled off area. He tried to breathe through his mouth as a pair of robots lifted a fallen wall and a gust of wind brought the stench of decay through the air.

"Ugh…sir?" Bertram tapped Gage's arm, offering a small open jar filled with gray paste.

Gage wiped a bit of the goo beneath his nose and the smell subsided.

"They really think they'll find anyone in this mess?" the steward asked. "Been six days since the place got hit."

"Civilians from the tsunami area fled to here, thousands thinking this area was safe." Gage looked up as

315

a shower of meteoroids traced thin white lines through the sky. "If their orbital warning system had been online, the loss of life would have been less."

"If the Siam knew a damn thing about orbital mining, a lot of things would be different," Bertram said. "The Admiral sent you down here to speak with the field hospital commander. Dare say he's in that awful big tent, sir."

Gage walked around the inner perimeter of the fence surrounding the field hospital. A hover stretcher floated past them on the other side of the fence, a dust-covered woman strapped to it.

"It rained two days ago," Gage said. "That upped the survival chance for anyone still in the rubble. The doctors are no doubt busy trying to save lives. I won't distract them now."

"Not to be morose, sir, but I doubt they'll be all that busy." Bertram turned away as a robot carried three more body bags to the collection area.

A small rock bounced off the fence. Gage heard a shout and another rock sailed through the chain links and hit his shoulder. He looked over and found a teenage boy waving at him from several stories up in a nearby partially collapsed building.

The boy pointed at one of the robots working across the street, then into the mess of wrecked concrete and quick-wall.

"Bertram, find a robot master and send a unit to that building. Now." Gage ran along the fence and then vaulted over a supply crate and into the road. He tapped a microphone on his chest and made his way up the slope of broken walls.

"What is it?" he asked, the microphone cancelling out his words and translating them into Siam for the boy.

"My grandfather! I see him inside," the boy said, the translation running through Gage's earpiece. He ducked his small face against a gap between the rubble and shouted off a rapid-fire sentence. "Your iron men, bring

317

one here!"

A chunk gave way beneath Gage's foot and went tumbling down the slope. He slowed his climb, kicking up more pulverized rock with every step.

"The rescue robots are a lot heavier than I am," Gage said. "Let me see." He stopped next to the boy, who was covered in dirt and ripped clothes. Gage tapped a button on the side of his hardhat and powerful headlights snapped on. He peered into the gap...and saw an elderly man lying on his side in a shallow puddle of rainwater.

"Save him, please," the boy said, shaking Gage's shoulder.

"Is he alive? Did he say anything to you?" Gage asked.

"I saw him move. I swear it."

The old man's arm bent at the elbow, then flopped back to the ground.

"Sir, I'm with an engineer," Bertram said through his earpiece. *"That building's standing by wishes and sheer luck. If*

they send one of their robots up, the whole thing is liable to come

crashing down."

Gage pressed his fingers to a mic on his throat.

"I've got a survivor on the third floor. I'll try and get him out. Send over a stretcher."

"Sir, the Admiral will be most cross with me if I let you—
"

Gage cut the transmission with a cock of his neck. He looked into the void between the collapsed walls again and saw thin bands of light coming through the back side.

"What's your grandfather's name?" Gage asked as he climbed around the pile of rubble and into what remained of a kitchen.

"Trai," the boy said.

"There are wooden shutters back here." Gage clawed away hunks of masonry and exposed dust-covered slats. "I can break this and get to him, probably. If things go wrong, you get out of here, understand?"

The boy shook his head.

"What don't you understand?"

"He's all I have left. My parents and my sister are in the bags."

"All right, son. I'll get him out of there." Gage lifted a foot and rammed his heel into the wood. It took two more kicks before the shutter snapped. He pried the slats open and tossed them aside until he had an opening big enough for him to crawl through. Gage slid into the opening and felt his fatigues tug and rip against a jagged piece of wood.

As he lowered himself into the dank cave between floors of the apartment building, his wide shoulders scraped against raw concrete.

"Why didn't I send that skinny kid in here?" he mumbled. "Looks like he could've crawled through a garden hose with room to spare."

He heard a groan just beneath his feet. Gage dropped down and splashed in the puddle. A tremor reverberated through the room and dust sprinkled around them. Slowly, Gage knelt next to the elderly Siam.

"Trai? My name is Commodore Gage with the Albion navy. I'm here to help," Gage half-whispered. He swept his hardhat lights down the man's body. Both ankles were wedged beneath broken walls. Blood caked the bottom of his legs and the smell of rot touched Gage's nose.

"If you could move, I guess you would have done it by now." Gage wrapped a hand around Trai's thin calves. The skin was fever hot and dry as a husk.

"Snowing. Snowing," the old man said.

Gage looked over the rubble pinning Trai to the floor. A chunk of outer wall had the man's ankles in a vise grip. Gage brushed away smaller rocks and gripped his fingers around the edge.

A rumble shook the building and a rock the size of his fist bounced off Gage's helmet, skewing it to the side.

"Right, this was not my best idea," Gage said.

"Snowing…"

"If we amputate, you'll be dead from shock," Gage said. "If we wait for the better trained sailors and better equipment from another rescue operation, the rest of this building will fall down. I'm left with only foolish, stupid options."

Gage tugged the rock aside…and nothing else fell around him. He grunted and pulled it off Trai's legs. Gage held the weight against his own chest, struggling to keep it from slamming to the floor and causing an avalanche.

"Move…your…" Gage tapped the side of his foot against Trai and he heard a wet shuffle as the old man crawled a few inches away. Gage set the rock back down with a thump. There was a groan and a crack broke through the floor.

Gage held stock-still, sharing wide-eyed panic with Trai. The water puddle drained through the crack, its spread slowing to a stop before it could reach the other side of the void. The old man tried to raise his head to look at his ruined feet.

"No, don't." Gage pushed his head back to the ground gently. He didn't need a medical degree to know gangrene had set in, but if he could get him to a doctor, the old man was sure to live.

"Albion, you hear me?" came from overhead.

"Yes. I'll lift him up—you pull him out," Gage said. A rope flopped to the ground, one end running up the gap. "Or that, yes."

"One of your drones brought that. Water too."

Gage ran the rope beneath Trai's shoulders and tied it into a knot over his chest. He lifted the old man off the floor, careful not to let his ruined feet touch the ground.

"Snowing," Trai said as he grabbed Gage by the collar with surprising strength, stopping his ascent.

"Head injury." Gage gently pulled the hand free and turned his head away as the mangled, reeking feet went past. He waited as Trai was pulled free, measuring the jump he'd have to make to pull himself into the escape route.

"Albion!" The teenager's panicked voice filled the cave and Gage winced as dust shook free. "Albion, my sister is alive!"

"Quiet," Gage hissed. "There's no one else. I'm sure."

"Grandfather says Tuyet is down there. She's small, crawled into a shrine box in a hole. Find her!"

Gage touched a fingertip to a screen on the back of his hand. "Translate Siam proper name: Tuyet."

"Snowing," quipped in his ear.

There were times the translation software failed to account for stress or injury, skewing what came through his earpiece. He made a mental note to have a one-sided conversation with the programmers if he ever got out of this building.

"I'll look around," Gage called up. He got down on his hands and knees and shined his hardhat lights along the floor. He found nothing but piles of dust. He looked around again…but found nothing.

The end of the rope fell back down. Gage wrapped the line around his wrist and felt a steady pull. A hover drone must have been anchored to the other end, one with more than enough pull to get him out quickly.

He tugged the rope…when he heard a sniffle. The rope burned his wrist as he let go, setting it loose as it rose up.

Gage pulled fractured concrete away from one side of the cave and found a broken hardwood case. Peering through a triangular break in the front, he found a little girl clutching a rabbit doll.

"Tuyet, I presume."

The little girl shivered and shrank into a fetal position.

"Been through a lot lately." Gage grabbed the ornate brass handle on the case and pulled it open, scraping the edge against the floor. "I can understand that you're scared of me, what with the uniform, green eyes, and that I must be taller than any Siam man you've ever seen."

The girl tucked her head against the water-soaked case.

"Forgive me, sweetheart, but we don't have time to do this the nice, calm way." Gage gripped her by the shoulders and pulled her out. She screamed and kicked out, missing Gage and hitting a packed mass of loose rocks.

A shield-sized hunk of wall slid free and fell toward Tuyet. Gage swung her beneath his bulk and took the hit to the side of his head, just beneath his helmet. Light flashed across his eyes and his limbs went numb.

Gage felt blood flowing down the side of his neck as his left ear rang like a bell. He kept the girl cradled beneath him for a moment, waiting for the next hit. A few moments later, he lifted his head as pain stabbed up and down his shoulder.

"You OK?" he asked.

She spoke, but there was no translation.

Gage gently touched the ear with his translator/receiver, and it came away with drops of blood. The girl looked up at him with wide-eyed terror, apparently uninjured.

The rope descended back down the hole.

"Let's try this again," Gage said.

****

Gage sat on a gurney as a doctor ran a scanner over the left side of his head. His shoulder was stained red; the broken remnants of his earpiece lay in a metal pan. Bertram stood in the doorway of the small treatment room, worry on his face.

"If makes you feel any better, I've seen much worse today," the doctor said.

"I'm sure there are others who need you more than I do right now," Gage said.

"Blood clots in the cranium are tricky things." The doctor held a metal pick to Gage's ear and his face pulled into involuntary ticks. "Don't want to let them knock around of their own volition. Bad things happen. You've had some very extensive reconstruction work done. Not recent either; must have been done as a child."

The doctor tapped the side of a lens over one eye. "Which makes no sense. No Albion surgeon would have touched a minor for something elective. Did your parents smuggle you to some back-alley place in wild space? No…this work is too good."

"Elective? I was on my bike. There was a tree. The tree won, or so I'm told. I don't really remember what happened."

"There are no healed fractures." The doctor touched the pick against Gage's ear, sewing a tear shut. "No bone realignment stents…curious. Suppose you can ask your parents once we're back home."

Gage held his tongue. That his father died before

he was born and his mother passed away decades ago was none of the doctor's business.

"So, what brings the Admiral's aide down to my little slice of heaven?" the doctor asked.

"Admiral Sartorius is concerned about Yorova Pox." The doctor's hands pulled away from Gage's face. "A corpse farther inland tested positive for the disease. The Admiral doesn't want panic spreading across the planet, so he's sending me to each field station to tell you to enact protocol zero if you come across any cases."

"The Pox hasn't been seen in this part of space for decades," the doctor said as he went back to mending Gage's face. "If it's been dormant for so long, the chance of mutation into something worse is…"

"Exactly. The settlement has already been isolated. The impact damage probably stopped the disease from spreading further. Computer models have the chance of it spreading in the single digits, but protocol zero is in effect."

"If I come across any cases, I'll send up the alert and stop anyone from leaving my facility." He picked up a sponge and dabbed it against Gage's neck.

"Christ…Yorova. Last time it made the rounds, it killed more people than the Reach Wars."

"I'm glad you understand," Gage said.

"Sir?" Bertram held two fingers to his earpiece. "Admiral Sartorius wants you back on the *Orion* immediately. Message is marked most urgent."

"Jesus, it's spreading." The doctor's hands fell to his side.

"If it was protocol zero, he'd say it was protocol zero." Gage pushed himself off the gurney. "Done?"

"Have Seaver finish you up in her sick bay." The doctor removed his gloves with a snap. "All that's left is cosmetic. Unless you want to keep the scars."

Gage looked at his bloodstained, dirt-caked uniform. He didn't regret saving the two Siam, but he couldn't be at the Admiral's side looking like this.

"Shuttle's inbound," Bertram said.

"Must be serious," Gage said. "Message say what the issue is?"

"No, sir, just that all the captains are recalled for conference. Highly irregular, wouldn't you say?"

Gage felt a tinge of fear spread through his chest. Highly irregular indeed.

CHAPTER 17

Jeneck tipped her teapot and filled Captain Ulrich's cup. She gave him a gentle smile and moved on to the next officer, Captain Vult of the *Ajax*. All the fleet's captains were gathered in Sartorius' ready room. All sat uneasily, and more than one tapped his teacup against his saucer in a dreadful display of manners.

"A full recall in the middle of sleep cycle." Ulrich sipped his tea and frowned slightly. "Bit more bitter than usual, steward."

"Apologies, Captain," Jeneck said and moved to the next captain.

"We're all here. What's he waiting for?" Vult

asked. "Captains only, no XOs, general recall of everything dirtside. Arlyss is moderately competent, but he can't juggle three squadrons of supply shuttles *and* ready the ship to weigh anchor."

"I'm less worried my executive officer will send the *Concordia* crashing into the planet. Though I did have to hit him with an alcholizer to clear his bloodstream before I left. That'll teach him to take another nip after dinner." Ulrich sipped his tea again. "Ugh, so bad it's making my tongue numb."

"Mine could do with a bit of sugar. It's not like Sartorius to keep us waiting this long." Vult glanced around the room. "You think he's holding us up for Gage? Where is that commoner? Playing in the dirt again?"

"Don't be so dismissive." Vult swirled his tea around, "I'd take Gage over any entitled Sanquay that thinks Mummy and Daddy's money means they deserve top marks come evaluations."

Jeneck poured a cup waiting on Sartorius' desk,

then set the kettle on a heat pad. She glanced around the corner to the Admiral's quarters, then turned back to the room of waiting captains. She cleared her throat and they set their cups and saucers aside as they rose to their feet.

A noticeably pale Sartorius came into the room and stopped behind his desk. He leaned against the lacquered wood top and stared at his tea for a moment.

"Sit."

The Admiral stood up and straightened the front of his tunic.

"I have just spoken with a member of the King's Intelligence Ministry, two of his sworn Genevan guards and a pair of fighter pilots off the *Excelsior*. I regret to inform you all that—"

The back door slid open and a filthy Gage hurried into the back of the room. Several captains twisted around to glare at him. Jeneck picked up a new teacup and started across the room when Sartorius stopped her with a raise of his hand.

"I must inform you all that Albion has come under sustained attack by an unknown enemy," Sartorius said. Protests came from the captains, and more than one went to their feet in alarm. "The information we have is fragmentary at best, but the Home Fleet's losses appear to be…total."

"We can't remain here." Vult stood and rubbed his throat. "We must weigh anchor and…" He coughed. "Pardon me, Admiral."

He opened his mouth again, but no words came out.

Captain Ulrich took in a strained breath. He raised a hand into the air, then collapsed.

Vult fell to his knees, both hands to his throat, gagging. A cough spread from one captain to the next as they fell over each other, knocking over chairs and shattering fine china against the deck.

"Gentlemen? Ladies?" Sartorius looked around in confusion. The only one who hadn't collapsed was Gage, who was loosening the collar of a captain in the back of the room. The Admiral raised a panel on his desk and mashed a blinking red button. He glanced up at the untouched steaming cup of tea on his desk, then looked at Jeneck.

His steward held a pistol leveled at his chest, a wicked smile spread across her face.

"*Nobis regiray.*"

Her pistol snapped twice and Admiral Sartorius fell against his desk. He slid to the ground, leaving a bloody streak across the lacquered wood.

Jeneck swung the pistol toward Gage and caught a spinning tea saucer between the eyes. She flailed back and bounced off a portrait of the *Thames*, first flagship of the Albion navy. The painting crashed to the ground.

She cleared her vision with a shake of her head and saw a blur of a charging body. She fired out of reflex, hitting the assailant in the chest and stomach. The bullets didn't send the man to the ground; instead, he kept right on coming and plowed into her. She went down under the dead weight and found herself staring into the already dead face of Captain Ulrich. Gage had used the body as a shield.

Kicking the pistol from her hand, Gage then sent a fist hammering toward her face, but Jeneck shoved Ulrich's body up with more strength than should have been possible with her thin frame and Gage's fist smacked against the back of Ulrich's head. The commodore stumbled as the corpse collided against his chest.

Jeneck kicked up into a squat. She sprang up, flattened her hand into a spear tip, and stabbed at Gage's neck. He deflected the strike, then rammed the palm of his hand against her chin.

Her head snapped back and she managed to twist aside just as Gage kicked at her stomach. The blow glanced off her hip, knocking one foot out from under her. She swung with the momentum of Gage's blow and jumped up, spinning around and launching a roundhouse kick at the man's head.

Gage ducked to the side, catching the edge of her foot against the top of his head. The force of the hit sent him face-first into the wall. She landed on both feet, then raised a foot to stomp Gage's skull into paste.

He rolled back, blood streaming down his mouth and nose.

Jeneck grabbed Sartorius' desk and lifted it onto her shoulder. Data slates and the poisoned teakettle slid off and thumped against the carpet. She smiled at Gage where he lay against the wall, the back of one hand against his face.

Gage raised her pistol and aimed it at her heart.

"What is this? Who the hell are you?" Gage asked.

"We are the yoke you've forgotten." Jeneck slowly raised the massive wooden desk just a bit higher. "We are your masters and you will be ruled again." She lifted the desk higher.

Gage shot her twice in the chest. She faltered, then laughed. The third round went through her eye and out the back of her head. She and the desk crashed to the floor.

"Admiral?" Gage kept the pistol on Jeneck's body as he went to Sartorius' side. He lay in a pool of blood, both hands against wounds on his sternum.

"Son…" Sartorius looked up, but his eyes had no focus. "Son, you're all that's left."

"Corpsman!" Gage finally heard the sound of fists banging against the ready room door. "Sir, hold on. We'll get you to sick bay. Albion needs you. We need an Admiral to get us through whatever's happening back home."

Sartorius brought a bloody hand up and pressed it against Gage's face.

"You're the Admiral…and the King." Sartorius' hand fell away.

Gage grabbed the limp hand before it could hit the ground.

"No, not me. Not me, sir. I'm not the one for this." He looked back to the room full of dead captains.

The doors jerked open a few inches as Bertram and a pair of men-at-arms pried the doors open with pneumatic jaws used by damage-control parties.

Sartorius' head fell to the side.

Bertram rushed into the room, then stopped, his face slack and eyes wide.

"Sweet mother..." Bertram tapped at his earpiece frantically as the men-at-arms went from captain to captain, searching for any still alive.

Gage closed the Admiral's eyes. Heat rose from Jeneck's body, like she was a piece of hot iron just pulled from the fire. Gage raised an arm just as her body burst into blue flame, scorching the desk and singeing the carpet. She was nothing but a blackened mass within seconds.

"Sir...you...you..." Bertram tapped Gage on the shoulder.

"Corpsmen...get the corpsmen up here. Tell Doctor Seaver there are casualties coming." Gage wiped blood from his face and got to his feet.

"They're all dead, sir," a man-at-arms said.

"Do it!"

****

Gage walked onto the *Orion*'s bridge, trailed by armed Marines. Commander Price, the ship's executive officer, turned away from the holo tank on the command dais to face Gage as he took the curved stairs leading up from the bridge deck.

Crewmen gawked at his bloodstained uniform and Gage saw fear writ across their faces. He rubbed the back of his hand across his mouth, feeling a trickle of blood from a split lip.

"I—I've monitored everything…sir," Price said. "Med bay doesn't have any good news. The poison's never been seen before. All were beyond saving by the time they—"

"You're the Captain of the *Orion* now," Gage said. "You understand that?"

"I've been the XO for a week," she whispered to

341

him. "Captain Simpson was about to fire me after I screwed up the last logistics push to—"

Gage grabbed her by the forearm with his bloodstained hand.

"You. Are. The Captain."

She bit her bottom lip and nodded quickly.

"There may be more enemy agents. I need you to get this ship locked down. Armed guards on every vital system. Set combat conditions. Your sailors know what to do; they just need your leadership to make it happen." Gage let her go. A corner of his mouth tugged down at the red smudge he left on her sleeve.

"Aye aye." Her features hardened and she turned around, put her hands on the railing around the command dais, and began issuing orders.

Gage looked over the control panels at the Admiral's station. He could pull up any data feed throughout the fleet and open a channel to any of the ships with a single touch. Gage took a deep breath, then tapped an icon.

Faces appeared in the holo tank as the second officers of each ship and Colonel Horton came online.

"Bloody hell, Gage," Barlow said, frowning at his friend. "You know you're on Sartorius' channel?"

Green lights came up next to each ship name on a smart screen. He had everyone.

"Albion is under attack," Gage said. "Admiral Sartorius and the captains—*all* the captains—are dead. Command of the fleet falls to me and each of you are now master and commander of your vessel."

"Dead?" Arlyss said the word like it was from another language. "This is ridiculous. You're obviously suffering from some sort of stress disorder from your last boondoggle planetside. Put Captain Simpson on the line so we can have you sent to a padded room."

Gage pressed his palm to a screen and a menu popped up in the holo. He tapped in an order and the portrait around each second officer blinked, then changed to a blue border of command.

"The *Orion*'s biometric controls know the captains are dead. Official command is now yours. Admiral Sartorius' steward poisoned them all, then murdered him. Her body…immolated after I killed her. We must assume there are more infiltrators. Every ship will adopt full combat readiness and prepare to weight anchor on my order."

"This is insane!" shouted Commander Erskine of the battle cruiser *Valiant*.

Gage found a video file in Sartorius' data buffer and opened it.

Camera footage from the *Joaquim* came up in the center of the holo tank: Daegon fighter squadrons in the skies over New Exeter. Home Fleet ships breaking apart in Albion's atmosphere. Hundreds of enemy ships emerging from slip space around the domed mothership.

"They call themselves the Daegon," Gage said. "I don't know much more, but survivors from Albion are here along with—" He stopped himself from mentioning Prince Aidan. That at least one member of the royal family lived would remain secret until he was certain another assassin wasn't lurking in the shadows.

"Get your ships locked down. The evacuation from Siam will continue. Colonel Horton," Gage said, swiping across the carousel of newly minted captains until he found the engineer, "leave the heavy equipment behind. Get our people off world as fast as you can manage."

"The Siam are already asking questions," Horton said. "There's no guarantee these Daegon will even come here. If we leave now, people will die by the thousands. You can't just—"

"Our first duty is to Albion," Gage said, "not Siam. Prioritize naval crew for return. I need our ships ready to fight."

"We're leaving billions' worth of equipment behind, but you're in charge." Horton threw his hands up in defeat.

"We have to go back to Albion," Barlow said. "Standard procedure. Any attack on the home world and all military assets will return at best speed."

"It'll take hours to pull a slip formula from the grav buoy," Gage said. "Focus on securing your ships and getting your crew off the surface until then. I'll speak with the survivors and share more when I have it. In the meantime, keep the situation secret. Sleeper agents may be waiting for word of the attack to strike. Gage out."

He closed the channel and thumped a fist against the control panel. A mountain of unknowns weighed on his shoulders. Who was the enemy? How long until they arrived here? What chance did his fleet of green crews stand against an armada of that size?

I'm not the man for this, he thought.

"Excuse me," came from behind where Tolan and Thorvald stood at the base of the stairs. "We overheard. Don't suppose that assassin went charcoal after he died?"

"She. You must be the intelligence officer." Gage

346

waved them both up the stairs. "You've encountered them before? How do we root them out?"

"Killing everyone to see who bursts into flames is a bit counterproductive," Tolan said. "I'm afraid we didn't learn much before we made it off world by the skin of our teeth."

"What about '*nobis regiray*'? She said that before she killed Sartorius," Gage said.

"I've heard that from their soldiers," Thorvald said, bending slightly at the waist in a bow. "Benjamin Thorvald. My gestalt recognizes you as Albion's regent until such time as…my charge reaches maturity."

"Protocol can wait," Gage said. "What I need is information. Were you followed? Tell me everything you can."

"Someplace more private." Tolan's eyes flicked over the bridge crew. "I've a spot in mind."

CHAPTER 18

Thorvald led Gage and Tolan into the shuttle bay where the *Joaquim* let off bursts of steam and cooling metal clicked. Lubricant pooled beneath the hull and dropped into small puddles. Amber lights along the bulkhead lit up and dimmed away, announcing combat conditions across the ship.

Gage, his skin free of blood, wore a fresh uniform—a skintight body glove and light armor beneath coveralls. An armored helmet and holstered pistol hung from his belt.

"Impressive," Gage said.

"Really?" Tolan raised an eyebrow at him.

"Impressive that it can break orbit. You've got the heir in that thing?"

"Didn't hear any complaints when it saved the kid's life or came bearing news. This gift horse may have a nag's teeth, but she gets the job done. Thorvald?"

The Genevan held up a hand and flashed three signs toward the ship's security cameras.

The ramp descended and Salis, holding a carbine, greeted Gage with a dirty look at his pistol.

"The regent," Thorvald said.

"Sire." Salis remained tense.

"Where is he?" Gage asked.

"Playing." Salis waited on the ramp until the three were inside and then closed the ship off from the *Orion*.

Thorvald led Gage to a cabin where Prince Aidan sat on the floor, a half-dozen carved wooden animals and dinosaurs in a semicircle around him. The boy didn't acknowledge their arrival. He glowered at the toys, then slapped one against the bulkhead.

"Bad!"

"We're eager to get him off this piss bucket," Salis said.

"And I'm eager to have my stuff back," Tolan snapped.

"Move him into the Admiral's quarters once…they need to be cleaned. Extensively," Gage said. "What of the King and Queen? Prince Nathaniel? Princess Daphne?"

"The Queen is dead. We witnessed her," Thorvald said. "The King stayed behind and is presumed dead. The castle's security systems read both Nathaniel and Daphne as deceased, but not witnessed. By Albion law and our charter, Aidan is the heir. You are the regent."

"How much did he see?" Gage asked.

"Too much," Salis said. "Nightmares. Outbursts. We're not experts in childhood trauma. The *Orion* has a complement of four psychologists, correct?"

"She does, but there is an issue of infiltrators.

Steward Jeneck was extensively vetted before being assigned to the Admiral. If these Daegon can get through that…I don't know who we can trust."

"If only we had a spy onboard," Tolan said, "one versed in counterintelligence and all things dirty tricks."

"I don't know what good you'll be," Gage said. "You were seen entering the bridge with—"

Tolan snapped his fingers and his face fell into loose folds, then morphed into patrician features. His visage molded into a poor approximation of Gage's face, then twisted into Thorvald.

"I told you not to do that," the Genevan said.

"Wait for it—" Tolan's voice perfectly matched Thorvald's, then he grew four inches taller. "That last part hurts."

"A Faceless," Gage said. "I knew intelligence liked to skirt the law, but this is too far."

Tolan morphed back into his original look, but one cheek drooped. He pressed the loose skin back with his fingers and clucked his tongue.

"You want to find the Daegon spies? Set me loose. I'll start with your men-at-arms and intelligence section. After all, if you don't have counterintelligence, you don't have much of anything. This steward, did she poison the captains?"

"How did you know?"

"It's what I would have done. I take it there's a sample of this somewhere? Med bay? Assassins prefer tools with a low probability of killing themselves before the job is done. I'd bet the Daegon agents are immune to this poison…which would make them unique compared to the average sailor, yes?"

"He is insufferable," Thorvald said, "but insightful."

"Get to it," Gage said. "I'll tell Doctor Seaver to expect you."

"Do keep this…" Tolan waved a hand over his face, "…our little secret, yes?"

"Fair enough." Gage looked at the Genevans. "I prefer you stay here until I'm certain the ship is safe."

Salis sighed heavily.

"I'll have armed guards posted outside the shuttle bay. There's no place safer for now."

"As you wish, sire," Thorvald said. "Which of us shall accompany you?"

"I don't need either of you. Stay with Prince Aidan."

The two bodyguards glanced at each other.

"You are the regent," Salis said. "Your safety is our responsibility. Our confidentiality and loyalty is total."

"I don't doubt your ability," Gage said, holding up a hand, "but having one of you hovering over my shoulder at all times is—"

"A necessity, so long as you suspect enemy agents in your crew," Thorvald said.

"Don't…don't you need to sleep? There are only two of you."

"Our gestalts can supplement our nervous systems. We can sleep while standing and with our eyes open," Salis said.

"I'm sure that's not awkward at all. Bertram will be jealous, but…Thorvald. Come with me, please."

Aidan started crying, demanding his mother.

"I'll see to him." Salis bowed to Gage.

The commodore's heart ached as the boy began sobbing. Aidan pulled into a ball and fell to his side, his head buried in his hands.

****

The *Orion*'s primary med bay was eerily quiet as Tolan walked past a surgical suite where a handful of doctors and nurses huddled together. They said nothing, occasionally pressing their fists to their lips where they puffed on nic-sticks hidden between their fingers. The silence…coping through nicotine (medical professionals were always the most unhealthy members of any crew, Tolan had noticed during his many years of service to the crown)…something terrible had just transpired in this med bay.

Tolan wore the same scrubs as everyone else in the med bay, and his face was morphed into a visage so bland it was meant to be forgotten. Human beings had evolved to recognize and remember other faces more than any other physical trait. Those few who went through the surgery and pain of becoming Faceless learned ways to trick others' memories with the right set of features or by changing just a few details when those fleeting glances surveyed a crowd.

This was not a time to be remembered, and on his way out of the med bay, everyone would see a different person than the one that came in.

He looked at a reflection on a window across from the chief doctor's office. Empty, but Tolan had an idea where to find her. He continued on, walking with the confidence of one who was supposed to be there, and stopped in front of the morgue. The door panel read it was locked from the inside.

Tolan put his palm to the panel and a thin metal transmitter embedded in his wrist sent out an override command. Bolts clicked as the door slid open. He stepped over the threshold and walked into a familiar smell of burnt meat with a foul copper tang.

The morgue had several rows of square lockers along the walls. One was ajar, and Admiral Sartorius lay on a slab, his uniform soaked in blood, eyes taped shut. Twenty bodies in black bags lay on gurneys along the walls, the dead captains waiting for return to their ships.

Tolan spotted a woman sitting next to Sartorius, her upper body hidden by the slab. The spy closed the door behind him and walked around the dead admiral.

Doctor Seaver sat with her head in her hands, a small metal flask pinched between a thumb and forefinger. The spy had a good view of a mess of gray-streaked black hair, but not her face.

Tolan crossed his arms and cleared his throat.

Seaver's face snapped up. Puffy eyes looked at him in a moment of panic as she clutched the flask to her chest.

"Who the hell are you and how did you get in here? I told the chief I needed to be left alone while I—"

"Tolan, Intelligence Ministry. I'm in acute need of your expertise, Doctor. Where's your lab?"

Seaver slid the flask into a thigh pocket and wagged a finger at him.

"This is my med bay and I don't care who the hell you think you are. You can't just barge in…how did you get in here?" Her words slurred ever so slightly and Tolan picked up a faint smell of vodka apart from the burnt meat aroma in the air.

"Tolan, Intelligence Ministry. I spend a lot of time where I'm not supposed to be doing things a lot of people don't approve of. The door was only code locked from the inside. Next time flip the manual bolts and it'll slow me down for about eight seconds. Did I mention an important task for the two of us?"

Seaver pushed herself to her feet and swept her hair away from her face. She was in her late forties and kept an athletic build. Her ring finger had a tan line from a missing wedding band. Tolan made a mental note to determine if its absence and the drinking were connected, or if she removed the ring whenever she had to ply her profession.

"I don't know what you want from me," she said. "All were unconscious and near brain-dead when first responders got to the Admiral's wardroom. Heroic efforts were…there was nothing we could do."

"Poison, yes?" Tolan nodded to the body bags.

"Whatever it was caused a complete neural shutdown. None of our anti-venom treatments had any effect."

"You have a sample of the delivery vehicle? The

tea?"

Seaver zipped Sartorius' body bag up quickly, then sent his slab into the wall.

"My staff are in shock," she said. "Now that I've had a minute to process all this, I need to attend to them. There's really nothing more I can share with you."

"I've come across this kind of enemy agent recently." Tolan sniffed twice. "If you've got the poison, we can run it across another genetic sample. Spies tend to have a resistance to any poison they use; cuts down on the risk of workplace-related accidents."

"Wait," she said, her eyes clicking from side to side. "When did you run across this before? Were you on that ship in shuttle bay twelve no one's allowed to talk about? What's going on back home?"

Tolan held his poker face. He was no doctor, but telling the truth would definitely harm his efforts to solve a very pressing problem. Married or recently divorced, the chances were extremely high she had loved ones back on

Albion.

"We can figure out what the killer had for breakfast later. Right now, Commodore Gage is concerned there are more assassins on his ship or in the fleet. I need you to take me to your lab and that sample of the poison."

"Actually, Mr. Tolan—if that is your real name— you can piss right off. There's no chance of a genetic sample from Jeneck. Whatever happened to her broke down every cell in her body. There's nothing to be learned in my lab, so I'd rather spend some time with better company." She tapped a finger against the flask in her pocket.

"Oh, what's this?" Tolan pulled a hand out of his folded arms. He held a small swab stained with blood that he'd cleaned off Thorvald's armor during their trip through slip space. "A blood sample from another enemy agent? Just what the doctor ordered."

He wiggled an eyebrow as she shook her head in disgust.

"Where did you get that?" she asked.

"It doesn't matter. Shall we get started?"

"Wait…how do you know I'm not another one of those…" she pointed to a closed cubicle, "those things."

"If you were, I figure you would have tried to kill me when I laid out what I know." Tolan took out his other hand, which held a small pistol. "Since we're beyond the not-going-to-kill-you phase of our relationship…" He brushed his hands down his sides and hid the blood sample and pistol with a sleight-of-hand trick, turning his empty hands back and forth in front of her like an amateur magician waiting for applause.

"Fine. Next door." She took a step forward and lost her balance. Tolan caught her and got a better whiff of the alcohol in her system.

"I have an alcholizer in my desk," she said. "Will straighten me right out."

"Physician, heal thy—"

"You don't shut your goddamn mouth—or you

breathe a word of this to anyone—and I will kill you and make it look like an accident."

"Doctor, I like you already."

****

Seaver placed the bloody swab into a tube, then slid it into a bio scanner. The double helix of a DNA profile came up on a flat screen. The doctor looked over the data…then turned to Tolan, who was a few feet away, his back to the wall and half-watching the shut door to the small lab.

"Where did you get this sample?" she asked.

"An unwitting donor. It's human, right?"

"Of course it is—why wouldn't it be? There's some genetic drift…but it's not from an artificial splice. I've seen markers like this from populations with long-term exposure to high radiation levels. But this isn't…" She zoomed in on a section of the genetic sequence and frowned. "High-rad worlds that have been settled for a long time—Mars, Etruscia—the current generation show

362

some evolutionary adaption to the environment. But this man…it's like he has a ten-thousand-year head start on those born today on Mars. Did he have purple skin, by any chance?"

"The implications of what you're talking about are interesting and horrifying," Tolan said, "but I need to find out if he has any friends on the ship. Check for antibodies, a genetic resistance to that poison, something I can use."

Seaver tapped a screen and a glass chamber holding Jeneck's teakettle lit up next to her.

"The ship's computer can restructure the sample to—"

"Yes, wonderful," Tolan said, tapping his foot. "Any new sailors in your med bay? Any acting strange?"

"11th Fleet was just re-manned for a five-year mission to wild space," she said. "Most of the fleet are new recruits with their training cadre, couple old hands for division chiefs and senior staff. Most everyone is either new to the navy or new to each other. I came on last minute after—"

A yellow text box popped up on the screen.

"All right…whoever you got this sample from has a resistance to the poison. Good lord—his white blood cells are on steroids."

"Is that enough to do a search through the ship's medical database? Find out who else is like this?"

Seaver turned to him and put her hands on her hips.

"You are aware of the Unalienable Rights Clause to our Constitution, aren't you? No Albion citizen will be subject to genetic screening or profiling without their express consent or a search warrant. I was beaten over the head with this in medical school from the very first day. If I violate the URC, my license will be revoked in a heartbeat and I am not going to give up the second-to-last thing in my life that—"

"Doctor," Tolan said as his bile rose at her objection, "I assure you this is a matter of life and death.

No one will fault you for sidestepping the URC for now."

"'Sidestepping'? It doesn't even matter. No one can even open the sealed files that have that genetic data without a writ from the judiciary or an admiral. The only admiral within a dozen light-years is cooling on a slab, so I guess we'll just stand here looking at each other like idiots until you finally leave my med bay."

"Computer…" Tolan raised his chin slightly and waited for a chirp from the speakers on the bio scanner. He concentrated on the muscles in his neck and felt his vocal cords tremble.

"Access subfile sigma-nine-bravo-two." His words came out tinny, the modulation changing from syllable to syllable.

"Command file active," the computer voice said.

"Authorization Sartorius, Gregory M. Remove all URC restrictions from medical and personnel databases through all 11th Fleet systems." Tolan's voice was normal again. "In fact, remove all URC restrictions."

"Acknowledged," the computer said.

"What the hell?" Seaver watched as additional windows popped up on her screen. "How did you…you can't…"

"One of the first things Albion Intelligence did after the URC was ratified was to build a back door into the system. For emergencies. Like this. It's all very illegal, but we in the intelligence community have always had a smile-and-nod relationship with the law. Now would you like me to tap in the search commands and give you plausible deniability or do you want to get this over with that much faster?"

Seaver looked at the poisoned teakettle, then through the one-way glass to the morgue where twenty-one men and women lay dead.

"You're sure there's a real risk and I can trust you to never speak of this to my colleagues? Emergency or not, doctors have ethics."

"I'm a spy. Of course you can trust me."

"Then I'll do it." Seaver reached into the DNA scan and highlighted parts of the sequence with her touch.

****

Wyman steered his fighter onto the guidance laser from the *Orion*'s forward flight deck. He cut his speed with a burst from his forward thrusters and his Typhoon shimmied from side to side.

"Not supposed to do that," he muttered as he re-leveled on the laser. Inside the landing deck, a post rose from the metal floor and two lit cones extended from the sides. The cones moved back and forth, signaling his landing was clear. Wyman coasted through the environmental shielding and sound returned from the outside world and through his canopy. He landed next to the auto-crewman, powered down his fighter, then pulled his helmet off and looked across the flight deck. A dozen Sparrow shuttles, barely large enough for two crew and a bit of cargo, shared the deck with him and Ivor as she came down next to him.

Wyman tapped his throat mic.

"Rest of the fleet captains are here," he said to his wingman. "Don't see the *Joaquim*, though."

"Remember what Thorvald told us?" she asked. "Not talking about a certain something on the radio? Him threatening to rip our lips off. Then our arms."

"He didn't actually say that last part. You're just making things up because he scares you." Wyman pulled a handle and his canopy came loose, then rolled to the side and into the fuselage. A hooked ladder attached to his cockpit and Wyman swung a leg onto a rung.

He stopped midway down. A scorch mark ran across the fuselage just beneath his cockpit, a near miss he didn't remember. One wing had a jagged forward edge, like a shark had bitten into it. He hurried down the ladder, not wanting another reminder of just how close he'd come to death in that last frantic dash from Albion.

A lieutenant commander in a flight suit waited for him at the base of the ladder. His collar was flaked with dry sweat and he wore an *Orion* ship patch on his chest.

"Ricks, I'm the ship's CVG," said the commander of the ship's void craft. "Saw you two coming in on the scope during my last run. You care to explain just what in the hell is going on?"

Wyman opened his mouth to speak, then snapped his jaw shut. Ivor came up beside him and gave Ricks a nod.

"Sir, the...other ship's been here for at least an hour. They didn't tell you anything?" Wyman asked.

"I don't know how the flight deck runs on the *Excelsior*," Ricks said, nodding to Wyman's patch, "but when every CVG I've ever met asks a direct question, they expect a direct answer. Not this dull surprise bit you two are playing. My ash-and-trash squadron is pulling personnel off the planet as fast as we can manage while leaving billions in equipment behind. And what the hell happened to your fighters? They look like you flew through a lightning storm."

"We're not supposed to say…" Ivor mumbled to Wyman.

"Tolan ordered us to stay quiet," Wyman said, his anger rising, "and we're off that freak's piss bucket of a ship, so to hell with what he wants. Sir, we need our fighters serviced and prepped for combat operations. Where are your Typhoon pilots? We've got gun camera footage and have worked out a couple maneuvers that might work against the Daegon fighters."

Ricks cocked his head to the side.

"It's Albion, sir," Ivor said. "The Home Fleet is gone. Cities burning. The Daegon know we came here and if they followed, they could be here any minute. We have to get ready to fight…or to run."

CHAPTER 19

Gage ran a hand through his hair and shook his head at President Hu's hologram.

"Yes, Madame President, I'm certain of everything I just told you. I don't know if these Daegon are coming here, but we're planning for it."

"My people are in desperate need of your assistance, and you're going to abandon Siam…leave the door wide open to these barbarians. We will not survive if—"

"Your world is indefensible," Gage said. "No orbitals. No forts. No ground-to-orbit weapons. Albion had all of this and it fell within hours. The Daegon may not have any grievance with you, just us. If we stay, you *will* be caught in the cross fire."

"Your engineers are still working on fifteen different sites and—"

"We will leave behind what we can. Some of the systems can run on their own. Water purification plants, a few of the construction robots. I will have my manpower back, President Hu. Do not press me on this."

She leaned back from the camera, her jaw working from side to side.

"Where will you go? Perhaps they'll allow you to demilitarize here if you surrender."

"Albion never surrenders. As for where we will go next, it would be best if you didn't know. We'll leave what we can in the orbital docks. I'll be in touch shortly."

Hu pressed her hands together over her chest and bowed.

Gage cut the channel and brought up a star chart in the holo tank. An orange ring around a white dot identified the Siam system. Slip streams traced from point to point, back to Albion, and into the shaded regions of different core territories.

"Captain," Gage said to Price, who was standing on the opposite side of the tank. "Captain?"

"Yes! Sorry. Still not used to that." She gestured in the tank and golden lines traced along slip streams away from the Siam system. Dashed lines connected to nearby stars without slip streams.

"The entire fleet can return to Albion in less than thirty hours," she said. "Least-time transits are to Port Arthur and Temecula in wild space, both at a little less than two days. Neither world has an anchorage agreement with Albion, but if we point the guns and ask nicely, I'm sure they'll come around."

"What's the shortest route to Indus space? Preferably a system with a major ISN base."

A moment passed before Price spoke.

"We're not going home? We're not going to

fight?" she asked.

"There are hundreds of Daegon ships over Albion. More arrived as the *Joaquim* fled, some on course to the colony worlds. The 11th can't beat them, not by itself. We have a mutual defense treaty with Indus and Cathay. If we get to their space, I—as regent—can rally them to—"

"We have a mutual defense treaty against the Reich," Price said. "Neither the Indies or the Kongs ever bothered to lift a finger against pirates out of wild space. It was never their problem. How are you going to get them to move against someone like these Daegon?"

"You saw the size of their fleet," Gage said. "They won't stop at Albion. It's only a matter of time before they attack deeper into the core."

"So what do we do? Go begging star nations to borrow their fleets?"

"Our options are limited, Captain. We can charge back to Albion and be blown to pieces before we're barely out of slip space and accomplish nothing. We…run," he almost spat the word, "and keep the flame alive. Call on our allies and lead a force to free our earth and skies. If you've another idea that can save our home, I'm open to suggestions."

"I'm sorry, sir," Price said, folding her arms across her chest. "Been a difficult past few hours."

"Help me here—find what I'm missing. We slip to Sicani, then we can make it to the New Madras. INS is there in force, easy transit to their capital on Vishuddha."

"Sicani? That's a Harlequin system. If I remember correctly, you are not popular with them. Even with a fleet at your back, there's no guarantee we'd get free passage."

"Pirates tend to be pragmatic when their backs are to the wall. It'll be in their best interest to get us to Indus…lessens the threat the Daegon will bother with them. Or we point the guns and ask nicely, just like you suggested."

"Or we go a rough transit to this red dwarf," Price

said as she touched a star in the holo tank, its name a jumble of letters and numbers, "and add three days to the trip without risking a shooting match. Last intelligence has the place in contention between the Harlequins and Wyverns. Which means we'll find two pirate fleets that want to shoot us or no one at all."

A pulsing red triangle appeared in the holo tank and a siren wailed.

"This can't be right." Price brought up an astrogation report and a wall of scrolling text appeared next to the nexus leading back to Albion. "The mass readings coming through are far higher than—"

"Cancel all outbound shuttles and prepare to weigh anchor," Gage said.

"Sir, we still have thousands of sailors on Siam awaiting pickup. Another turn of the shuttles and we could have them all," she said. "Just a little more time, please, sir."

"You heard me. Pull a slip equation for Sicani and

pass on the orders to the rest of the fleet," Gage said.

"Yes, sir."

Gage watched as almost fifty Daegon linked-diamond ships emerged in a tight formation. That they'd managed to arrive with such precision almost made Gage envious.

"Sir, we're being hailed," said a lieutenant near the command dais.

"Send it to me." Gage straightened up and let his breath leave his chest slowly.

A black screen opened in front of him. A Daegon in blue armor and a helmet with metal slats down the sides and over the nose appeared. Behind the slats, an obsidian carved face mask of a man stared at Gage. Behind the Daegon was pitch black. He lifted his helmet up and Tiberian looked at Gage with curiosity.

"I am Tiberian. I am here to claim you."

"Brought an awful lot of friends for a simple pickup," Gage said. He lowered a hand beyond where the camera could see it and snapped his fingers at the comms officer. The lieutenant gave him a thumbs-up.

"Albion is ours. Your fleets burn in the skies. You may surrender and live as thralls to us, but if I am to spare any of you, I will have the child. Alive…or dead, if you've already chosen to take the royal name for yourself." Tiberian smiled, flashing perfectly white teeth beneath his dark lips.

"I'm afraid I have no idea what you're talking about," Gage said.

There. Tiberian's eyes glanced down. He was reading something. Unless the Daegon had mastered a way of sending information to a ship in slip space, then he must have just received some new information.

"Lying thralls have their tongues cut out. The *Joaquim* is aboard your vessel. The last of Albion's royalty is with you. Stop toying with me and I will see you whipped in the vise for your insolence. You may keep your tongue since you did not know the penalty."

"We've never seen your ships before. Never seen humans with your…deformities." The word earned a snarl from Tiberian. "Who are you and by what right do you think you can attack us?"

"We are your masters. For thousands of years, you toiled under our yoke, rightly guided to a glorious future. When you proved unworthy of us, we left you behind. Now look at you—look how far you've managed to crawl forward after so many years. Pathetic. We've returned to take up our mantle and cast down your worthless leaders. You will be ruled, and you will be grateful for it."

Gage felt a hand tapping his right calf. The intelligence section had what they needed.

"We were quite happy with how things were. Return to Albion. Take yourself and the rest of your kind and go back to whatever hole you crawled out of and pray we don't come looking for you. This is your last chance."

Tiberian chuckled. "I will flay the skin from your body and serve it to my—"

Gage cut the transmission and looked down at a pair of naval intelligence officers.

"Rogue transmission out of dorsal battery seven," one said. "We don't know what it said, but it was directed to the enemy fleet."

"Send Tolan to deal with it. Let him know a prisoner we can interrogate is better than a corpse."

"Goes without saying, sir," the other said.

Gage reached into the holo tank and spun the projection around. The Daegon would reach Siam orbit in less than an hour at their current speed. He tapped the planet, and a screen came up showing he still had 4,533 personnel still on the ground.

He opened a channel to Colonel Horton. The exhausted-looking engineer appeared seconds later.

"Colonel, I see you're still in Lopburi."

"First in, last out. Sappers lead the way, sir," Horton said. "I take it this isn't a good-news call, considering how the civilian news channel just shit itself."

"We have to leave. We can't beat what's coming for us and I do not believe in glorious last stands so long as there's a chance at victory…no matter how small or far off."

"My soldiers and I will go to ground, see how we can make these Daegon bastards' lives hell for as long as we can. Albion's light burns."

"The light burns. I will return for you. Godspeed."

"Godspeed."

Horton cut the channel.

"Captain Price, set course for the Sicani system at our best speed. Have every ship prepare their own slip equation. I doubt these Daegon will let us go without a fight," Gage said.

"Aye aye…what of the shuttles still on their way?" she asked.

"Shields must go up in…fifteen minutes. Any shuttle not docked by then will have to turn back. Tell them to hurry." Gage flipped a cover off a red and white button that would cut into every single communication frequency and speaker in the fleet. He touched the button, preparing a speech he never thought an officer of the Royal Albion Navy would ever have to give.

****

Crewman Clyde shifted his shoulders within his void combat uniform. Every sailor learned to live with the constant weight on his body, the never comfortable hygiene codpiece and the itches beneath the vacuum-resistant light armor that could never be scratched. Wearing his void suit with no known point, though, was a source of stress and worry for him.

His station was at the base of a plasma cannon set in an armored turret, sitting in a raised metal chair bolted to the side of the weapon that must have been designed by the comfort-adverse engineers that made his void suit. The ten-yard barrel extended through an enviro-shield and into the void. Clyde double-checked the roller assembly that moved the cannon forward to its combat position and pulled it back into the more protected carry position within the *Orion*'s hull. He looked down to the armored hatch where the plasma munitions were kept. As one of the many assistant gunners in cannon station B-8, it was his job to load the weapon and keep her firing through any engagement.

He looked up at Master Chief Eisen, sitting in the command station nestled against the ceiling behind the weapon where he could survey the entire crew. He'd been unusually quiet since the alert order came down.

Clyde touched the helmet hanging from a hook on his chest and twisted it around to check the charge on the air scrubbers—still green. Master Chief Eisen had retold a story of his early days in the service when a shipmate had trusted, but not verified, her gear and had to breathe vacuum after a power-coil accident left her floating in the void. She'd gotten her helmet on in time, but the faulty scrubber killed her long before search and rescue found her.

Siam's horizon filled the bottom of the view from the open gun port. That he actually wanted to go back dirtside to help the locals surprised him. Digging through rubble and building shelters was a good deal more satisfying than the shipboard life of drills and catching whatever cleaning details Eisen had waiting for him and his fellow sailors whenever they thought they'd catch a few hours of free time.

"Now hear this! Now hear this!" boomed from the speakers in the ceiling and from his helmet. Amber lights on the walls went red. The ship was now in combat condition alpha. Clyde lifted his helmet onto his head and sealed it against his neck guard with a twist. He looked over the side of his chair to Overton, the youngest member of the cannon team responsible for loading the charges into the weapon's breach, and saw red blinking lights on the back of his helmet.

"Overton, check your seals," Clyde said, thumping

a heel against his seat.

The sailor twisted his helmet back and forth and the lights went green.

Clyde dared a look up at Eisen, half-expecting the Chief to be flying over the railings to beat the life out of Overton for making such a mistake…but Eisen remained at his station, tapping furiously on a data slate. He wasn't even wearing his helmet.

"Thanks," Overton said. He looked at the Chief, then whispered, "Do we say something or…"

"Just man your station," Clyde said.

"This is Commodore Gage," came through Clyde's helmet. *"It is with great sadness that I share this news with you. Albion is under assault from an enemy we have never faced before now. Home Fleet is gone. All but one member of the royal family is known to be dead or missing."*

Clyde froze in disbelief, struggling with what Gage was saying. The world was everything—his family, his entire life—and now it was under threat?

"This some kind of a joke?" asked Harris, standing on the other side of the breach from Overton.

Clyde hushed him with a pointed finger.

"What's more," Gage said, *"enemy agents have infiltrated the Orion and murdered our admiral…and every ship's captain. By the naval regulation and Albion law, I am taking command of this fleet and every free Albion citizen until relieved by a superior officer or the royal family."*

"It's a goddamn mutiny," Harris said. "That common-born Gage must think we're a bunch of idiots. He knows he'll never make admiral, so he's going to take us into wild space, turn us all into pirates."

Clyde ignored Gage as he continued speaking.

"You were down there with Gage," he said to Harris. "He strike you as the kind of officer that would do what you just said? He's got more integrity and courage than any of the high-born fop officers I've served with since—"

"Ready the cannon!" Eisen shouted.

Clyde turned to his station and activated the screen connected to the ship's gunnery section. A cursor blinked, but there was no firing data to execute. Clyde hit a refresh button…and got nothing.

"…cannot make a difference if we return home. It is not for us to surrender or throw our lives away, but to fight. Albion's light burns through us, those of us still free."

"Raise one plasma munition," Eisen said.

The rest of the crew repeated the command and Overton flipped a switch on his station. The deck vibrated as an auto-loader arm beneath their feet removed a plasma charge from its armored casing and carried it to the hatch leading up from the magazine. All munitions fired by the cannon were instruments of destruction. A lucky hit by an enemy could result in the premature detonation of the rounds, which would end very badly for Clyde and the rest of the team…and those nearby. The extensive armor plating around the weapon turret and magazine mitigated much of the risk, but Clyde's heart began pounding as the munition neared the hatch.

"Special firing instructions," Eisen boomed with a command tone. "Do not load."

Clyde repeated the words, then did a double take at his screen. There were no such instructions from the gunnery command.

The hatch slammed open and a metal cylinder with thick bands around either end rose out of the floor. The metal iris on the cannon's breach widened and the cannon adjusted its width to accept the plasma round. The round should have loaded within a second of coming up from the magazine. Now, with the munition exposed and the hatch to the rest of the rounds open, cannon B-8 was in an achingly vulnerable position.

"...*have allies in the core worlds, allies sworn to aide Albion in her time of need. We will call upon their strength to—*"

"Chief, no firing instructions received," Clyde said, tapping the refresh button on his screen again.

"Comes straight from the bridge," Eisen said.

"Open the override hatch on the munition and prepare to make adjustments."

Overton stepped back from the plasma charge.

"Chief? Are you serious? That's an ordnance specialist task. I can identify faults, but I'm not rated to make any sort of—"

"Open the override hatch!" Eisen half-rose from his seat and one hand went to the pistol holstered on his thigh.

"We carry the last surviving member of the royal family, and it is our duty to protect Crown Prince Aidan with our lives."

"Order received." Overton took a metal punch key from his belt, pressed it into the round, and twisted it to the side. A panel slid open with a snap and a touch screen blinked on.

A chime sounded in Clyde's ears; he'd finally received word from the gunnery section. On his screen, a message rolled across in plain text: UNAUTHORIZED WEAPON ACTIVITY. CHECK FIRING. FREEZE.

Clyde slowly sent one hand to his own holstered pistol, hidden from Eisen's view by Clyde's seat. He carefully unsnapped the flap over the handle.

"Override access exposed," Overton said, his hands opening and closing rapidly.

"Enter the following code," Eisen said.

Clyde gripped his pistol and felt a slight vibration as it chambered an energy bolt.

"Overton, belay that order," Clyde said.

"As you were, sailor!" Eisen rose to his feet, hand on his pistol. The entire gun crew shrank away from the furious chief. "Overton, this is wartime. You will follow my commands or your insubordination before the enemy will be dealt with. Enter the following code: Alpha-Nine-Delta-Seven. Now."

"That's not the command from gunnery, Chief!" Clyde's heart pounded in his ears. What was Eisen trying to do to them?

"Overton!" Eisen drew his pistol but kept it

pointed at the deck.

"Chief…" Overton looked back and forth from Eisen to Clyde. "If there's a mix-up somewhere…I don't even know what that code does!"

"Don't do it." A drop of sweat ran down the side of Clyde's face. He'd known Chief Eisen for almost a year, a straitlaced sailor as he'd ever met. None of this made any sense.

"Chief," Overton said as he stepped back from the munition, "can we—"

He jerked back as energy bolts slammed into his chest and exploded out his back. Blood splattered against the open breach and Clyde's faceplate.

Clyde ducked down as Eisen turned his weapon on him. A round hit the headrest and ripped it off the seat. Clyde lurched out of his chair and fell to the deck. He rolled to the side, fumbling with his pistol. The sound of more pistol fire broke out around him as he finally drew his weapon from its holster.

Harris was crouched behind a metal spar attached to the cannon. Blood ran freely from a shoulder as he fired blindly over the spar.

Clyde brought his pistol up to Eisen's command nook…but he was gone.

He didn't hear the shot, but he felt the impact against his helmet. The bolt struck just above the reinforced glass visor and snapped his head back like a kick from a mule. The world went sideways and when his eyes refocused, he found himself looking at the ceiling as the scent of burning hair filled his helmet.

His pistol was still in his hand.

"…and I say to you that we will fight. Fight against this foe until Albion is free. No matter the pain. No matter the price."

Clyde sat up, his vision swimming. Eisen was at the plasma munition, his back to him, Harris and Overton dead at his feet.

Clyde tried to aim his pistol, but his arm felt like it was made of jelly and the pistol seemed to have a mind of its own as to where it should point. Clyde pulled the trigger. The energy round zipped past Eisen's head and bounced off the plasma shell.

Eisen jumped back and swung his pistol toward the dazed sailor. He didn't see the turret doors open. He didn't see Tolan and a team of men-at-arms standing behind him, nor did he see when the spy released three crawfish that streaked across the turret and latched on to Eisen's back. He did feel the electric shocks as they ripped through his body.

The Chief's armor absorbed much of the onslaught, but his jaw clenched and he groaned in pain as he stumbled forward, dropping his pistol next to Clyde. Eisen fought through the pain and broke into a jog, heading right for the enviro-shield between him and the void. Ducking his head, Eisen charged through the shield and tumbled into hard vacuum. Without his helmet, death would come quickly and painfully.

Clyde fell onto his side, flopped a hand at the

plasma munition, and managed a slur.

Tolan came over and knelt next to him.

"Well…shit. So much for a prisoner. You OK?"

A flood of vowels came from Clyde's mouth.

"I can see your scalp, but not your skull or what's inside," Tolan said, shrugging his shoulders, "so I guess you'll live. Brave move shooting the plasma charge to throw him off. I'll make sure Dr. Seaver checks those brass balls of yours to see if they're still intact."

"Help…my team," Clyde said before falling back onto his elbows as the room started spinning faster.

"Medical's on the way." Tolan gave him a pat on the shoulder. "Good job, kid."

CHAPTER 20

Gage watched the approaching Daegon force in the holo tank. Three battleships, each slightly larger than the *Orion,* and a dozen cruiser-sized escorts made for Siam. They'd come out of slip space with little velocity but were accelerating far faster than Gage's fleet could manage.

After watching the gun camera footage from Ivor's and Wyman's fighters and gleaning every bit of the Daegon capabilities from what they and the other survivors remembered, there was little doubt his fleet stood little chance in a stand-up fight.

He zoomed out, taking in Siam and the nearby nexus points. He double-tapped the *Orion*'s icon and time plots traced from their position to each of the escape routes. The holo tank added a pursuit path from the Daegon force. Spinning X's on the escape routes showed where the Daegon would overtake the 11th. Only one route offered a chance to enter slip space without a prolonged engagement.

"Captain Price," Gage said, sweeping aside all the possible routes but one, "order the fleet to weigh anchor and set course for the Sicani System. Full engine burn, lens formation. The supply ships and the *Hephaestus* to the nexus at best speed; they're a good deal faster than us and I don't want to worry about protecting them."

"Sicani System. Aye aye, Commodore." There was a slight pause before her answer, as if she wanted to argue or mention something pertinent, but Gage knew what she meant to say. Sicani was a Harlequin system, and Gage had a death mark on his head there.

The *Orion* rumbled forward as her engines flared to life. Gage felt sick to his stomach as Siam fell away from the forward windows. The world was nearly defenseless, and he was responsible for over two thousand sailors and engineers that would be left behind.

"Commodore…" A junior lieutenant at the astrogation section waved to him. "Commodore, the grav buoy is transmitting data to the Daegon fleet. They must be working up a slip equation to follow us."

"Can you disable it?" Gage asked.

"Negative, it's under Siam ground control." The lieutenant glanced at her screen. "They're pulling more data than usual. Their jump computers must not have any historic data on file…maybe six more minutes until they have enough to follow us."

"Guns, target the grav buoy and prepare to destroy it on my mark. Comms, get President Hu or their ground control station on the line and tell them to shut the buoy down." Gage waited as both sections went to work.

"Commodore," Price said, "I agree with your course of action, but I would be remiss if I didn't tell you

397

that destruction of a grav buoy, no matter the circumstances, is a war crime."

She was right, of course. Without a grav buoy, any ship that arrived in Siam space would have to return immediately to the last star they had a jump equation for or be stranded for months as onboard graviton seismographs rediscovered the pathway to another place. Destroying Siam's grav buoy would isolate—and devastate—the planet.

"No word from Hu or ground control," the comm officer said.

"Gunnery, transfer command authority to the cannons with the firing solution to my station," Gage said. New screens popped up a moment later. He jabbed a finger into the blinking icons labeled FIRE and watched as yellow bolts leapt away from the *Orion*'s gun batteries and destroyed the buoy over Siam's north pole.

"This was done under my decision, my authority, my responsibility," Gage said. *I may be damned for this in the future, but if the Daegon follow us to Sicani, then all will be lost,* he thought.

"Enemy fleet increasing speed," Price said. "I say you caught them off guard, sir."

"If we manage the jump to Sicani, they won't be able to follow us, for a while at least," Gage said. Given the superior Daegon technology he'd seen thus far, he had a feeling they could overcome the lack of a grav buoy much faster than he could.

"Lens formation complete," Price said. "Activate shields?"

"No, keep power to engines. We've time to light them before we're in weapons' range," Gage said. In the holo tank, the 11th was arrayed in a lens with the curve toward the gaining enemy, the *Orion* in the center and the three battle cruisers *Ajax, Concordia,* and *Storm,* around the flagship. The frigate and destroyer squadrons formed concentric rings around the larger capital ships.

On his order, the ships would activate their shield

emitters and put up an energy wall between them and the enemy…a wall with weak points behind each engine array. Most star navies pursuing a foe with shields up would try to overtake them from the side, force a broadside duel. Gage felt he was about to learn a very important, and painful, lesson in Daegon tactics and capabilities.

Minutes ticked by…and the Daegon fleet adjusted course to swing closer to Siam.

"Daegon commander is hailing you, sir," the comms officer said.

"On my tank." Gage stood up straight and clasped his hands behind his back.

Tiberian appeared, shaking his head.

"I misjudged you, Gage. Albion was a just star nation, renowned for her honorable commanders…but I can appreciate a shrewd maneuver. Time for one of my own. Power down your ships and disable your weapons immediately or I will bombard what little remains of this…Siam. Many active Albion power signatures and communications relays are still there. How many men did you leave behind?"

"The planet is defenseless. I will order those left behind to surrender so long as you promise to treat them like proper prisoners of war. I do not know what you Daegon think to gain from this aggression, but murdering civilians from orbit is—"

Tiberian's transmission cut out.

"Get him back," Gage said. In the holo tank, the Daegon fleet spread apart as it sped closer to the planet.

"No answer, sir. Shall I raise Colonel Horton?"

Gage's hands balled into fists. Tiberian already knew he had men and women on the surface. A transmission to Horton now could be traced, pinpointing the engineer's location for a Daegon strike.

"No, don't open any hails from the planet. It only puts them at risk," Gage said.

"Nuclear munitions detected!" Commander Clark, the gunnery officer, shouted. "Two of the Daegon ships are hot, sir. Weapons are not in transit."

He'd left men behind. Committed a war crime. Now this Tiberian had a knife to Siam's throat and put their fate in Gage's hand. With each step, Gage felt himself moving further and further from the ideal naval officer he'd wanted to be since he was a boy. There were millions of people on Siam, far fewer in his fleet…he wasn't sure which decision would weigh heavier on his soul.

"President Hu is hailing us," Captain Price said.

"Don't answer," Gage said. "The Daegon are doing this, not us. I'll not be blackmailed into surrender, not when we can't trust them to spare the planet."

"Nuclear launch detected," the gunnery officer said. Small icons bearing the ancient symbol of a radiation hazard sprang from two Daegon ships, fanning out and toward Lopburi and the last few densely populated towns.

Gage never took his eyes from the holo as the warheads streaked toward a populace that had already suffered so much…and watched them explode. The holo tank traced out the effects of the blast waves and what little remained of Lopburi was annihilated in seconds. He thought of the little girl, Tuyet, and her grandfather and hoped they didn't suffer long.

"Fusion warheads, sir," Clark said. "I'll log the effects for later study…and as evidence to the rest of the core nations."

Gage managed a nod.

"Enemy readjusting course," Price said. "They slowed themselves down. They'll be in torpedo range within ten minutes. At current speed, we can make the slip jump in…twenty minutes."

Focus, Gage told himself. *The fleet needs its leader.*

"Order all ships to ready individual slip jumps," he said. "We won't be able to enter en masse once we engage the enemy. We will regroup once we reach Sicani space."

Price nodded and tapped instructions onto her screens.

To escape with as many ships and lives as

possible, Gage knew he had to slow the Daegon down. The less time his ships were under fire, the better chance the 11th had of reaching Sicani. Gage opened a tight-beam channel to the *Retribution*, one of his frigates.

Commander Barlow came up in the tank.

"Thomas? I mean, sir?" Barlow asked.

"I have a dangerous mission for you Michael," Gage said. "I need someone aggressive and brave and you're the best officer for the job."

"You want me to do a dangle, don't you? The same thing old man Bancroft said was the stupidest maneuver he'd ever heard of. I'm glad you called me. If you'd asked Dillard over on the *Firebrand*, I would've been insulted. Just my ship or my squadron?"

"Both squadrons; this is no time for subtlety. Time your attack to the first torpedo salvo. Inflict what damage you can, then make for the nexus. Hit and run, Mike," Gage said.

"You think I'm going to get stuck against their

battleships while I'm commanding a frigate? You said you wanted someone brave, not suicidal. I'm well aware you've the Crown Prince aboard the *Orion*. We'll give these new bastards a bloody nose, teach them what it means to fight Albion's finest hunter-killer squadron. See you in Sicani," Barlow said and cut the channel.

The fleet's six frigates broke from the formation and flew perpendicular to the path leading to the Sicani nexus. They'd stop beyond the known range of the Daegon vessels and keep pace with the enemy, daring them to break off and engage. Barlow would either strike the enemy with the devastating lances the frigates carried or retreat just out of range if the enemy tried to fight them, remaining a potential threat that could attack at any time.

Barlow had to either inflict damage and slow the foe, or draw off enemy ships to improve the *Orion*'s chances.

"Gunnery, ready a torpedo salvo. All ships and all tubes. Wide dispersal pattern," Gage said.

"Standard mix of laser and high-explosive warheads?" the gunnery officer asked.

"No…" Gage thought over the few minutes of combat footage from the *Joaquim*. "High explosive only. Load laser for the second salvo. All torpedoes."

"But that's—"

"Three-quarters of our laser inventory, I know. See to it—I'll explain in a moment." Gage turned his attention back to the holo tank as the ordnance sailors in the *Orion* and the battle cruisers readied the torpedoes. Each type of missile utilized the same body, but the warheads were interchangeable. Standard ship-to-ship engagements mixed the warhead types in the hopes the more destructive (and exceedingly more expensive and delicate) laser warheads could land a hit.

Gage waited as torpedo tubes across the fleet reported loaded and ready. The temptation to constantly issue orders to feel in control was almost palpable, but a commander that wanted to win a battle needed to issue the right orders at the right time, not give off a stream of micromanagements that could get jumbled during the fog of war.

Power fluctuations came off the Daegon battleships as their forward batteries prepared to fire.

"Light the shields!" Gage ordered.

The *Orion* groaned as her acceleration decreased and the inertial dampeners shifted power to the shields. The emitters in the four capital ships threw up a circular energy wall behind the fleet. The ring of destroyers shrank slightly to take refuge behind the wall; none of the smaller vessels carried emitters powerful enough to lend to the shield wall or take a direct hit from a capital ship's broadside.

Fire erupted from the Daegon battleships and hundreds of blue bolts streaked through the void, dissipating against the shields in fading ripples.

"Shields holding," Price said, "but they're down to 82—now 74 percent and falling fast."

"Gunnery, loose torpedoes," Gage said.

Armored hatches across the *Orion*'s dorsal and ventral hull slid aside and magnetic rails inside the launchers spat torpedoes into the void. The weapons flew clear of the shield wall, then the internal engines kicked on. The torpedoes' path bent toward the Daegon vessels and accelerated.

"Laser munitions loading," the Clark said. "Full salvo ready in three minutes."

"Hold salvo." Gage gripped the sides of the holo tank as the torpedoes streaked toward the enemy. Their course began to waver as the cannon fire from the Daegon shifted from pounding the Albion shields to the torpedoes. Gage hit a button on his console and a freeze-frame of the moment pulled to the side of the tank.

Half the torpedoes succumbed to enemy fire before smaller point defense lasers erupted and annihilated the remainder in seconds. None of the weapons even came close to lethal range where afterburners would kick in and drive the warheads into their targets like a bolt shot from a crossbow.

"Gunnery, set offset engagement for the next salvo to four hundred kilometers," Gage said. "Target the battleship to their left flank."

Clark did a double take at Gage, then nodded quickly.

Gage opened a channel to the *Retribution*. "Barlow, this is your moment."

"Engaging." The six frigates turned on a dime and accelerated toward the Daegon ships.

Daegon fire shifted to the edge of the shield, concentrating on a small area just behind the destroyer *Saber*. The shield edge buckled and frayed apart. Cannon blasts smashed through the *Saber*'s engine block and ripped out her flank. The ship canted to the side, then cracked in half. The Daegon kept up the assault, blasting the vessel into fragments.

"No lifeboats on the scope," Price said.

The next salvo flew away, and almost a hundred laser-tipped missiles closed on the enemy as Gage thumped his knuckles against the holo tank.

"Gunnery, continuous launch of all remaining torpedoes. Smaller vessels are the priority for laser warheads," Gage said. His maneuver would either even the odds for escaping or do nothing more than waste lives and munitions. The next few seconds would tell.

The laser torpedoes closed and the energy batteries within the warheads overloaded into focusing crystals angled toward the targeted battleship. Coherent beams of searing light stabbed through the void and traced crimson lines across the ship's shields. While nearly half the lasers missed at the long range, enough landed to have an effect. The Daegon shields glowed, forming a shell of swirling light as the onslaught overloaded the forward emitters. A pair of lasers ripped through the shields and into the leading diamond. The beams exploded out the bottom, shattering the armored sides. The last of the lasers scored hits up and down the hull and energy reading from the ship fell to zero.

The stricken vessel lurched to the side, then drifted off the pursuit path, trailing air and debris.

Gage ignored the cheers from his bridge crew as the Daegon fleet spread out. Their concentrated fire against his shields slackened, turning to the torpedoes launching from his ships every few seconds. The enemy tried to knock them down as soon as they cleared the shield wall with far less success than before.

"Not so confident now, are you?" Gage said to himself.

The Daegon ships to their right flank spread out as a few of the missiles closed…just as the frigates began their attack run. With their light shields and lances that ran the length of the ships, they were something of a glass cannon in any stand-up fight. The Albion admiralty strived to assign only the most aggressive (some said bloodthirsty) officers to command frigates and Gage waited to see if

Barlow and the others would live up to that reputation.

The smaller enemy vessels on the outer edge kept their fire directed against the incoming torpedoes closing on the battleships, ignoring the incoming frigates. Gage's brow furrowed in confusion—did they think the frigates weren't a threat?

Lances with more destructive power than the laser torpedoes from the *Retribution* and *Firebrand* struck a smaller Daegon ship. The two beams hit within a few yards of each other and ripped through the shield and into the hull. The ship exploded and wreckage bounced within the still-active shields, leaving a pill-shaped mess behind as the shields faded away.

The two frigates fell back as the last four ships sprinted toward a battleship's flank. The giant ship turned its cannons on the attackers, striking the prow of the *Huntress*. A hit broke through the hull and her engines gave out. Three frigates charged through the fire from the battleships and surrounding smaller vessels, then activated their lances. The beams converged against the shields over the battleship's engines. The shields buckled under the onslaught…but held.

The three frigates looped away, retreating for open space. The *Retribution* and *Firebrand*, their lances recharged, dove toward the battleship and fired. The beam from Barlow's ship powered through the shields and carved through the engines. Thruster nozzles the size of destroyers broke free and went tumbling end over end. The battleship slowed and fell out of the formation. Daegon cruisers slowed and closed around the battleship, forming a wall with their own hulls between the larger ship and the retreating frigates.

Gage opened a channel and said, "Well done, *Retribution*."

Barlow came up in the tank. A small fire burned behind him and sparks showered onto his head and shoulders.

"There's no response from the *Huntress*," Barlow

said. "She's dead in space, but there are life signs. Permission to—"

"Commodore! Slip signature forming around the pursuing battleships!" Price shouted.

"What?" Gage looked away from his old friend to the mass of Daegon ships. Readings on the two battleships wavered…then the ships and several escorts vanished.

"Where'd they go?" Price asked.

"Contact! Thirty degrees mark twenty!" the helmsman called out.

One of the Daegon battleships was ahead and just below the fleet's path…and it was racing right toward them.

"Shields forward! Evasive maneuvers!" Gage's order came as the battleship opened fire.

With their shields concentrated in the wrong direction, the Daegon's cannon fire punched against unprotected hulls. Armor plating along the *Orion*'s forward section buckled, and each hit sent a tremor through the deck that felt like a giant stomping toward Gage.

The *Orion*'s cannons opened fire, sending back a pitiful answer to the enemy battleship's onslaught.

The battle cruiser *Storm* took direct hits to the command superstructure, each strike deforming the armor around the bridge like a sledgehammer to thin metal. A shot hit the cannon turret just at the superstructure's base and the magazine full of plasma shells within the turret ignited. The explosion ripped the bridge away and knocked the ship off course.

The *Orion*'s shields finally shifted to cover the forward third of the ship, absorbing some of the punishment.

"Flight deck alpha is offline," Price said. A damage report came up in the tank, pulsating red spreading from the prow to the forward cannon batteries. "Hull breach from decks three to nine. Turrets B-3 and C-4 are…destroyed."

"Concentrate all fire on the battleship," said Gage.

The deck lurched aside as a power coupling along the outer edge of the hull exploded, sending off a shower of sparks and armor plating into the void.

"Sir, the *Storm*," Price said.

The mortally wounded battle cruiser's engines flared, sending it hurtling straight toward the enemy battleship.

"Her bridge is gone," Gage said. "Who's steering her?"

"The engine room could do it," the helmsman said. "Can control everything but guns from there."

The battleship tried to steer away, but the massive ship was a lumbering beast compared to the smaller *Storm* as it closed. The Daegon pounded the *Storm*, blasting her hull into a battered mess. The battle cruiser's engines sputtered and faded out, but momentum carried the *Storm* forward and into the battleship's flank. The *Storm* broke against the shields, tearing along the energy shell like a predator's claws down bare flesh. The shield flickered and what remained of the *Storm* impaled itself into the enemy hull. The battleship's fire slackened and energy readings from the ship dropped to almost nothing.

Whoever had sent the *Storm* to its destruction must have known the ship was doomed and decided to make her last moments count. Gage wished he knew the name of the brave soul responsible, but the battle continued.

"Reform the fleet," Gage said. "Someone tell me where that last battleship went."

"There," Clark said as he tapped one of his screens, "near the nexus point to Sicani and with several escorts."

The enemy vessels appeared in the holo tank along with an alert message over the nexus. Gage frowned at the readings.

"Astrogation, care to explain this?" Gage asked.

"It's a low-level slip frequency, sir." The lieutenant peered at her screen. "And I'm getting a weird resonance in our own engines…graviton readings from the nexus are fluctuating. I don't think we can leave, sir. Some kind of jamming I've never seen before."

"Enemy fighters in the void," Price said, "and missiles, all vectoring toward us."

"Launch all fighters." Gage's hands maneuvered the holo tank as blinking red icons of fighters and larger missiles tracked away from the last Daegon battleship and several of the escort ships clustered around it. The missile tracks moved slower than Albion torpedoes and faster than the spear-tip-shaped fighters…but not by much.

The Daegon force was several hundred kilometers from the nexus point and nearly stationary. Gage had a straight shot to their escape…but the door was slammed shut.

Gage touched a fighter in the tank as it flew from the *Orion*'s second flight deck.

****

Wyman gripped his control stick, appreciating acceleration's press against his body as his fighter raced toward the approaching swarm of Daegon missiles. He was well trained in interdiction of enemy fighters, but shooting down the incoming torpedoes was going to be a challenge.

"You never mentioned the enemy using torpedoes," Ricks said through the squadron's network.

"Didn't see it," Ivor said. "Our torps—and any other core-world torps I've ever heard of—are a lot faster than theirs. It doesn't make sense to me."

"Easy kills," Wyman said. He maneuvered his fighter alongside Ivor's and the rest of their new squadron, the Reavers.

"Stand by," Ricks said. "New instructions from the Admiral—Commodore—whatever…we're to bypass the incoming bogies and hit the battleship. Red Arrow squadron will join us. Rest of the fighters might if they can get all the debris out of the way from their flight deck.

Primary target is their slip generators. *Orion* needs that destroyed or we're not leaving this garden spot. Freak Show, Briar, what does it look like?"

The squadron banked to the side as Ricks sent out a new flight path that curved around the incoming fighters and missiles.

Wyman looked at Ivor in her cockpit. She looked at him, then raised her hands and shrugged her shoulders.

"Edgy," Wyman said, using Ricks' call sign, "we don't know. Didn't get a close look at their cap ship hulls during the dogfights."

"Our slip generators look like nacelles and are on the outer hull," Ivor said. "I know it's hard to believe these Daegon are human, but they've got to follow the same laws of physics as everyone else. Graviton waves are so weak you can't detect them through any armor or within a hull. I bet we can find them if we look in the right place."

"Let's go sniffing around that monster," Wyman said. "Sure they won't mind one bit."

"You have something constructive to add to this mission, Freak?" Ricks asked. Wyman shut his mouth.

"Slip generators need some shielding from engines," said a pilot, call sign Tanner. "And offset depending on how hot the engines are…bet we find their generator on the fourth or fifth diamond from the engines."

"A concentration of point defense turrets," Wyman said, "it's a critical system. It'll be protected. If we take more fire than usual from an area, that's a hint. See? I'm helping."

"Sure hope you two are right that our guns can get through their shields," Ricks said. "Else this is about to become a stupid way to die."

Wyman looked up as Daegon fighters and torpedoes flew past far overhead.

"Lot of contacts," Wyman said. "Sure hope the destroyers and the flak can handle it."

"How about we worry about our own problems?"

Ivor asked.

"Red Arrows to the forth diamond, Reavers to the fifth," Ricks said. "Arrows will work back toward the aft if they come up empty. We work toward the fore. Any questions?"

"Bogies, coming right for us," Tanner said.

Ten Daegon fighters flew between the escort ships.

"Phalanx," Wyman said, "we need to watch for it."

Cannon blasts came off the outer ring of escorts. Blue light washed over Wyman as they zipped between the squadron.

"Ready missiles," Ricks said. Wyman chose an approaching fighter and activated one of his Shrike missiles.

"Tone," Ivor said. Other Reaver squadron pilots repeated the word as they locked on.

Wyman felt a tinge of fear as the Daegon fighters

snapped away from each other and their edges glowed bright.

"Move. Move!" Wyman pushed his control stick down and sent his fighter into a dive. He rolled to the right as a solid beam of energy ripped through space in front of him. He continued rolling and missed the phalanx beam by a distance he did not want to dwell on.

He pulled up and found the enemy squadron flying at minimal power. He locked a missile and let it fly. A dozen more Shrikes joined his and annihilated the enemy in a ripple of fireballs.

"Hot damn," Ivor said. "It worked."

"Lost one," Ricks said. "Vulgar, form on my wing. Get through the picket ships and remember the mission."

Wyman fired up his engines and soared forward, snapping over an escort ship firing wildly at the incoming Typhoons. Double-barreled turrets on the battleship opened up, clipping Wyman's wing and ripping a Shrike from its mount.

Wyman banked to the side and dodged another blast that would have blown him to fragments. The blast hit a picket ship and punched a dent into the hull.

"Freak?" Ivor asked.

"Fine. Just fine." Wyman accelerated toward the fifth diamond, keeping a few seconds behind Ivor. "Didn't like that missile anyway."

"Not getting any fire from the escorts," Tanner called out. "Anyone else?"

"Negative." Wyman jinked to the side, watching as a turret struggled to keep up with his maneuvers. "Nothing from behind."

A fireball erupted overhead. Wyman glanced up and saw one of the smaller ships breaking apart as shots from the battleship chased after Red Arrow fighters, impacting the spreading cloud of debris.

"Shit rolls downhill in this fleet," Ivor said. "Think I've got something. Freak, let's cut over."

"On your wing." Wyman followed her over the

battleship, its hull shimmering beneath active shields. He ached to strike at the exposed tubes running between where the diamond tips met, but that wasn't why he was there.

They crested over the top of the ship…and found another flat hull section.

"I see it!" The words were full of static as a Red Arrow pilot joined the Reaver network. "Third diamond, forward left—" The transmission ended with a squeal as a fireball erupted just off the battleship's side.

Ivor and Wyman turned toward the engines and saw a torrent of fire rising from a cluster of point defense turrets on the Daegon ship. Red Arrow pilots dove at the hull from well above the shield wall, firing their cannons that sent high-velocity slugs through the shields. At their present distance, a direct hit would take a miracle. Two more Typhoons exploded as the defenders found their range.

"Not going to be easy," Ivor said.

Wyman dipped his nose down to dodge a double bolt. He looked at the battleship and saw a hexagon the size of a soccer field on the same hull plate as the defense cluster protruding from the hull near the turret.

"That's a shield emitter. I've got an idea." Wyman pulled up and into a loop, then dove straight down on the hexagon. He fired, unleashing the full fury of his guns. Bullets sent ripples through the shield wall as they passed through, then punched into the hexagon. Electricity snapped out like lightning along the base of a thunderstorm. Wyman's dive took him straight down…and right past the shield layer.

He pulled up and flew a few feet over the hull on his way to the slip drive.

"I can't tell if you're a damn fool or a friggin' genius, Freak," Ivor said as she joined his wing.

"Make up your mind after this works…or doesn't." Wyman put a hand on his manual thruster controls.

The Red Arrows kept up their attack high above, holding the defense turrets' attention as the two survivors from Albion closed on the target.

"Going tail up," Wyman said, "in three…two…mark!" He pressed two fingers against thruster controls and pressed them up. His tail kicked up, angling his nose down toward the hull. His Typhoon flew perpendicular to the hull and over a point defense turret. A mound rose off the hull as light swirled beneath the semi-opaque glass.

Wyman fired, blasting gouts of crystal into the air, but the slip drive kept swirling. He flipped an override on his missile system and set the Shrikes to point detonations, turning the exquisitely engineered hunter-seeker missiles into very dumb rockets. He launched the missiles and watched as they closed on a section of the slip drive being pummeled by Ivor's guns.

A missile exploded on the surface. The second broke through the glass. A flash broke along the slip drive, then the light faded away.

"Genius!" Ivor shouted. "I take back every bad thing I ever said about you."

The defense turrets exploded. Great gouts of flame billowed out of the holes and died in the void.

"All craft, this is Edgy. *Orion* says the nexus is clear. Disengage and get back to the ship or be left behind."

"Don't have to tell me twice," Wyman said as he steered toward the *Orion*'s beacon and rocketed away.

CHAPTER 21

The *Orion* shook beneath Gage's feet as Daegon fighters cut across her bow, pounding her shields as they sped by.

"Torpedoes incoming!" Clark called out.

"Redirect fire to intercept." Gage looked out the windows and saw a trio of torpedoes heading straight for his bridge. Shields melded around the missiles as they pushed through the barrier. A flak turret on the *Orion*'s forward edge lifted and sent up a curtain of fire that clipped a missile. It tumbled end over end and broke into pieces. The remaining torpedoes' thrusters ignited…and angled down, right where the command superstructure met the main hull.

As the two missiles struck the hull, Gage flinched, expecting a life-ending explosion. The weapons were embedded in the hull, and gas escaped around the tipped armor until emergency force fields squeezed around the breach. Debris from the destroyed torpedo crashed against the bridge's windows, skittering across the glass and around the side. A bit of wreckage hit and left a red streak as momentum carried it along the glass.

Gage jumped off the command dais and ran to the port window, catching a good look at the object—a severed arm.

"Those were boarding torpedoes," Gage said. "Why didn't they strike at the engines or…Price, send men-at-arms to deck three. They're going for Prince Aidan."

He pointed at Thorvald, who'd stood near the lift doors in silence like a sentinel throughout the battle.

"Go. Protect the Crown Prince."

"I cannot leave your side." Thorvald shook his head slowly.

"I do not matter. Aidan is the last of the royal family and you are sworn to him. Now go!"

Thorvald leaned to the side to step away, but his feet remained locked to the floor.

"Why are you fighting this?" Thorvald asked aloud. "Our duty is clear." He raised one foot with difficulty, like a powerful magnet was pulling it down. He broke loose of whatever was holding him and went into the elevator.

His armor rose up his neck and set into a helmet as the doors closed.

"Who was he talking to?" the communications lieutenant asked.

"Helm! Time to slip space?" Gage grabbed the railing on the command dais and vaulted back to the holo tank.

"Four minutes…if we're lucky."

****

Bertram gripped his rifle as the sound of weapons fire echoed through the walls of the Admiral's quarters. He looked down at Prince Aidan, in a bespoke armored vacuum suit made from the *Orion*'s foundries, one hand held by Salis.

The Genevan had her pistol in hand, watching the barred doors intently.

"Nanny Salis, what's that noise?" Aidan asked, clutching his plush dinosaur against his chest.

"Never you mind, young master," Bertram said. "Just…pipes. Yes, pipes that the lay-a-bout crew haven't got around to fixing."

"Do not lie to the child." Salis cocked her head to the side. "Is there another access way to this room?"

"The bulkheads are armored, reinforced, and we have a separate life-support system. The only way in is through those doors," Bertram said. "And the young master has been through more than enough in the last few days to—"

"No fighting!" Aidan stomped his foot.

"It's not fighting when Mr. Bertram explains to Nanny Salis—who's been on an Albion warship for all of a few hours and thinks she knows how everything works—that everything is going to be OK." He looked at Salis and practically growled, "Won't. It?"

Rounds hit the outer wall, hammering out dents that sent the painting the *Thames* crashing to the floor. Aidan clutched Salis' leg.

"Do not lie to the child." Salis' armor formed a helm over her head. "They're coming."

"What do you mean? I don't hear any more…pipes. The men-at-arms must have—"

A yellow circle of hot metal appeared on the wall, wide enough for two men to climb through at a time.

"Down." Salis pushed Aidan to the ground, then grabbed Bertram by the throat and used him as a human shield for the Prince.

"Don't. Move." She hooked a heel against Sartorius' battered wooden desk and kicked it toward Bertram. An intricately carved drawer face stopped an inch from his face.

The bulkhead within the metal circle jiggled forward as something hit it from behind. After the second blow, it slid loose and a pair of Daegon warriors pushed it forward, slamming it to the deck with the clang of a church bell. Salis shot both the warriors, who collapsed beneath the breach.

A metal ball flew through the breach and bounced off the metal circle.

Salis jumped into the air, spun, and landed a kick on the ball, sending it back the way it came.

The grenade exploded in a wave of light and a thunderclap of sound that fluttered Bertram's ears. Salis staggered back, shaking off the effects a moment later.

Blue-armored talons grabbed the edge of the breach, and a Daegon swung into the room. He landed flat on the floor and sprang straight up, faster than Salis could adjust her aim. The Daegon hit the roof and gripped it with claws on both hands and feet. It sprang from the ceiling toward Salis, its arms extended at her throat.

She fired a round that sparked off the Daegon's chest. Her free hand shot up, grabbed him by the wrist, and ducked, swinging the enemy down like a sack of potatoes against the deck. She stomped a boot onto his neck and shot him twice in the head.

A shot from behind hit her in the lower back, leaving a gouge along her armor. She cried out in pain and swung around, firing wildly. A bullet struck the desk and cracked the wood into splinters.

More of the taloned Daegon crawled into the room, gripping the walls and ceiling like spiders. Salis leaped to the side as a regular warrior leaned around the breach and fired on her. She aimed at the warrior when a Daegon jumped on her, its limbs wrapped around hers, bending at impossible angles with metallic snaps. The two fell to the ground, Salis struggling mightily but unable to move more than an inch at a time. A taloned warrior snatched her pistol away and squeezed it until the weapon shattered.

One let off a hiss of Daegon language.

Claws slammed onto the desk and tossed it against the bulkhead, revealing Bertram, who had Aidan pinned to the wall, the steward's bulk blocking the Prince from view.

"You'll-you'll not have him!" Bertram stammered. Four of the taloned Daegon formed a semicircle around the steward. One laughed and clicked the tips of his talons together in anticipation.

"Bastards will have to go through me first!" Bertram tried to bring his rifle to bear, but it was yanked from his hands in an instant. A Daegon snapped the weapon in half.

"Close your eyes, young master. I'll keep mine open for the both of us."

A Daegon reached for Bertram. Cyborg eyes

glinted beneath the faceplate as it came closer. There was a snap, and the warrior's head exploded, sending a messy smear of blood and blue armor burst across Bertram's face.

Thorvald charged into the room and shoulder-checked a taloned warrior off its feet, then swung a fist back into another and cracked its helmet open.

Salis roared and broke an arm free. She cocked a thumb up and drove it into the faceplate of the Daegon restraining her. Her digit broke through and speared the warrior's eye. The Daegon let her go and scrambled away from her.

Thorvald swayed back as claws swiped at his face and shot the attacker in the chest twice. One round shot out the Daegon's back, sending a spray of black fluid against the wall. The Daegon hissed and jumped onto Thorvald, its talons catching the Genevan by the wrist and pulling his arms apart. The clawed feet clamped onto his chest and ripped downward, rending Thorvald's armor. He jerked to the side and his pistol went flying.

Salis snatched the pistol from the air and turned it on the Daegon holding her fellow bodyguard. She shot it through the temple, then shot the warrior with a thumb-sized hole in its mask through the same hole.

The final warrior tried to flee past Thorvald. He slammed his hand against the Daegon's throat and raised it into the air, driving its skull into the deck, crushing it with a wet crack.

Salis stumbled against Thorvald. Her armor pulled away from her head and she looked at Bertram.

"The Prince?"

Bertram, who had held very still during the melee, leaned away from the bulkhead. He turned around and found Aidan squatting against the wall, his eyes closed and the dinosaur clutched to his helmet.

"Can I look now, Mr. Berty?" the boy asked.

"No." Bertram pulled the boy close and kept his head buried against his chest. "You keep your eyes closed for a bit, young master."

The lights flickered and a deep thrum rose through the ship.

"You hear that? We've gone into slip space," Bertram said. "We're safe now." He looked over at the Genevans. "We *are* safe now?"

"That was the last of them." Thorvald took his pistol from Salis and looked down at the scars on his armor.

"Are we going home now?" Aidan asked.

"Not yet, lad. Not yet."

CHAPTER 22

Gage turned a corner and slowly walked down the corridor leading to his quarters. He half-slumped against the bulkhead and put his chin to his chest. His head felt like it was stuffed with cotton, his limbs weighed down by fatigue. Three sleepless days of emergency repairs, failing engines, and a fire on four decks that refused to die until mere hours ago.

He'd just finished a tour through med bay, where Doctor Seaver and her teams had been working even harder than him.

Gage wiped the back of his hand across his face, feeling the coarseness of a budding beard, then he swiped his palm over a panel next to a door, and it slid aside with a hiss. As the Admiral's aide, he rated a one-bedroom berth with a small desk and a lounge area with seating for several visitors. He entered and cracked the seals on his combat jumpsuit, getting a whiff of several days of accumulated funk.

"Sir?" Bertram came from around the kitchen partition, holding a silver tray with a small teakettle and a covered dish.

"Bertram…" Gage's eyes struggled to focus as he flopped down on a couch. He ran a zipper down the side of his uniform and let the chest covering flop open, exposing a body glove beneath. "I need you to…something."

"You need to eat, sir." The steward put the tray down on a coffee table and removed the covering. A flatbread chicken parmigiana sandwich and french fries gave off a whiff of steam.

Gage's eyebrows twitched, suddenly aware of just

how hungry he was. He snatched up the sandwich and took a giant bite, eating in a most undignified manner for an officer.

"As we're no longer on alert," Bertram said, "I'll lay out a shipboard uniform for you. The sonic shower is ready at your leisure."

Gage mumbled as he ate. Once he was halfway done, he set the sandwich aside and turned to the fries, which came with a dipping sauce made of ketchup and mayonnaise that was uniformly reviled beyond Albion.

The pitter-patter of feet came from the bedroom. Prince Aidan, wearing pajamas and rubbing sleep from his eyes, ran up to Gage.

"Who are you?" Aidan asked. Salis and Thorvald stepped out of the bedroom and took a post on either side of the doorway.

"I'm Commodore Gage." He cleaned his hand with a napkin and extended it to the boy, who shook it firmly.

"Is this your room?"

"The Admiral's quarters require extensive repairs…and cleaning," Thorvald said.

"No, this is your room for now," Gage said to Aidan. "I have some of my things in here, which I'll have moved."

"When are we going home?" Aidan asked.

Gage put his hands on his knees. "I don't have an answer for you, my Prince. We'll need some help to do that."

"But we *will* go home?"

"On my honor."

"I'm going back to sleep. Thank you for the room." The boy ran back into the bedroom and Gage heard a thump of a little body jumping onto his mattress.

Gage sighed, then looked at his half-finished meal.

"You two eaten?" he asked the Genevans.

"Do not concern yourself with our well-being, Regent," Thorvald said. "We are here to protect you

443

both."

"I don't need protecting," Gage said, stretching out on the couch. He yawned and tucked a pillow beneath his head. "Figure out what to do with you two…morning."

Bertram came out of the kitchen with a bowl of ice cream. He grumbled at the sight of the sleeping Gage, then policed up all the food and took it back to the kitchen.

"Two people are coming," Salis said.

There was a crash of dishes and Bertram rushed through the sitting room and out the door. He found Price and Clark in the corridor, both holding several data slates.

"May I help you, madam? Sir?" Bertram asked.

"We need the Commodore to approve these personnel transfers," Price said. "Then there's the matter of our munitions."

"Begging the good captain's pardon, but is anyone bleeding, on fire, or at risk of either of those conditions?" Bertram set himself in the open door.

"Step aside, steward," Clark said. "These need the Commodore's…actually, maybe they can wait." He stepped back, a bit pale.

"Commodore Gage has a standing practice of allowing his subordinates to make their own decisions so long as they follow his guidance," Bertram said. "I'm certain you can manage for a bit."

"Yes, thank you." Price nodded quickly and walked off with Clark. Bertram watched them go with a smile.

"Mr. Thorvald. Are you standing behind me?"

"I am."

Bertram turned and got a good look at the gouges running down the Genevan's chest.

"I could have handled that all on my own, thank you very much."

"No doubt."

"You're going to tell me how the two of you manage to hear every mouse fart and move like smoke.

Now step aside and let me attend to my officer."

Bertram squeezed around the Genevan and went to the sleeping Gage. He removed the Commodore's boots deftly, a maneuver he'd practiced over the years at Gage's side. He took a handkerchief from a pocket and wiped a smudge of blood from Gage's face. Bertram gave his head a gentle pat, then returned to the kitchen.

CHAPTER 23

No matter how many times Tiberian walked the grand court of the *Sphinx*, the majesty of the engineering, the vision, the purpose of it all never failed to fill him with confidence. Obsidian floor plates were carved with great moments from Daegon history, from the first rulers to the first kingdoms to Awakening, Landfall, the Defeat of Death, and the declaration of the Final Crusade. The fall of Albion would become part of the history of every great House…an accomplishment he'd put in jeopardy through failure.

From this, the highest point of the mothership that dominated over the ruined city of New Exeter, one could survey much of the planet, the first to return to Daegon domination.

Tiberian made his way to the base of a stairway leading up to a golden throne, the back of which was to him. Regal statues of bulls, lions, and other beasts molded from gold and silver lined either side of the stairs. The animals shifted their pose as he went to his knees: snouts bared teeth, claws raised to strike—all now embodied a primal rage.

She was angry.

Tiberian pressed his knuckles to either side of his knees, then bent his forehead to the ground. He held the bow for a full minute, then slowly lifted his shoulders up. The golden chain and lockbox holding his Charge dangled from his neck.

Metal cuffs snapped out of the floor and pinned his wrists to the floor. Tiberian kept his head bent, waiting for his fate.

"You return," came a lilting voice from the

throne. "You return with fewer ships and without the last of this world's pretenders."

"There is no excuse for failure, Baroness."

A slight breeze scented with flowers and sword oil caressed his face. The sound of metal clinking against stairs came closer.

Tiberian knew his death could be moments away. He took comfort in the coming closure. Imagining his fate during the return from Siam had been worse than the moment the *Orion* slipped through his fingers.

The sound of steel sliding against steel tickled his ears. He kept his gaze to the floor and extended his neck, giving her an easy strike.

The tip of a blade floated in front of his eyes. The blade grew red hot, burning his blue skin ever so slightly. The edge touched the golden chain of his Charge, then flicked aside, taking the necklace with it.

"Look at me, Tiberian."

He raised his head. Baroness Asaria was as

beautiful as ever. Armor clung to her body like it was painted on. The intelligence protecting her shifted the plates over her arms, stomach, and thighs like waves lapping against a beach, giving tantalizing glimpses of the flawless blue skin beneath. Gold and platinum wire woven through her hair glimmered beneath the stars above Albion. Eyes the green of the deep jungle looked at him with pity. One hand held her sword, heat emanating from it even as it cooled, the other held his Charge.

"I am disappointed in you." She wove the chain around her fingers and gripped the golden box against her palm. "You were to cast down the pretenders. Our spies assured us the world would not resist once their 'king' and his ilk were gone. I witnessed your bravery, your fury, in the castle. I was so certain you would lead the next phase of the Crusade…and yet one escaped you. I could take your head, mount it at the base of my throne as a warning to your brothers still fighting on the surface. Or I could melt your Charge and see it poured down your throat."

The Baroness squeezed her hand into a fist and the golden chain softened, then changed color to slate gray. She dropped a new Charge in front of Tiberian. What had been gold was now iron.

"You have not failed…completely," she said. "The mongrels believe their pretender king and family to be dead. Resistance crumbles across every front. Soon we will transform them into proper thralls, but if they have reason to believe they are not beaten…This is the first world of the Crusade. The rest of the un-ruled nations must see what awaits them, see that submission is the only way to survive and that those in our thrall are treated to their usefulness.

"Can you imagine, Tiberian, if our House fails here? If the other Houses can blame their failures on our poor showing? We would be left with nothing but scraps once the Crusade ends. We've planned our return for hundreds of years. Would you see me rule over a backwater, become the laughingstock of the other

Houses?"

"Never, Baroness."

"Your charge is incomplete, not failed. You will have the resources needed to hunt down this child and bring back the broken hull of the *Orion*. I will hang it in the sky where every mongrel can see it and know that they are defeated. Then you will return to the head of my House."

"As you command." Tiberian felt a wave of anger at the sight of the iron Charge. It was almost an insult for him to be given a tertiary task in the grand scheme of the Crusade. He would bring Aidan—and the damnable Gage—to her for a public execution or he would die trying.

The restraints unlocked and sank back into the floor. He stood up and Asaria ran her fingertips down the side of his face and over his lips.

"Don't force me to choose another as my consort," she purred at him. "You've always been my favorite."

"If you allow, I will leave now."

She clicked her tongue, then patted the flat of her blade against her calf.

"And do what, Tiberian? Blunder about wild space burning worlds until you stumble upon the *Orion*? No, I've a guide for you. Someone we found in the castle dungeons."

A hatch slid open at the base of the stairs and an elevator rose, holding two guards in obsidian armor and a man in ragged clothes, his hands bound at his waist. Every part of his body was as dark as the abyss; even the sclera of his eyes was pitch-black.

A guard kicked the back of the dark man's knees and sent him to the ground. One grabbed him by the scruff of his neck and pressed his head to the ground; the other put the flat of a serrated bayonet against the base of his skull.

"Such an abhorrent alteration to the human form," Asaria said, "but useful."

She flicked a finger and the guards pulled the prisoner to his feet, keeping his eyes off the Daegon nobles.

"Name yourself," Tiberian said.

"Ja'war." He lowered his head even farther. His voice sounded as if several men were speaking at the same time.

"This Ja'war knows wild space quite well, doesn't he?"

"None know it better than I, mistress."

"You will aid me in finding the *Orion*," Tiberian said. "Do this and you will be raised over the other thralls."

Ja'war looked at Tiberian, and his skin changed, melding into a perfect match for Tolan.

"Let me kill this one, and that's all the reward I need," Ja'war said.

"Go," Asaria said. "I have less patience than mercy."

CHAPTER 24

Gage leaned against the command deck railing, watching the kaleidoscope of bent starlight of slip space rotate beyond the *Orion*.

"Slip transit in three…" the astrogator said.

Real space swept over the ship and her slip bubble faded away. An ocher and beige world hung in the distance.

"No sign of the rest of the fleet," Price said from the holo tank behind Gage. "But there is a significant orbital presence over Sicani Prime."

"Three hundred million people down there,"

Gage said, "and none of them will be happy to see an Albion warship in their space."

"Scanners have hull matches on several known Harlequin vessels…multiple families. You know them better than I do, sir," Price said. "What does this mean?"

"If they're not fighting each other, then it means they've banded together against a common foe—which could be good for us, could be bad for us."

"*Ajax* just came out of slip space. Nineteen thousand kilometers away," the astrogator said. "More coming, very spread out."

"Go into slip space sloppy, come out sloppy," Gage said. *We're lucky we made it at all*, he thought.

"Three battle cruisers just broke orbit and are on a course for us," Price said, highlighting the tracks in the holo tank with her touch. "They'll get here long before the *Ajax* or anyone else can link up. If we weren't still limping from that last fight, it wouldn't be much of an issue, but now…"

"We're being hailed," the comms lieutenant said. "A Captain…Loussan."

Shit, Gage thought.

"Commodore," Price pursed her lips, "isn't that the pirate that put the death mark on your head."

"He is," Gage said, "and I'm sure he's still angry for the beating I gave him the last time we crossed paths. No running from this. Comms, send it to my tank."

A screen appeared displaying the image of a man with long blond hair spilling over bejeweled epaulettes and a magenta doublet. A scar over his eye marred what would have been an otherwise handsome face.

"Albion vessel, you have strayed too far from home," Loussan said with a flourish of heavily ringed fingers. "If you've come looking for trouble, you've certainly found it, much more than you look capable of dealing with…"

The pirate's eyes narrowed. He leaned toward his camera, looking intently at Gage.

"You…" His lips pulled back into a sneer. "I've waited a long time for this."

The channel cut out.

"Harlequin vessels are raising shields…powering up weapons," Price said.

"That went as well as expected," Gage said.

THE END

The Story continues in *The Long March*, coming April 2017!

FROM THE AUTHOR

Richard Fox is the author of The Ember War Saga, and several other military history, thriller and space opera novels.

He lives in fabulous Las Vegas with his incredible wife and two boys, amazing children bent on anarchy.

He graduated from the United States Military Academy (West Point) much to his surprise and spent ten years on active duty in the United States Army. He deployed on two combat tours to Iraq and received the Combat Action Badge, Bronze Star and Presidential Unit Citation.

Sign up for his mailing list over at www.richardfoxauthor.com to stay up to date on new releases and get exclusive Ember War short stories.

The Ember War Saga:

1.) The Ember War
2.) The Ruins of Anthalas
3.) Blood of Heroes
4.) Earth Defiant
5.) The Gardens of Nibiru
6.) Battle of the Void
7.) The Siege of Earth
8.) The Crucible
9.) The Xaros Reckoning

Made in the USA
Coppell, TX
24 September 2020